"Brent Terry is that rarest of [illegible] a gifted prose stylist with vision and high moral purpose. His writerly eye is acute. His instinct around a sentence is virtuosic and masterful. In **The Body Electric,** Terry takes us on a journey from the palpably familiar to the deliciously imaginative realms of truth. Reading this lush and lyrical novel is a visceral experience; it feels like waking up and stretching. A marvelous debut."

—Chris Torockio, author of "Floating Holidays" and "The Soul Hunters"

Wry and elegiac, erotic and inventive, Brent Terry's The Body Electric is a pulsing, thrumming novel. "Lightning strikes and strikes and strikes," he writes, reminding us that life itself is a live wire, dangerous and utile and ultimately, miraculous. Terry's kinetic prose unspools a story about the complicated business of being alive, of chasing ghosts, of catching ghosts-- and of letting ghosts go.

—Jill Alexander Essbaum, NYT bestselling author of "Hausfrau"

The Body Electric

Brent Terry

THE BODY ELECTRIC

Published by Unsolicited Press
Printed in the United States of America.
First Edition 2020.

Attention schools and businesses: for discounted copies on large orders, please contact the publisher directly. Books are brought to the trade by Ingram.

For information contact:
Unsolicited Press
Portland, Oregon
www.unsolicitedpress.com
orders@unsolicitedpress.com
619-354-8005

Cover Design: Kathryn Gerhardt
Editor: Jay Kristensen Jr.
ISBN: 978-1-950730-35-3

For Terry and Frank

Happily there is this sure We,
Happily there is this love,
This chosen ambiguity,
Until the weather knows its mind...
Meanwhile this lifetime—
To succeed never beyond the weather
Until it turns to death,
That perfected deliberation.

—Laura Riding, "Though Gently"

If lightning
loved me, it would be sewn
with tongues, it would open
my mind to the sky
within the sky.

—Bob Hicok, "Pilgrimage"

I remember
How the darkness doubled
I recall
Lightning struck itself

I was listening
Listening to the rain.
I was hearing
Hearing something else

—Television, "Marquee Moon"

Before

YOU WANT TO lick her neck.

You register everything: her hands balling into loose fists as she drives them forward, the way they flick open when she draws them back, the fine spray of sweat that flies from her fingertips and rains upon the synthetic surface behind her. Coming into the backstretch, the farthest she'll get from where you sit panting, her running looks effortless, but as she moves nearest to where you sit, you can see the little imperfections, wee signs of a toll you understand all too well: the slight roll to her shoulders as her upper body seeks to drive the tiring legs, the labored breathing, how she forces each exhalation with a little *fshoo* sound (I know, pal, *endearing*), and inhales deeply, greedily—*desperately* sucking oxygen from the thin Colorado atmosphere. But her face is nearly impassive, her considerable discomfort registering only in a look of minor puzzlement, a slight furrowing of the brow.

That first time, at the track. It must've been about a hundred ten degrees, you, lying there on the dying infield grass in a pool of your own fetid sweat, finished, completely freakin' fried. A delicious pain: the all-encompassing throb, headful of heartbeat, eyeful of swarming blue specks: the fading blindness of the last straightaway. Big-ass water bottle vs. the unslakable thirst. There you lie, exposed and sunblasted in the oval's shadowless interior, gasping, stupefied by heat and exhaustion as this—yeah, I know, sport, this *vision*—in sports bra and bun-hugger racing shorts jogs up to the starting line, presses her watch, and without further ado, commences to freakin' fly. With absurd grace, she circles the track all breakneck and shit, and you go from intrigued to engaged to riveted. There are some fast girls in this town, but *this*...this is ridiculous.

And beautiful...? Angelic arias with Stradivarius and Stratocaster; sudden salvo of feathery, cherubic shafts. Palpitations, etc., etc....love at first sight and all that.

Am I getting this right?

She flies past the starting post at the end of her first lap; you start your stopwatch. You think, *She can't be going as fast as it looks*; you think maybe the heat is making you hallucinate. (You think, *My God, would you look at that ass!*) The weather is weirdly humid for Colorado, and sweat, which normally evaporates immediately here, glistens on her legs, soaks her lavender running bra to a deep purple. You watch the moisture fly off the end of the single braid into which she has tied her long, dark hair, the dip of the head and shoulders as she crosses the line, hands spread slightly: the finish lean of racers and interval runners everywhere. You bob forward in concert, unthinking, *simpatico*, glance at your watch at the exact moment she stops her own. She *is* going as fast as it looks.

She slows, catches a spike, staggers just a bit, hands on knees, gasping hard, then straightens and starts off in a slow shuffle to jog a recovery lap. Briefly, her glance sweeps over you, catches you staring like a goob. You nod, attempt a smile that says *I'm a brother in arms; I feel your pain,* not: *I want to lick your neck.* Real slick, sport, and from her, not a glimmer of response before she shows you her heels, glides off into the heat like a freakin' mirage.

Part One: Thunderstruck

. . . just as the tastiest sandwich
is the pilfered sandwich, the tastiest kiss
is the kiss stolen behind the drapes at the party,
lips devoured like canapés, the feasters groping
backlit unknowingly on someone's terrace
where lightning licks the last morsel of song
from the throat of the nightingale.

—T. Finnegan McGuinn, "Rancid, Gladys" (2003)

Finn

LIGHTNING STRIKES AND all the prepositions change. Bolt from the blue and *nearby* becomes *away*. *Before* is replaced by *behind*, by *after*, and, more suddenly than blinking, life is all *between* and *beyond*; *except* and *since* and *until*. What about *by*? What about *for*? About *like* and *near*? Those are gone, pal—literally in a flash—and what are you left with, but the one preposition that in the end defines you.

Without.

It's the word that governs your every breath, screams in your ears, makes up the cramped two-syllable barracks you share with your army of ghosts and voices. *Without* (which is the opposite of *within*...oh, you remember *within*?). Like it was yesterday, don't you, sport? Frozen on your tongue like a kiss: you *within* her, inside her body, her mind, snug as a bug in the Persian carpet of her heart. And she was curled up, all cozy in you too, but a sucker punch at the speed of light and—*bam!* —she is gone, and you can't follow, and you have been left behind, left *without*.

And *without*, while we're at it, is the opposite of *with*. Once, you were with her, and then, quick as a flash, she is gone, and you are alone. *Without*: it's the ozone whiff in your nose, the electric hum that keens through your sleepless nights, the inescapable, impossible gravity of your days. It's the coffee spoon of your hours, amigo—seven years' worth—and it's a motherfucker.

Which is why you find yourself sprinting through this meteorologist's wet dream: trees bent double, whitecaps frothing Lake Harriet; wind and thunder and the clatter of garbage-can lids like something by Berlioz, courting, as you always do, the million-volt sayonara, the sweet, shared fate—the only possible act of bonding left for the two of you—as all around you the sky explodes like an artillery barrage, a mad ballet of birches and ashes and maples illuminated in hallucinogenic flashes, spasming strobe-lit in the evening of middle afternoon.

Transformers explode with boom and sizzle. Arcs of green flame. Cascading sparks. Minivans and SUVs creep along the quickly flooding parkway, the faces of children staring at you through fogged-over windows in gape-mouthed amazement. And stare they should, because you, my friend, have gone certifiably batshit, a regular occurrence when air masses collide and the wind fills with hail and electricity, your channel changed by a sudden drop in atmospheric pressure. You've gone from mild-mannered poet, lovable recluse, to the man who would be Mercury. Into the deluge you charge, lunatic with a taste for lactic acid and oblivion, chasing thunderbolts down the same street Sophie took: mythic dead-end with a third rail to blast you all the way back to Olympus.

Is this how your world ends? Not with a whimper, but a bang? Are you an arrow of flaming love shot heavenward from Cupid's quiver, voltage-enhanced, martyr of your own myth? Or are you just a skinny, lovesick sap? Are you some new Odysseus, soaked, tied to the mast, searching for the way home? Or are you just all wet?

* * *

THOMAS FINNEGAN MCGUINN—Finn, to everyone save his mother, who to this day calls him Tommy—has the company of two private demons as he charges over the bike path and past the ghostlit band shell. One, born of bone-deep anguish, is his silent, vicious taskmaster. The other, spawn of instinct for self-preservation spiced with cynicism, fights a losing battle with the first. One demon drives him to this dangerous dance; the other gives him shit about it.

He runs blindly, yet picturesquely: driving his arms, springing crisply from his toes. Past the small marina he flies, past a symphony of wind and rigging he does not hear, through chill, calf-deep water that doesn't impede him, buffeted by gusts he does not feel. He is unaware, but he is running as fast as he ever has: sub-fives for sure. He is going to feel this tomorrow.

In mid-stride, his world explodes: searing flash, then concussion that plucks him from low-altitude orbit and splashes him down like a shotgunned duck into the mud next to the path. Not twenty meters away, an old birch has been neatly split by the bolt. Still joined at the base, one half teeters north, the other totters south, bark blackened, embers sizzling at its ruined core. Finn picks himself from the muck. Spots dance before his eyes. His ears ring. Both knees are bleeding, and somehow, there's a cut on his forehead.

Where am I? How the hell did I get here?

He knows, of course. This has happened before. Usually he finds himself climbing the steps to his porch as if awakened from a truly awesome occurrence of somnambulism, freaked and dazed. Never, though, has he come so near to being struck down, to getting just what his demons told him he was asking for.

***

HOURS PASS. THE heartrate slows. A prodigal son comes home to himself. Bruch violin concerto on the stereo. Chinese takeout. Three bottles of dry hard cider and a slight, sweet buzz. The mania that had earlier propelled him now spent, he sprawls in his chair on the screen porch, feeling slack as flat soda. He scratches the tufted heads of his Wheaten Terriers, Frank O'Hairy and Seamus, cracks open a fortune cookie, lets the thin paper strip, its bit of ancient wisdom, trail unread to the floor. Absently, he pops the cookie into his mouth, chews without tasting, gazes out the window to the sky beyond his backyard.

Gravity champions over him. He feels drugged, balloon-like. His head nods heavily atop his shoulders like that of a bobblehead doll. Numbly he chews; numbly he takes in his limited view: birds dive-bombing clouds of small, dusty moths. Squirrels. Bats flitting through a latticework of leaves animate his slim swatch of sky, its angry grey-green giving over to a mood indigo: distant flashes from receding thunderheads racing eastward, taking it out on Wisconsin now, taking the edge off the evil humors that had possessed him two hours before. He stands, totters for a moment like a newborn giraffe, and steps out onto the lawn, bending to stretch his run-sore hamstrings, picking up as he does so a few small branches, the odd flyer windripped from some telephone pole (LOST CAT: Black and White, Named Scrapper—!REWARD!). From the slats of his fence, he peels soggy supermarket circulars, junk mail addressed to his neighbors, the usual debris left behind by a storm.

Absently, he patrols the perimeter, stooping and plucking as dusk descends. The dogs chase one another, roll in the wet grass. He wonders if Scrapper has made it home. He wonders if the basement has flooded. Water oozes between his bare toes. Small things chirp and whir. The air bursts with the aroma of moist earth and damp bark; the woodsy odor of ash and maple. Lilac, mock orange, honeysuckle, the pink-champagne smell of a flowering shrub he can't quite name. The faintest hint of mesquite barbecue smoke, like a memory of long-ago good times, bites at the back of his tongue and disappears.

Hint of fabric softener. Quick whiff of skunk. Stumbling through the hangover of his earlier exertions, these things he both does and does not notice. The legions of evening shoulder past while he murmurs vague apologies. Snippets of Joshua Bell's violin escape his living room and sail away on the slackening breeze, joining the whisper of branches, the faint crackle of ever more distant thunder.

Receding too are the voices of his demons, so loud just hours before, now a sizzle on the periphery, a pair of aging widowers overheard bickering from down the street. They'd be back, sure as shit, the next time colliding air masses brought heavy weather, and just as sure, he, Finn McGuinn, would be doing their bidding, casting his willow tree body into the tumult with reckless disregard for health and well-being. His neighbors, spying on him through cracks in their closed curtains, would shake their heads and mutter.

"There he goes again, crazy bastard."

"Guy got a death wish, or what?"

If they only knew.

I am demented, thinks Finn, not for the first time, and mounts—wincing at the pain in his knees—the steps to his porch, where his cell phone has just begun ringing.

* * *

"OUT PLAYING WITH electricity?" asks Beannie without preamble.

Amanda Sue "Beannie" Drinkwater is one of his two oldest friends—his only remaining friends, were he to be honest. She and his other childhood chum, Gizmo Hornaplenty, had been keeping a close eye on The Weather Channel, and upon Finn, for seven years, ever since the accident, ever since his acquisition of certain talents, his subsequent compulsion to go for hard runs during dangerous thunderstorms. Whenever hot and cold air clashed over the Upper Midwest, pelting the Twin Cities with hail, torrential rain, and vicious lightning, Beannie or Gizmo (or both) would get on the horn and make sure their old buddy Finn still counted among the living.

"Whatever do you mean?" Finn's voice oozes innocence.

"Listen, fuckwit, I'm sitting here watching pictures of street flooding in St. Paul, hail ripping the shit out of Minneapolis, and the most hideous lightning I've ever seen blasting some place called Wayzata. And I'm all too familiar with you and your fucking suicidal tendencies, buster, so you can spare me the Scarlett O'Hara crap."

"I went for a run in the rain. I'm fine."

"Glad to hear it."

Her voice is a stew of exasperation, feigned nonchalance, and relief. For years, Beannie's mix of bravado and sometimes spectacularly foul language had veiled the note of worry in her voice, mitigating somewhat the undertone of fear, thus blunting his awareness of the burdens he had placed upon his friends through his unique, if unwanted, set of circumstances.

These calls both embarrass and comfort him. The near-certainty of the call, the by-now-ritualized banter, give Finn someplace solid to hang his emotional hat after what is still a disquieting occurrence. His "thunderstorm fartleks," as he has come to call them, his inability to resist the force that sends him into the deluge, come near to unhinging him every time, and the phone calls, along with a stiff drink or four, the playing of some favorite piece of music, always help him regain some measure of equilibrium. He doesn't mention the lightning strike.

* * *

BEANNIE AND FINN first met in Hampden, Vermont, on September 4, 1973. The air, holding on fiercely to summer, was hot and redolent of goldenrod. (The grownup Finn sneezes at the memory. *Bless you,* says Beannie.) It was the first day of Kindergarten, on a raucous school bus, the pair making their maiden voyage to North Hampden Elementary, where they would spend the next six years becoming like peanut butter unto jelly. Both wore stiff, new school clothes, and both were secretly relieved to be separated briefly from young mothers ravaged by the grief of losing their babies. Each possessed a relentless curiosity, a keen intellect, and a precocious wit. Neither was in the least apprehensive about beginning school. Both preferred chocolate cupcakes to Twinkies, both despised the hideous pink and coconut of Sno Balls. Still, the relationship did not begin well.

Finn's stop was one of the last, and having extricated himself from his mother's trembling grasp, he mounted the three steps to find the bus full nearly to its capacity of seventy-two riders. The bus smelled like pencils and soap. He moved down the aisle looking for a place to sit, his metal *Flintstones* lunchbox held straight out before him in a Frankenstein's Monster pose to avoid smacking any of the sundry knees, elbows, and shoulders that protruded into the narrow passage. About halfway back was an empty seat next to a girl who appeared to be his own age. She sat staring fiercely straight ahead, her Monkees lunchbox clutched tightly to her starched white blouse, a riot of red curls protruding from her cap—a loosely knit, rainbow-striped affair, somewhere between skullcap and stocking hat in design—constellations of freckles fairly throbbing across her pale cheeks and pixie nose.

"Can I sit here?" he asked.

She shrugged in answer, casting a single, disdainful glance his direction, before continuing to bore holes in the green vinyl seatback ahead of her. He considered the empty seat, the forcefield of rage that had kept even the sixth graders at bay. He pondered the dearth of other seating possibilities, and casting his own shrug in return, sat. They rode the last ten minutes to school in a little bubble of silence, floating along in the general cacophony of the bus, neither child acknowledging the other until, as the bus pulled up in front of the school, Finn spoke.

"Thanks for letting me sit here," he said, and, already polite to a fault, stepped back into the aisle, allowing her to precede him from the school bus.

Again, the glare, before marching to the front and off the bus.

"She doesn't like you."

Gilbert Hornaplenty, stating the obvious, smiled sweetly and exited in the girl's turbulent slipstream. Finn stared after him, stupefied. What was up with these people?

"Move it, dork!" came a voice and a shove from behind, and thus, Finn stumbled out and into the blinding sunshine of his elementary-school career.

* * *

"HEY, EARTH TO Finny…anybody home?"

"Sorry, drifted off for a minute, there. I was just thinking of our first day of kindergarten."

"Ah, the inauspicious beginning. God, what a raging little shit I was that day!"

"I'm almost ready to forgive you."

Beannie sighs. "Isn't it funny how well we all remember that bus ride, even Giz, who was really just an observer at that point?"

"Well, we do have a lifetime's worth of joint memories we can trace back to that exact moment in time. It's really pretty amazing to think about. Who knows, though…if that cute little blonde girl hadn't resisted my advances over finger paints later, everything may have gone differently, and that bus ride would be just another forgotten moment among millions."

"Mmmm, yes, the blonde. Just the first in a litany of hopeless romances, and with li'l old me always there to pick up the pieces."

"So true. But it was at recess that The Three Musketeers were really formed, remember?"

"God, the beanie incident. Of course I remember, and the second one of the day for me. I fought Mom tooth and nail to be able to wear that thing. Then I took it out on you."

"I still remember the name of that kid who stole your hat: Todd Sperlock. In high school he fancied himself quite the ladies-man."

"We girls called him Todd, Todd, Gift from God."

"Or Todd Spearcock."

"Ha! I'd forgotten that one, but I do remember you and Gizmo pounding that fucking, glandular thug, getting my beanie back, and getting suspended from school, all on your first day of Kindergarten."

"My mom was so pissed. My dad tried to act mad, but I could tell he was really proud of me."

"His little man. And hey, speaking of Giz, have you talked to him lately?" asks Beannie.

"We had a conference call with our publisher last Thursday, but not since. He's up to his ears in his project at The Tate."

"And up to his ears in some Brit hootchie, I'd guess."

"Goes without saying."

"I just got off the phone with him, by the way. Before I called you. He says get a fucking treadmill."

"Bite me," says Finnegan sweetly.

"Sorry, not my flavor. Speaking of which, I have a date, so. . .ta, darling!"

The line goes dead.

* * *

THE NEXT MORNING, Finn finished his run as he had started it: gingerly. The muscles he had so traumatized through his helter-skelter twelve miles the previous afternoon had loosened as he eased into a slow seven, but the fresh scabs on his knees had split and begun once again to bleed. For the first mile or so, he winced with every stride, especially running up steps or hopping curbs, and his legs became encrusted with blood from knee to mid-shin. Pedestrians eyed him with alarm. He cast them a *Boy, am I clumsy* smile and a shrug. But the morning was bright and unseasonably cool, fresh-scrubbed from the storm, blessedly free of humidity and alive with the sounds and smells of early summer. On flat stretches, where he could forget about the burning of his knees, he floated along in the happy fog of the super-fit, taking it easy, soaking up sun.

He cleaned his wounds in the shower, hissing at the sting of soap and hot water, watching the scabs and new blood swirl down the drain. He dried off, then sat on the edge of the tub, smearing his knees with antibiotic ointment. The lacerations weren't deep, just messy and annoying. The ointment would keep them supple and resistant to cracking as they each bent and straightened, some five hundred times every mile. He neatly taped gauze over the clean wounds, and checking over his handiwork, grimaced at the thought of putting on pants.

It had been some time since he had looked at his knees closely, and as he finished tending to his new wounds, he was faced with the scars of some old ones; injuries that were not so healed as they appeared. Not by a long shot. Seven years after the accident, the cuts had faded to thin, pale ridges of tissue that ran in haphazard, ragged lines across both kneecaps, a roadmap to a place long abandoned: desiccated and tumbleweed-strewn, a ghost town his demons would not let him leave.

* * *

THE DAY HAD been hot, the kind of Colorado July afternoon where bare skin sizzles, where throat and lungs chafe on the thin, dry air. The sky over the red cliffs was a pale blue, almost white at the horizon, an opalescent azure directly overhead where the sun hung, beating down on the two runners without mercy. It glinted from the wave-riffled surface of the long, narrow lake below them, the water tormenting them with images of unattainable coolness. A dry wind rustled through prairie grasses, sagebrush, and yucca. Across the lake, the rust-colored cliffs gave way to blue-green foothills that climbed toward the high mountains, snow still visible on their summits. Below the dam, the town stretched eastward onto the plains, dancing off toward Nebraska through waves of glimmering heat.

A hawk sailed the thermals. Not a cloud in the sky—still, from somewhere, the distant rumble of thunder.

* * *

IMAGINE YOU ARE the hawk.

Imagine you are watching the runners—man and woman; husband and wife—as they follow the narrow red ribbon of trail: past the football stadium, the rodeo arena. Watch as they skirt the shallow pond, with its fishermen and herons, pass through the prairie dog town and switchback through a stand of pines up the steep hill to the road that runs the five-mile length of the reservoir. Imagine their voices as they tease one another, complain about the heat, make plans for a party later. This is the scene Finnegan gazes down and back upon, sitting on the edge of a bathtub, looking across time like a storybook wizard with a magic mirror.

"Sophie," he whispers.

Imagine the runners turning onto the pavement. The man says something to the woman. They reach out and clasp hands briefly, then separate and are silent, except for their breathing, which is now audible, even from this distance. They have accelerated and begin to move quickly along the ridge. The man reaches out again, gently touches the woman's tanned shoulder, then begins to move slowly, almost imperceptibly away. The runners fly down the first of many familiar hills, then across the flat expanse of the first dam, and begin to climb the brutally long, steep grade on the other side. They are running fast, but the man is moving slightly faster, and gradually telescopes away.

Imagine that from your hawk's-eye view you can see the storm coming, see the far-off thunderheads rolling in over Long's Peak, lightning flickering deep in their bellies. You can hear clearly the crackle of thunder as it chases the light over the miles and hills and canyons, to where you circle—watching the progress of the runners, riding your invisible columns of air under a crystal sky.

Imagine then a flash, blinding even in the bright sun, and then a booming explosion, the concussion from which you can feel even at this remove. The world tumbles and tilts below you as you struggle to right yourself on this sudden wind. You settle, bring the runners again into view. The man is running, staggering really, back down the hill, back toward the woman. He is bleeding. He stumbles. Once, twice, three times he falls. The woman lies on the yellow center stripe. One of her shoes lies, sole up and smoking, on the lakeward shoulder of the road, the other in the weeds on the opposite side.

A smell of ozone and something burning. Utter silence. The woman lies motionless in the middle of the road. The man drops at her side, touching and pleading. He pushes on her chest, bends his mouth to hers. Then, as the man begins to scream, imagine yourself tack away on an updraft and glide off, seeking shelter from the approaching storm.

Imagine.

* * *

LIGHTNING STRIKES AND strikes and strikes.

Sophie seven months dead. The sunburned summer of wailing and sedation bleeds into a grim autumn of early snows and suicide watches which gives way to a winter of creeping numbness. In Boston, Gizmo and Beannie and Hendrick's Gin carry Finn through a nightmare Christmas, and in Vermont, his mother mothers him shakily into the New Year. The world sings *Tommy, can you hear me?*

Back in Colorado after the holidays, he stops drinking and resumes teaching, moves wearily, insubstantial as a shade along the corridors between lecture halls and workshop rooms. He prepares diligently, critiques his students' work with a keen and gentle insight, attends to committee work faithfully, if numbly. He runs twice daily and pays his bills on time. He mostly remembers to eat and shower and shave.

He teaches his classes and goes home each night to sit in a pair of warmup pants and Sophie's old Tufts sweatshirt, staring for hours at the television or the mountains or the same page of a book. He does not write. He chews his pasta and salad; he swallows. He does *not* glance at the empty place at the dinner table. In the evenings, he never ventures past his porch. He falls asleep in his chair. In/out he breathes. He cultivates dust bunnies and shadows; tends to the void like a gardener.

* * *

Am I pathetic?
He wonders.

* * *

THERE IS ZOLOFT for the depression, Ambien for the insomnia. For loneliness there is music, the television, the telephone. There is food for hunger—for thirst, drink. More drink for forgetting. For sustenance there is poetry, and for simple survival, of course, there is running. But for The Glimpse there is nothing, nothing at all.

* * *

BY FEBRUARY, HIS friends declare him AWOL and decide drastic measures are called for. Thus, at nine o'clock one bitterly cold evening, the wind piling frozen tumbleweeds against the side of his house, a posse of runners, graduate students, and younger English faculty descend unquietly upon Finn's small bungalow, a ragtag little army of the ectomorphic and literary sweeping in as from across the blizzard-ravaged steppes. They fishtail onto his street from all directions, led by the ancient red Saab of one Dirk Maraschino—associate professor and writer of flash fiction, champion snowshoe racer, self-styled leftist desperado, and undisputed darling of the graduate students. The happy mob enter with the most perfunctory of knocks and proceed to swarm the living room like a band of drunken Cossacks, leaving paintings askew and boot-track-shaped snow piles on the hardwood floors. Maraschino, smiling expansively through his bushy, bushy black moustache, his stunning eyebrows arching like a pair of steroidal caterpillars, shoves a parka at Finn and says in his best phony Russian accent, "Am afraid you must come viss us."

Finn acquiesces with little resistance and less enthusiasm, dons the parka against the driving snow, and trudges wordlessly to the waiting Saab. Undaunted by Finn's less than enthusiastic reception, the ten-odd conspirators joyfully follow Maraschino's lead, his chief deputy, a goofily grinning, goateed-and-ponytailed adjunct named Bob, going so far as to duck Finn's head, policeman style, through the rear car door. The well-meaning and decidedly testosterone-enhanced assemblage proceeds to kidnap him to a local club, where a raucous Groundhog's Day party is in full swing, and where, after an icy and terrifying ten-minute thrill-ride, he finds himself amid the by now unfamiliar din and revelry, shell-shocked and blinking like the aforementioned Pennsylvania rodent, certain he casts no shadow at all.

* * *

INSIDE THE STATE Armory, titanic speakers crash dance music down on the heads of a surprisingly robust Tuesday crowd. Sodden undergrads, newly in thrall of legal hooch, dance with loose-limbed abandon in puddles of spilled beer, while graduate students and younger, hipper faculty cultivate their highs more sedately around widely scattered tables, and venture in twos or threes to the verges of the dance floor's pulsating mob. The bare brick walls of the cavernous former warehouse are covered in an odd assortment of old license plates, spent artillery shell casings, National Guard flags from seventeen states, a stunning array of classic BB-guns, and various small farm implements.

The *pièce de résistance* of this décor is a refurbished WWII-era B-24 Liberator. Hung from the rafters as if roaring over the heads of the dancers, it leads the charge in the nightclub's war on sobriety, its bomb-bay doors open and filled with speakers that rain down devastation upon young ears and brain cells. Disco lights rotate and strobe, strafing the dancers with tracers from its machine-gun turrets, while a lovingly repainted woman—mostly nude, with antigravitational 1940's breasts—winks and smiles lasciviously from the plane's nose.

Finn gapes, blinking at his surroundings like some nocturnal marsupial awakened by Armageddon. Not having planned this mission much beyond arriving at the bar's threshold, his captors commandeer a few tables, and after making some nervous, inaudible small talk, deliver unto him a pint of Fat Tire and some pats on the back, then disperse with self-congratulatory swaggers, joining the erstwhile-holiday melee. They tell him to try and have some fun, maybe bust a move or two. They vow to check back from time to time, then leave Finn sitting—aghast, alone, and surrounded by a small mountain of winter coats—at a table on the glittering periphery of the dance floor, his bewildered face sparkle-lit, as if swarmed by a thousand psychedelic fireflies.

Gee, he thinks, *thanks a million.*

He gathers himself a bit, adds his parka to the pile, and makes for the stairway, which leads to a sort of balcony that horseshoes the bar and houses a smattering of tables, a few arcade games, some decrepit, butt-littered plants. The balcony is sparsely populated. A few couples sit at the tables talking. Frat boys play drinking games. A group of students throw darts; others lean on the railing, watching the dancers below. Here, where the light and noise are slightly less mind-shattering, Finn intends to compose himself, develop a neato survival strategy that will see him through the evening and keep him from appearing insane, at least until his friends can deliver him safely home to his tidy little cocoon of despair. It will, he thinks, be a strategy hinging heavily upon pinball and repeated pints of his favorite local brew, which he plans to consume while hiding behind a large ficus near the window.

Before he can even begin to implement his daring plan, it is shattered by a blast from the past, a bristling nimbus blowing tipsily in his direction on a stiff breeze of thunderous funk. A navel ring ensconced in a tanned ripple of abdominal muscle sparkles in the discolight. Thin-but-muscular legs emerge tautly from a just-the-right-tight denim miniskirt and plunge earthward in a series of lewdly flexing and relaxing curves, disappearing eventually, socklessly, into a pair of classic blue-suede adidas.

Danger, Will Robinson.

She dances along unsteadily, dragging many sets of eyeballs upward from the dance floor, and bringing to the balcony a new meaning for the term *scenic overlook.* She is the picture of indifference, keeping the beat while somehow managing to sing along with the house mix and noisily suck the dregs of a margarita through a tiny straw.

Nikki Desmond...fuck.

He sees her coming before she sees him, but there is nowhere to run and—since she is between him and the ficus—nowhere to hide. *Isn't she cold, dressed like that?* he wonders. She looks up from her drink, eyes going wide with recognition. A glimmer of predatory glee flashes across those eyes before she reigns it in, replacing it with the more appropriate look of sisterly concern.

"Finn! My God! How *are* you?"

Nikki is a runner, and a good one: a strawberry-blonde Brit from the Lake District, with a taste for mud, hills, potent drink, and, as he'd found out one regrettable evening, occasional rough sex with a fellow harrier. He chases away the troubling image of the Union Jack, tattooed high, high on one inner thigh, the Jolly Roger similarly emblazoned upon the other, her invitation to *run these bastards up the flagpole*. Their one night together after the U.S. Cross Country Championships in Portland had left him bruised, carpet-burned, and doubly sore, but had amazingly convinced her that here, finally, was *the one*. He'd tried to gently disabuse her of this notion in a candlelit tête-à-tête that evolved into an ugly and embarrassing scene, which had taken place in this very bar. Peppered with lively and ornate British swearing, much of it brand new to the ears of the gathered Colonials, it had been a memorable exchange, and one that, to Finn's eternal embarrassment, instantly gained a permanent place in local running lore.

Shortly thereafter came the fateful track session that sealed his romantic fate. After a whirlwind courtship Finn married Sophie, and Nikki, admitting defeat with uncharacteristic grace, went back to nasty races on turf and even nastier rolls in the hay. Now here she is again, joined in a duet with Prince, singing "Sexy MF" and practically licking her lips as she reaches out to embrace him. Finn winces. He sweats. He swallows hard. He feels like a man wearing a bacon suit thrown into a cage full of underfed tigers.

* * *

Which may have proven less painful than what happened next.

* * *

...SO SHE WRAPS you in her arms and it is ten thousand no ten million volts it's all jolt it's an electric chair bear hug baby and you are the doomed man the dying man the frying man twitching in convulsive writhing neon fucking spasms your head exploding like a burst transformer oh pain and pain and pain and pictures from somebody's noggin not your own and what the fuck is this why is she in your head why these memories of Daddy the sick fuck and what he used to do and ohshitohshitohshitohshit someone please pull the plug take the fork from the socket don't want to be the lightning rod the pain oh fuck leave her alone oh Jesus let go of me Nikki please—but you are a rag doll in a twister and the world is a lightning bolt and you're riding it straight to hell—oh Nikki let me go oh please oh shit oh sweet Jesus fuck—can't anyone see you are dying…?

* * *

ALL NIKKI KNEW was the second she touched him he jerked rigid in her arms, his eyes rolling back in his head, streams of gibberish spewing from his tongue, then a desperate thrashing to get away. She could have sworn she saw sparks. It was like a tent revival laying-on-of-hands gone horribly awry. She screamed, letting go of Finn, who slumped to the floor, bringing forth both bouncers and the heretofore-merry troop of kidnappers, who saw immediately that something was most definitely amiss with their charge. A crestfallen Dirk Maraschino, moustache drooping, looked at the crumpled poet and wondered at the magnitude of his miscalculation. The newly monk-like Finn, abducted from his echoing monastery of grief, had crumbled like a stale cookie in the light and noise of the real world, not to mention the fact that Finn and Nikki, who under the best of circumstances had mixed like petrol and a Zippo, had gone up like a firebombed Kuwaiti gusher. The entourage split into two groups: one leading the trembling Finn to a nearby chair, where he hunched, spent and shivering, the other tending to a shaken Nikki Desmond, who was feeling a strange stew of emotions. She was both shocked and afraid, concerned and miffed. Her touch could incite such a response? Not the intended effect. Not the intended effect at all.

* * *

"IT WAS LIKE being electrocuted while watching scrambled porn," Finn told Gizmo on the phone the next day.

Gizmo almost laughed—such colorful imagery rolled effortlessly from the lips, the pen of his friend but even Gizmo could see that this was no time for mirth, and he choked back his chuckle before it could emerge.

"Remember that ungrounded freezer in your barn, how we used to hold on to the blade of a shovel, then grab the freezer door handle, see how long we could hold on, how long we could stand the shock?

"It became our undergraduate metaphor for life, if I recall. And I remember that you're the masochistic little bastard who holds the record. That could explain a lot, come to think of it."

Finn ignored the barb.

"Well, imagine that shock, multiplied by a hundred, while at the same time—I swear to God—bright lights, explosions, flickering pictures of what seemed to be *her* childhood, what something told me *was* her childhood, flashed through my mind. It was scary; it *is* scary. Jeez, Giz, did that really happen to her...and what's happening to me?"

"I don't know, man. I do know that I've been your friend pretty much my whole life. I know that you've always been more sensitive to other people's shit than most...more than what's good for you, if you ask me. Now you go through this horrible tragedy with Sophie, go into seclusion, then get dragged out to a fucking nightclub with no warning. *Then* you get cornered by an old lover...unexpected intimate contact...hell, I think your wiring just blew there for a second. Finn, I *know* you. I know how much you loved Sophie." He paused. "I know your future was locked in, in your mind, in your heart. There were no alternate scenarios. Now she's dead and you have no clue how you're supposed to exist without her. Under the circumstances, I think you're doing pretty well." He paused again. He couldn't resist. "Seeing visions, hearing voices, but doing pretty well."

"Thanks, bitch, you're such a comfort."

And really, he was.

* * *

Daddy did, daddy diddled, daddy did
me darling, when I was a girl.
He planned it, he planted it, he placed
his tic, his tic, his talk, his time bomb,
he buried it deep, and when it went off
oh, oh, oh, when he got off,
his little girl got offed, got early old,
but boy she buried that big-old boom...

WHAT ELSE COULD he do, really, but write it down: the shock, the horrible pictures that flashed and flickered in his mind as Nikki held him, all twitching and overcome? Actual or not, the images felt real, passed on from his former lover like a virus or a gift, and how else for a poet to deal, but to put them down, writhing and ugly, on paper. What to do but attempt to frame the experience—his experience, hers—snatch a snippet of context from the ethers, to tell the truth by creating a fiction, to plug into the mainline and channel this bitter monologue loosed from the mouth of a babe.

* * *

HE CALLED IT The Glimpse and it wasn't a one-time thing.

From that first freaky night forward, every other human being on the planet had become a literal live wire, and any physical contact caused Finn to perform the same spastic St. Vitus' dance he had affected that night with Nikki. Each embrace held the promise of a technicolor electrocution, every handshake a joy-buzzer shockgrip, a cosmic practical joke, and Finn was not fucking laughing. Finn knew that electricity was everywhere: that currents flashed and pulsed through every cell in his body, that every subatomic particle held or passed on a charge, that great magnetic and electric fields pulsed through space, shaping the future of the universe and bending time itself. He understood that all the cosmos, from the smallest bits of his body to the vastest reaches of space, blazed and sizzled and flashed like an unimaginable Las Vegas, so given his recent past, it didn't surprise him that he was the epicenter of some bizarre electromagnetic phenomenon.

That didn't mean it didn't piss him off.

He resented the physical pain, the exquisite and often public embarrassment, the unwanted intimacy of seeing someone else's laundry, long hidden from everyone, even themselves for all he knew, suddenly aired out in all its grotesque grandeur for him alone to see, fluttering above the garbage-strewn alleys of his synapses, accompanied by a jolt that etched the image of it permanently on the canvas of his traumatized gray matter. *I have my own problems to deal with right now, thank you very much.* And just when he had begun to stick a tentative toe back into the pool of life, the last thing he wanted, really, was some electric shitstorm blowing in and blasting to hell his chance at the everyday comfort of a little human touch.

He remembered back in elementary school, how someone (usually Giz) would get the whole class to join hands and shuffle across the carpeted floor of the classroom to build up static electricity. Then the person at the head of the line would touch the metal vent of the air conditioning system, bringing a jolt that would pass unfelt through each child save the one at the head of the line (guess who?), who would be the beneficiary of a shock that would detonate in his hand, shoot up his arm and leave his fingers tingling for an hour. And now Finn, who had been showing signs of emerging from his den of bereavement and resuming life as a social animal, found himself on the receiving end of some electrified cosmic game of crack-the-whip, singed and sizzled and utterly without a clue, growing aloof, ever more separate as the world became a great conga-line of people scuffling across a vast expanse of carpet, storing up static electricity and suppressed memories with which to blast him back to his hermitage, his emotional hidey-hole.

The second time it happened, he was in his cramped campus office, with its jammed bookshelves, Frank O'Hara and Steve Prefontaine posters on the door, walls crammed with Sophie's paintings and drawings, The Posies' "Dream All Day" on the stereo quietly. A former student with a copy of her first published poem. The quick hug, the same electric maelstrom in his head; not so traumatic, these pictures, a shouting match with a young man, sobbing on a front porch, traffic passing in the slush, but still he shook and stuttered and struggled with explanations and apologies. The third time, a handshake with the dean, flashing images of a casket, an old woman...*mom!*...an attic with hat boxes and old photographs, a heart not his own skipping a beat. He feigned a coughing fit, pretended the flu.

He waited for it to stop. It didn't. One after another they came, these fellow citizens, unwittingly offering up what they had buried deepest, and Finn stood like a one-person receiving line, accepting the handshakes, the embraces that felt like blows.

* * *

SO WHAT DO you do now, sport?

You withdraw. You write. You change; your poems change. Your playful, sorrow-tinged lyrics—which no less than Kenneth Koch had once called *beguiling invitations into the funhouse, the mirrors reflecting dazzling wit and devastating, unsentimental sorrow*—these lyrics, they stop puppying about, morph into something darker: a world of exposed viscera and flayed nerve, where you serve up the truth raw: blood red, but seasoned with a mélange of sweet sympathy. So you open a vein; out spills book number two: it's *The Smell of Something Burning,* and with your poisoned pen, you build yourself a freakin' symphony—a rock 'n' roll temple, a darkened stage from which to howl your hosannas of personal and planetary apocalypse.

You are a dervish, amigo; you're freakin' Zorro. You thrust; you parry. Your lyrics twist like a knife in the gut. Your swirling, elliptical mini-epics, beautiful and hard as hell, are miraged Parthenons of language, language that crumbles like ancient steps beneath the feet, leaving no option but to keep on climbing, up, up into your devastating rhetoric, your soaring lyricism.

Make the leaps, you tell them, *or fucking fall.*

You left them dazed and confused, didn't you, sport? Offered them a glimpse into your world—*take it or it leave it*—and while some turned away, heartbroken and unable to continue, some limped on through the terrible beauty of your burning vistas, staggering and awestruck: onward, entranced by your landscapes, your freakin' blade still twisting in their guts.

But you didn't write this for them, did you, pal?

Oh, you raged; you ranted. You wrote feverish true gobbledygook. You sounded like the love child of Sylvia Plath and John Ashbery and Joey Ramone. Your poems rocked and flayed, serenaded and seduced—you played with them, didn't you: you sang them a lullaby—oh, you cooed and you wooed them, feted and fucked them senseless. Then you left them, all alone, to their own sweet dreams, to *your* tortured nightmares.

The little magazines eat this shit up, don't they? The prestigious small presses duel for the opportunity to publish you. *The New York Times* gushes; *Rolling Stone* runs a short piece about you and your rockstar pal, Beannie. You are long-listed for a Pulitzer, short-listed for a National Book Award. You actually win some smaller prizes, a few grants, read at festivals and universities and bookstores large and small. You make a little money, gain what small acclaim a poet can achieve in this world, give interviews and answer some fan mail. The hipsters dig you. You are *Da Bomb,* you are thirty-one and oh, how she would have loved this shit, and, oh yes, the university coughs up a full-time offer. Other colleges and universities get in line. You are courted, you are coddled; you are beset, and you are besieged. You smile for the camera and you answer the questions, you: polite and erudite and broken. Oh, everyone loves a plucky survivor, and they love you they love you they love you. They do.

And you? You do not want this, you are null and you are void, you are numb and, believe you me, you are no one they want to know. You are called into the storm by the voices of killer clouds and you answer them with your stripped-down body, your flying feet. You play matador with thunderbolts, you *kamikaze* the ack-ack from atmospheric gunships, offer your throat to the wolves with teeth of flame. You beg to be taken, don't you, sport? But taken, alas, you are not.

So you suffer the slow electrocution of handshake and hug. You endure the megawatt twitching, the pornographic, flickered freeze-frame until you can endure no more. You smile and you bow and you look one last time at the high mountains, gleaming and ice-topped at midsummer still.

Goodbye, you whisper... *Sophie, goodbye.*

Shut softly, sport, the door behind you; to this life, bid a fond *adieu.*

* * *

HE CLOSES HIS eyes, puts his finger on a random name on a list, makes the call. *How soon do you want me there?* He fills his truck with gas, with possessions, points it east, he drives across the flatlands of Nebraska, the rolling hills of Iowa, turns north at Des Moines, drives until he sees the silver coil of the Mississippi, the twin sets of skyscrapers shimmering in the humidity. He tries not to, he really does, but he thinks, yes of course he does, of another summer not so very long ago.

* * *

THE MAN HE was then sits in the sun-ravaged infield, stretching, guzzling water, watching as the woman systematically runs herself into the same gibbering mush he is only now coming out of. He sits transfixed as she clicks off all eight of her eight hundred-meter repetitions—the exact workout he has just run. She runs each of the first seven intervals within a single second of the same five-minute-per-mile pace, the discomfort he knows she must be feeling never showing as she moves around the track, seeming to float above the surface rather than running upon it. Nothing in her manner betrays the terrible toll of this exertion, nothing save a creased forehead and that look of puzzlement that is, to him, already endearing. It is only as she finishes each rep that the cost of the effort shows: the gauntly attractive face etched with salt and anguish as she coasts to a staggering stop; the tottering for a moment in an agonized duckwalk, hands on knees, gushing sweat, her breath coming in ragged, raspy bursts as she begins to ease into the one lap recovery jog she takes between the two laps of self-inflicted torture.

He feels an odd sense of intimacy as he sits, watching her run. It is only the two of them, nobody else being courageous—or stupid—enough to do a track workout in the obscene late afternoon heat, and only one can truly know what the other is feeling. Though he is unsure of how aware she is of his presence, his unwavering interest, he feels none of the voyeur's sense of distance, of safety from being seen, as he sprawls, consciously willing her through each painful lap. He gazes on unselfconsciously, the drama that unfolds before him holding him rapt. He is both observer and participant in this drama. Even as he hangs on the edge of his grassy seat, waiting to find out what happens, he knows how the scene will end.

He has fallen, he thinks, a little in love.

Sophie

SHE FIGHTS OFF the fatigue that threatens to overwhelm her, keeps it at bay like a menacing but familiar dog that snarls behind the invisible fence of her own hard-won fitness. With three hundred meters of her last 800 remaining, she drives her arms a little higher, springs even more forcefully from her toes. A voice in her head hollers, *The last one is always fastest, bitch...always!* The strange, self-loathing voice, loosed from some vile cesspit in her subconscious, never fails to rise up late in a brutal workout, scream obscenities in her head. Blue specks begin to swim before her eyes: incipient tunnel vision, a total blackness that has never yet come, though she teases it ever closer. Down the backstraight she flies one last time, and into the final curve, fighting: fighting to hold form, fighting gravity, fatigue, the terrible heat. Fighting also the other voice, the one that says she's worked plenty hard today, to go ahead and coast the last hundred.

In answer to the voices, she explodes from the final corner, throws everything she has left into a finishing sprint that comes from someplace deep and foreign, someplace she, as hard as she trains, visits very seldom. The blackness of tunnel-vision comes thundering down, racing her to the white line that gives her permission to stop. She thinks only of her form, the picture in her head of herself running, strongly, *perfectly,* through the line, and keeps the blindness at bay—barely—until she does just that. Through the fog she looks at the time on her watch. *2:14. Sheee-it-fire,* she thinks, her last semi-coherent thought before she staggers to the grass and collapses in a heap.

She never really loses consciousness, just lies there in the thunder of her own heartbeat, letting pain swat her around a bit, like a doomed mouse in the paws of a cat, absently watching the slow progress of a single high cloud across the cruel blue expanse of sky. After a few moments, she has regained enough strength to raise an arm, looking again at the time on her watch. *Jeez-Louise, where did that come from?*

Suddenly, a shadow creeps the length of her supine body and across her face. She looks up, still too tired to truly be startled. A young man stands over her—she thinks only, *finally, some goddamn shade.* Her still-fogged gaze travels from the untied laces of a pair of Adidas racing spikes up tanned, hard shins, calves and thighs, the sweat-soaked green shorts, across the flat, rippled stomach, small-but-defined chest, skinny arms and shoulders, to the face: bright blue eyes and goofy grin framed by barely tamed drying reddish-brown locks. His black Oakley shades are pushed up on his forehead. He is backlit, the sun just behind his head making a halo. He looks like a malnourished angel.

His eyes twinkle with merriment and concern. He is holding toward her, she finally notices, a full and condensation-sweated water bottle.

He really *is* an angel.

It takes her a moment to realize that this was the guy who was wrapping up his own workout (dude was *fast,* and completely blown-out, glassy-eyed, a sight that had filled her with apprehension) as she prepared to begin hers, the guy who seemed so interested in her intervals. The guy, a voice inside her head suggests, for whose benefit that last, hell-bent hundred meters may have been. And then, the angel speaks.

So, he says, *you gonna live, or what?*

***

TWO HOURS LATER, they are ensconced at a back booth in the shadowy, cool depths of the Rio Grande Cantina, sucking on icy mango margaritas and inhaling bowls of deliciously salty chips and homemade salsa, the intense discomfort of the workout dulled to an insistent hunger, a nearly unquenchable thirst. Their arms and legs buzz with a low-grade electric fatigue; taut muscles twitching beneath their skins. They are tired, content, and a bit drunk to boot.

***

AFTER DRINKING HALF of the liter bottle of water he had offered and dumping the other half over her head, Sophie begins quickly to feel better. Mr. Angel asks if she wants to join him for a cool-down, and she eagerly accepts. It is her first run with another person in the week (and 97 miles) since she had moved to town, and she relishes the company. She refuses to admit to herself that she finds this friendly, fast fellow a little bit cute.

They cruised through an easy six miles, keeping the run to the shady neighborhoods between campus and City Park. The streets were wide, flat and tree-lined, and filling quickly, as afternoon melted into evening, with runners and brightly clad cyclists on expensive bikes heading for the roads and trails in the foothills west of town. As usual, Sophie felt crappy for the first mile or so, her body struggling to process all the lactic acid and other waste products that filled her muscles after the track session. Soon, however, her legs once again beginning to feel like her own, she settled into a relatively easy seven-minute pace, and set about getting to know her skinny new companion, who strode along beside her without apparent effort (though he *must* be feeling just as ragged as she), gabbing unapologetically, relishing his role as tour guide.

She found herself amazed, as Finn seemed to know about every third runner they passed. He waved, called out "howdy" to runners of all ages and sizes, and for many, had more specific greetings.

It was all, "Hey, Sara, how's the knee?" (to a petite, gray-haired woman wearing a Chicago Marathon t-shirt and a Cho-Pat strip below her left kneecap), and "Nice 10K up in Estes, Doug!" (to a large man wearing new, high-end Asics and a madly beeping heart monitor). Or, "Twenty at Horsetooth, then the barbecue at St. Clair's Sunday, right?" This, to a lithe and tanned couple coming at them around City Park Lake.

"You bringing your artichoke dip?" asked the man, whose angular build and floppy blonde hair made him look like a surfer from the Santa Barbara summers of Sophie's youth.

"Only if you marinate some of those wings of yours," answered Finn. Sophie was suddenly ravenous.

"Deal," answered the surfer.

The woman caught Finn's eye, looked at Sophie, who was still politely glancing at the blond man, then gave a quick double bob of the eyebrows, silently asking, *So, who's the babe?*

They were all kind of running in place, as runners going in opposite directions, wanting to say hello, but not really interrupt their run, often do, which let Finn off the hook, long introduction-wise. Surfer looked at Sophie and asked, "Are you coming to the barbecue?"

Finn gave her a hopeful nod, and she said, "Uh. . .yeah, sure, I guess so."

"Cool, then we'll interrogate you there," and to his girlfriend, "Shall we, my love?"

And the two sets of runners were off, briskly and in opposite directions.

"The King and Queen," said Finn, "Rex McMichael and Rachel Barnett," nodding in the direction of the receding couple. "Wicked-good steepler, he, and seventeenth at XC Nationals last year. And she just ran two-forty-one at Boston."

Sophie considered this a moment before responding, "Seventeenth huh? Not bad." She glanced at him sidelong. "That put him what, eleven places behind you?"

She grinned at the look of happy surprise on his face.

"Well, my dear," he said (it came out "my dee-yah"—slightly Kennedy-esque—as he added a little extra juice to his disappearing New England accent), "it seems you have discovered my secret identity. I did indeed participate in that particular footrace. But I must clarify: 'twas a mere ten places that separated young Rex and myself."

They ran another moment in fatigued, contented silence before he continued, "And forgive me for not remembering exactly"—a sudden flash of recognition widening his eyes—"but as I recall, you finished in the low-teens at that same meet, correct?"

It was Sophie's turn to look at Finn in surprise.

They continued around the park, looping its golf course and passing the lake once more on their way back to campus. The small lake was at its summer, after-work busiest: alive with raucous geese and stately swans, model sailboats bobbing in their feather-strewn wakes. High-school boys, shirtless in baggy shorts or low-slung jeans, and girls in bikini-tops leaned against cars, sipping soft drinks or taking surreptitious swigs from hidden beers. Car stereos blasted Primus, Bob Marley. Clusters of runners stretched in spots of shade, waiting for late-coming members of the group, and cyclists pumped up tires and made last minute adjustments to gear. The air rang with the laughter and shouts of children and was thick with the sweet perfume of Russian olive.

They spoke less as they neared the end of the run, heat and fatigue once again taking their toll, but they moved along in a companionable silence, as if they had been training together for years. Slowing to a walk as they entered the parking lot behind the track, Sophie realized that, as glad as she was to stop running, she wasn't ready for the afternoon to be over. A pleasant combination of wistfulness and low-grade lust washed over her as she watched Finn grab her gear bag, as well as a couple of cold bottles of Gatorade from a cooler in the back of his dusty black Toyota pickup. She couldn't help noticing the defined, elongated muscles of his back gliding along under the tanned skin, how his ribs were visible between his back and rippled abdomen as he leaned into the bed of the truck. She fought back the sudden urge to reach out and touch him there.

"So..." He gazed at her, handed her a Gatorade, perhaps reading her mood, and thus overcoming his habitual shyness, asked, "If you're interested, there's a place in Old Town serves

up some passable Mexican, and more'n passable fruity drinks of the tequila persuasion...um, after many glasses of cool water, of course."

Was she imagining things, or had his accent just gone all genteel, a cool Carolina?

He grinned at her with a sort of lopsided goofiness that made her inexplicably happy, and she smiled back.

"Tequila, huh?"

"Jose Cuervo, sports drink of champions!"

"You've twisted my arm. Give me an hour."

* * *

SUNDAY EVENING: POST-run, post-barbecue, post-coital bliss. Sophie wakes purring, stretches like a cat. Ecstatic, wee shudders sizzle along her spine. Whispers of a twilight breeze rustle the curtains, tiptoe along her flushed, bare back and shoulders. Goosebumps, and a quick frisson: an adrenaline thrill as she remembers where she is.

She feels the warmth of Finn's breath on the back of her neck, the easy weight of his arm draped across her naked hip. She opens her eyes, gazes at his thin wrist, its watch-shaped tan-line a stark white next to the permanent red-brown of his hand and forearm. He lies behind her, half spooned, half sprawled, so relaxed as to be boneless, sleeping with happy abandon. The sheets that drape them, haphazard and worn, are a faded purple, and clean, and smell of the same wind that sweeps through the backyard linden and across her naked skin: prairie and mountain and mesquite smoke—summerhot bodies, soap, and shampoo. The sharp spice of sex.

She follows the shape of him down, to where his skin disappears under the sheet. Over her shoulder she watches him, notes the slow rise and fall of chest, the flickering kaleidoscope of light and shadow as it moves over his body like a caress. She breathes in his every angle and curve, takes the sense of him into her, impresses every cell of him onto the canvas of her memory. Soon enough, she will take up pencil and pad, paint and brush, soon enough she will translate this man, this moment, this emotion into a painterly language, but for now it is enough to inhale him, to memorize him. For now, it is enough to snuggle back into him, to feel him rise again to the touch of her, and as he wakes with a sigh of sweet surprise, to welcome him, with a sigh of her own, back home into her body.

* * *

AT A SPARKLING 7:30 that morning, the air filled with sage-scented breezes and the notes of redwing blackbirds ringing from the wetland behind the house, she had joined a group of about thirty runners in the large and shady front yard of one Saxony Bliss, local attorney, 2:45 marathoner, and president of The Rock Runners, a large, serious, and hard-partying local running club. If Peter Pan's Lost Boys included women, and all were decked out in microfiber shorts, state of the art trainers, shirtless, or wearing brightly colored running bras, this is what they might have looked like. There was a definite whiff of eternal youth in the air, though some of those present had advanced irrevocably beyond the threshold of middle age. Though joking and jovial, they were lean and hard, forged into edges and angles over tens of thousands of miles. This group would brook none of Captain Hook's shenanigans. They would chase both Hook and his pirate crew down, happily fuck them up, then maybe get in a quick ten before celebrating over nachos and beer.

The runners milled about exchanging muted greetings, draining to-go cups of coffee and tea, or swigging from bottles of water while stretching halfheartedly, stewing together in excitement and dread. The twenty-plus miles that lay ahead of them were hilly and sunbaked, and not even the spectacular views of lake and mountain would provide much uplift near the end, when even the fittest of them would be fried to a crackly crunch. It was cool yet in the shade, with dew on the grass. An early morning breeze played through the leaves and brought a fleeting chill they would all look back upon with longing soon enough.

But the company was good, the scenery even better, and barring a total bonk, even the pain would be sweet when at last it was over. Sophie introduced herself, exchanged pleasantries, relishing the easy acceptance offered her by the group. After a few minutes, she felt a light hand brush her elbow, and there was Finn, shirtless and grinning.

"Here we are again, just like Kansas, proving that Missouri loves company," he said, arms wide to indicate the collected runners.

"And speaking of misery," piped in Rachel Barnett, who had just arrived and stood pulling her hair into a scrunchy, "two-plus hours of Finn's bad puns. As if eighty-degrees and endless hills aren't bad enough."

"Just a little humor to take a gal's mind off her problems," retorted Finn, pouting extravagantly.

"*Little* humor is right," she snorted, drifting with Finn, Sophie, and a slow-waking and heretofore silent Rex onto the empty Sunday street, settling into a relaxed trot amongst club runners of various ages and abilities, an egalitarian tableau that would be sundered soon enough, as the gazelles among them found a pace that suited them, one that would see them pretty much rocket away from the fit, but less genetically gifted members of the group.

Soon the foursome, plus a couple of others—college runners staying in town for the summer—were well clear of the rest and sailing along at a brisk, but not yet taxing pace. After the customary few minutes of bitching about running-related ailments, the band ran along in silence for a few moments before Rex, wide awake now, called out, doing his best John Cleese: "It is time to begin the Spanish Inquisition!"

And just like that, he and Rachel were off, throwing themselves enthusiastically into the task of learning all there was to know about their new training partner.

"What," screeched Rex, ever-accelerating and still in character, "brings you among us?!" His eyebrows twitched suspiciously. "And how"—before she can begin to answer— "long are you planning on staying?!"

Sophie began to talk, but once again, he interrupts her.

"And what, pray tell"—this much more quietly and conspiratorially— "are your intentions regarding Mr. McGuinn here. . .ehhh?"

Both Finn and Sophie begin to object, but Rex and Rachel scream, in unison and unconvincing Cockney, "There is no talking during the Spanish Inquisition!"

The quartet (the college runners having dropped back, either from embarrassment or fatigue) are soon, due to hysterical laughter, reduced to a stomach-clutching, though still fast trot, thanks to a twenty-minute group recitation of favorite Monty Python skits, still having learned nothing about the new runner in their midst. They run in silence for a moment, attacking the summit of a long hill, before Rex resumes the chase.

"Seriously Sophie, what's your story?"

So for the next hour (and nine miles) Sophie, oddly comfortable with these new friends, throws caution to the wind and tells, with breaks for oxygen and concentration on climbs, her tale."After my parents died," she begins, noting a trio of quick intakes of breath...

* * *

SHE EXPLAINS HOW she had graduated from Tufts two years previous, on a picture-perfect May morning, the air fragrant with apple blossoms and weed, the occasional slow, early bee alighting on the lip of a champagne bottle, joining 824 of her fellow graduating classmates in spilling out into the waiting throng of family and friends. She tells them how she had expected to find her parents—mother a journalist, father a photographer, freshly arrived from Montreal, where they had been on assignment—waiting for her. She was met instead by Jimmy Callahan, her coach, and her beloved painting professor, Chaim Brodsky, both looking uncomfortable in coat and tie under their professorial regalia, each taking her gently by an elbow and leading her away from the crowd and to a bench littered with petals in quiet pocket garden behind the chapel. She tells her rapt and ambulatory audience how the happy shouts and peals of laughter had drifted in on the perfumed breeze, tells them about the accident that, late the night before, had killed her mom and dad: the sleeping trucker, the car taking flight from a New Hampshire highway and coming to rest, twisted and burning among saplings and new green leaves along the fourteenth fairway of a sleeping suburban country club.

"So you're running with an orphan: Little Orphan Sophie." She manages a sad half-smile. "Anyway, I couldn't face grad school after the accident, so I just drifted for a while. I stayed with friends, spent a few months with my grandparents in Cambridge and Santa Barbara. I cried and watched TV and ate Ben and Jerry's. Never went near my training shoes or a paintbrush. Then, one day, a high school cross country team ran by the house. They were laughing and giving each other shit, and I tell you, I almost ran to the door and yelled for them to wait for me. So I started running again, just put on my shoes and stumbled off the porch like a fat little zombie. God, I'd forgotten how much I loved it! I felt like started to wake up. I started to paint again too. It was, all of it, the running and the painting, like fingers thawing after being frozen: you know it's going to get better, but that doesn't mean it doesn't hurt like hell."

The others mumble encouraging noises between increasingly labored breaths, so she continues. "I was ready to get going but had no idea where to begin. I felt bad, mooching off people, but spending the life insurance money or inheritance felt ghoulish. Finally, my grandparents had a sort of intervention. They told me the money was a blessing, that my parents loved me and wanted me to go after what I wanted, so I should ditch the guilt, get the hell off their couch, paint and run and start living again. Jimmy and Chaim said they were sure that between running and painting I could probably earn enough to squeak by, even without my parents' money. So, I am skipping grad school, at least for now, and giving it a go. It was the only thing that felt right."

Sophie stopped talking. The morning was growing increasingly hot, and they were beginning their ascent of the last major hill, a mile-long slog up a ten-percent grade that climbed from the dam, with its views both of town and the lake, across which they had just sped, to the top of the next redrock ridge. The climb—a monster the locals had dubbed "The Dam(n) Hill"—required all of the runners' focus and made talking impossible. They toiled on, the silence broken only by the trilling of meadowlarks, the distant chatter of prairie dogs, and their own ragged exhalations.

"So," she said, after they had crested the hill and begun the long, gradual descent back towards town, "I had been here to Fort Collins for a running camp during college, and remembered being mesmerized by the light, the scenery, the openness of the people, and one morning, I woke up and just knew. The next day I drove out from Boston. I took two weeks, just driving, running, staying places that were weird or pretty or interesting. I raced a high school hotshot around the parking lot of a truck stop in Pennsylvania—poor kid: testosterone poisoning—helped feed flood victims and about a million fucking mosquitoes at a Red Cross camp in Rainy River, Minnesota, and went to a rodeo in Buffalo, Wyoming. Chuckwagon races...who knew? Finally, I pulled into town, checked into a hotel, and just collapsed for forty-eight hours. That was eleven, no, twelve days ago."

She paused, placed a finger to the right side of her nose, blew a ladylike chunk of snot from her left nostril, and continued. "Then I met Finn here, and the rest is history." (This bit of expectorate bravado made something double-clutch in Finn's chest.)

For a moment, no one spoke, and Sophie, fearing she'd said too much, began to apologize. "Oh crap," she sputtered, "I'm sorry. Too much, too soon. I'm being inappropriate." (To herself: *Go ahead. asshole, scare them off with memoirs and pity parties...fuck!*) Embarrassingly, tears began to form, threatened to spill down her sunburned and run-flushed cheeks.

Finn was the first to jump into the breach.

"Oh God, no, Sophie...shoot, we were just thinking, just absorbing it all! It was a lot to take in all at once, and well, I'm honored—we're all honored—that you felt comfortable enough to talk to us. And besides, we asked for it. Hell, the first time Rex here ran with us, he told us how he went to fart on a run once and filled up his tights...now *that's* inappropriate!"

Rex threw a laser-guided elbow into Finn's solar plexus, then produced a sudden burst of speed. Finn responded with a burst of his own and a deft, two-handed tug at the back of Rex's shorts, leaving him bare-assed and suddenly shackled, shorts around his knees, a situation Rex seemed in no hurry to rectify. He held the pace with tiny strides, the very picture of nonchalance.

Sophie howled, the tension evaporated, and the foursome chattered like jays. The late-run cocktail of endorphins and cannabinoids had kicked in, pickling their brains to a happy, exhausted stupor. Sophie felt…what? Content? No, more than that. Here she was, hurling herself through the landscape at ten miles per hour, hot, tired, and a thousand miles from anyplace she had ever called home, and she was filled with a sensation that was entirely new. Flying along under the endless expanse of western sky, suffering and laughing with newfound friends, Sophie realized with something akin to shock, that she felt…*happy.*

* * *

AND THEN: SEATS in the shade, copious cold beverages, mountains of food, a cacophony of laughter, conversation and music, the shrieks of happy children, all in the manicured backyard of one Jon St. Clair, godlike in these parts: recently retired road runner *par excellence,* maybe the best American runner of the previous decade, still cocky and boyish in greying bangs, perhaps the only Yank with the *cojones,* week-in and week-out, to take it to the legions of Kenyans and Ethiopians who dominated the U.S. roads from sea to shining sea. Sure, he took his lumps, but then he dished them out too, and it made him both a tidy living and a living legend in a city and state where top runners were household names. St. Clair had been a bit unlucky in that he most excelled in the distances between the ten thousand meters—the longest Olympic track race—and the marathon, which was the only Olympic race run on the roads. Nobody dominated road races of twelve to twenty-five kilometers like St. Clair, and in ten-milers and half marathons, the first-place check almost always went home in his pocket. But the crown jewel, a spot on an Olympic team, had eluded him. No matter. Today he was a man at peace, king of his castle, comfy in a faded race T-shirt from the Lilac Bloomsday 12k, flipping burgers, brats, and chicken breasts, and telling war stories with equal dexterity.

Sophie Ringrose, in khaki shorts and faded race T-shirt of her own (Codfish Bowl Cross Country 1992) rehydrated with water and a sweating glass of iced tea, sat behind a plate piled high with all five food groups—and then some—in the shade of a small grove of transplanted aspen, eating like a stevedore and talking to a revolving group of runners, all of whom seemed thrilled to have her around. Food, fatigue, and all this instant acceptance left her in a daze of fuzzy contentment. Still, there was something missing...and here it came now.

"This seat taken?"

Without waiting for a reply, Finn slid with a sore groan onto the picnic table bench beside her, depositing before him a pair of plates loaded with cantaloupe, strawberries, chips and dip, and two massive cheeseburgers, with everything. Somehow, he had also managed to carry a bottle of water and a can of Dr. Pepper.

"Hungry?" Sophie nodded at his plate.

"Growing boy," he said, tearing into a burger, dripping ketchup down his chin, and emitting a moan of almost sexual pleasure.

"I bet you are," she said, maybe a bit more provocatively than she had intended, and as he raised his eyebrows, she dug into a mound of potato salad just to shut herself up.

She was saved by Rex and Rachel, who eased onto the bench across from them, then dove with only a nod for greeting into their own meals. Between mouthfuls, the foursome continued the conversation begun out on the road. Laughter was the order of the day, and by the time the shadows started to lengthen, blanketing them in mid-afternoon shade, Sophie, who had suffered with them under a brutal sun, who had laid bare her soul, and who had broken their bread, had become one of the family. Soon, Rex and Rachel, on some unseen signal, departed for home, leaving Sophie and Finn alone at the table. One by one, the other partygoers receded into the periphery, then vanished altogether from their consciousness. As they talked, their legs brushed now and then under the table, and eventually they left them there, touching from hip to ankle, and hot. She traced the quivering muscles of his quadriceps with a fingertip, looked into his eyes with a gaze full of question-marks, and they had to get out of there fast.

His house was closer than her hotel, and they drove there in his truck (she hoped he had stopped for red lights), the bucket seats and gearshift thwarting her desire to kiss him, to touch him in immodest fashion. Vaguely, she remembered him parking, holding her hand up the walk. He held his front door open for her. She entered. He followed her in, began to say something welcoming or gentlemanly or something. She covered his mouth with her palm: *no more talking*. She put her hand behind his head and pulled his mouth to hers. She kissed him hard, then led him down the hall, where she hoped his bedroom would be, like it was the most natural thing in the world.

* * *

AND IT WAS. Though her last two years were consumed by the grieving solitude following her parents' death, and her time at Tufts was spent mostly on the roads and trails and tracks of New England, or in a studio with her paints and brushes, leaving her with precious little time or energy for sexual adventuring, an erotic buzz had sizzled between she and Finn almost from the second they met, and it had made her brave. So here she was, leading an (incrementally) older, vastly (she was certain) more experienced man, a man she had really only just met, to bed like she had done this sort of thing a million times. She didn't think twice as she practically dragged him down the hall, worrying briefly that she might lead him into a closet, though given the rising level of her desperation, a closet would do just fine.

Halfway down the hall, Finn stopped, pulled her back to him, pressed her against the wall and kissed her again, giving her an inscrutable look. Then, for the first time since coming inside, he spoke.

"Uuhmmm..." he said.

She looked up at him, riveted by panic, a sudden sinking feeling. *Jesus, did he want to stop?*

"Uh, yeah, I was just thinking..." *(Oh,* ***hell*** *no,* she thought, *thinking is* ***not*** *what you should be doing right now.)* "We both just ran twenty miles, and I for one, am feeling a little gamey, so..."

Her knees almost buckled, such was her relief. She did not let him finish his sentence. "Where's the shower?"

Now he was leading her, to the end of the hallway and into the sunny bathroom, where with no further ado he pulled her T-shirt over her head and eased the tight running bra over her sweaty breasts and off, thumbs lingering only briefly over nipples, and pulled her shorts and panties to the floor. She stepped out of them and quickly returned the favor, removing his T-shirt and shorts with only a little nervous quivering, a slight struggle with waistband and cock. He turned on the water, tested it and stepped in first, then took her hand and helped her into the tub, and she found herself immediately pressed to the cool tile wall under the showerhead, warm water cascading over her head and down her body, as she caressed his back, clutched his ass, pulling him close. His hands were in her hair and he kissed her with a desperation of his own, like he needed to drink of her to survive. Then he pulled away, smiled at her devilishly, reaching for the rack on the wall behind him. Turning back to her, he held a bar of soap in one hand. The other he held behind his back, and said, with another in his repertoire of accents (Pakistani?), "It is time, now, for the...LOOFAH!" Which he produced from behind his back and brandished with glee.

And lord, could the man wield a loofah. He proceeded to soap and scour her into a frenzy—as if every nerve were not already on high alert—lathering and scrubbing, then kissing the spots he had just washed. This was brand new, this ecstasy of erotic exfoliation, and she gave in completely to the sensation of being washed, scoured, made ready. Her newborn skin came alive under the slick of soap, the firm insistence of his fingers and lips and tongue. And he was kissing her *everywhere,* the sensations wet and electric. When his lips brushed the hollow at the front of her hipbone, her run-weary legs shook, her knees nearly gave way, and she collapsed into a world of pure sensation, out of her mind, yet coherent in a brand-new way, acutely aware of every sensation being sent brainward. And then Finn, his own washing accomplished in a much more utilitarian manner, toweled her dry and took her to bed.

The sheets were unbelievably soft and cool against her skin, which was played over by jacaranda-perfumed breezes, the shadows of lightly billowing curtains, by Finn's fingertips, his lips, his teeth, and tongue. Sophie surrendered completely to sensation, opened herself to him in every sense of the word, gave herself over to instinct. She sacrificed thought on the altar of sensation; every synapse on fire with singing colors and eddies of electric breeze; undone by a tongue that traipsed and wandered, by fingers that played and probed and lingered over her flesh.

It was like music, and she wasn't sure if she was the player, the instrument, or the notes being played. She was all three, and all at once. She was a poem, a painting, a dance that unfolded to a twin drumbeat primal and primeval: a circling and a twining. She was half of an ancient beast conjured to life by firelight on cavern walls as low moans and gutturals echoed among shadows that snaked over the figures of wild things and long-dead gods. It was natural; animal, this *pas de deux,* and the lovers, athletes at home in their bodies, fell easily into taking their pleasure and giving pleasure in return.

Sophie's conscious self, her inexperienced self-consciousness, had been drowned in a perfect storm of emotion that had devoured all thought. Unapologetically, she took what she wanted, gave orders and directives, then happily submitted to Finn's own fierce want. He was gentle and he was wild; he led and allowed himself to be led. *More,* she cried, and more he gave; and when, overcome by it all, she lay sobbing, he held her until her fires flared again and she urged and begged, demanded and pleaded. Once patient, she was suddenly insatiable. She clawed his back, nearly drawing blood. She grasped and pulled and engulfed, drawing him toward her center. She raged and thrashed and bit, whimpered and cried out and sang. And he joined her in song.

They were motes in a maelstrom, and they tumbled at the mercy of a wind of their own making—now hot and raging, now gentle and meandering—and as afternoon turned to evening and a cooling breeze blew in through the lindens, finally, she was satisfied. A feeling of fullness and languor came over her; her limbs were as filled with sand, her head impossibly heavy upon the pillow. She had run, she had eaten, and she had loved. And now, as the nightbirds began to sing and the streetlights came on down the block, she curled tightly into her new lover, and sated, she slept.

* * *

SHE AWOKE TO the sounds of children playing in backyards, silently rejoiced as they ignored their parents' calls to come inside, thrilled as they wrung every minute of play from the too-short season, the syncopated percussion of their basketballs echoing from floodlit driveways, the wheels of their skateboards rumbling, their sneakers slapping and skidding on concrete, their shouts and bursts of laughter ringing through the air from all around. The window was open also to the smells of flowers and barbecue smoke, to moonlight and streetlight and the transient illumination of headlight beams. And as she awakened more fully, she became attuned to the rhythm of Finn's breathing, slow and steady in sleep. She savored the new tenderness of her feelings for him, just as she savored the tenderness—soreness even—of all the parts of her body so unused to the kind of electric friction they had just undergone. She thought of how, as athletes, they were so aware, so comfortable with their own bodies, and how, with the right person, that comfort could so easily transfer itself to the body of another. She thought also of how, as a runner, the best times were often those spent on the thin line between pleasure and pain, in the pleasure *of* pain, experimenting with new dimensions of sensation. Now she knew it was also that way with a lover.

This had happened fast, had begun to happen, she supposed, when he had handed her that water bottle at the track. This was something different for her, for both of them, she suspected. This was something *big*. Her heart began to beat fast, like in the seconds right before the gun went off to start a race, though it wasn't adrenaline fear that caused this elevated heartrate—well, not entirely—but rather anticipation of what this all meant, of what would come next. Finn sighed in his sleep, *(Jesus! somehow)* hard again next to her, and as she snuggled back against him, easing him once again inside her, the pain was most pleasurable indeed.

* * *

AFTER MIDNIGHT, THEY woke again, to a silence dotted with crickets, birdsong, the odd creakings of his old Craftsman bungalow. A car eased down the street, trailing fragments of Latin jazz. Far off, a train whistle keened. They lay silently for a while, holding hands and listening to midnight's starlit sonata. Sophie realized she was ravenous, the previous afternoon's feast long burned away by subsequent exertions. Her stomach rumbled, breaking their reverie.

"I know!" Finn said. "Let's get you something to eat."

He handed her a pair of faded blue boxers and an old T-shirt with Gaunt is Beautiful printed on it. The clothes smelled of the dryer and cedar shavings. He slid into yellow and blue tartan boxers, a beaten Ramones tee, then they padded to the kitchen, where she sat at the table, one leg tucked under her, as he rummaged through the refrigerator, made a salad of tomatoes, mixed greens and cucumbers. He sliced hunks from a loaf of bread and a wheel of Vermont cheddar, collected a pair of plums from the crisper, a pitcher of sweet sun tea, then joined her at the table, where for a while they ate, greedily and without talking. The air turned cool here after dark, no matter how hot the previous day, and the slight chill of the breeze ghosting the kitchen curtains felt good against her flushed face, arms, and legs. As their initial, desperate hunger was satisfied, they settled into a sleepy rhythm of eating (somehow, half a chocolate cake arrived and disappeared) and talking, easily and of nothing of great import, unself-conscious after what had transpired earlier. After they had eaten and talked themselves into an exhausted fog, he piled the dishes in the sink, took her hand, and they stumbled back to bed, where they fell, immediately and entwined, into a deep and dreamless sleep.

* * *

AND THEN SHE was awake, instantly invigorated by sunshine and subwoofed Wu-Tang Clan from the kid next door's classic Camaro, the clatter and basso profundo of a garbage truck trundling up the alley, the cooing of a mourning dove, a quick whiff of bacon on the breeze. After waking Finn for a sweet, slow reprise of the previous evening's activities, Sophie yawned, stretched extravagantly, and rose, naked, rumpled and refreshed. She rummaged through Finn's dresser, found a pair of worn plaid Bermuda shorts, slid into them, cinching them tight with one of his belts, then checking herself in the mirror on the back of his door. *Hmmm, not too bad.* She then pulled on the Gaunt is Beautiful shirt. Finn lay gaping in happy awe. From the bathroom, she called to him, helping herself to an extra toothbrush, "C'mon slugabed, get some clothes on, I have something to show you. Oh, and bring your car keys."

Finn, still suspended in a web of post-coital, newly-awakened stupor, struggled to switch gears, to match her bright, *up-and-at-'em*-ness.

Slugabed?

She laughed as he yawned, ran his fingers through his sleep-mussed hair, and rose with a creaky groan. "Old age is a bitch, dude…right?" She tossed him his Ramones shirt and flounced back into the bathroom for a pee and to figure out what the hell to do about her hair.

He sighed and struggled into his clothes, and not trusting himself to drive before his first cup of tea, surrendered the keys to his truck to a miraculously groomed and whistling Sophie, her ponytail protruding from the back of one of his many baseball caps, then stumbled after her out the door and down the walk, muttering loudly enough for her to hear, "No way am I going to keep up with her this morning."

"Buck up, Boyo," she chided, "caffeine awaits." And sure enough, a stop by Rocky Mountain Bagels for a huge mug of English Breakfast with cream and sugar, a gigantic Americano for her (*Espresso, oh yes, oh yes, oh yes,* she moaned), and huge blueberry bagels with cream cheese brightened his outlook considerably.

A few minutes later, they were flying up Rist Canyon, dashing through early morning shade cast by rock walls and dense stands of conifers, then spilling out into patches of astringent sunlight. The interplay of shadow and light, the alternating sensations of warm sun and cool breeze through the open windows, the flush of new love, filled her blood like a drug as she negotiated the narrow road's curves, an intoxicant so pure she felt not quite of this world. She had to concentrate hard just to keep the dusty black pickup on the road.

She could not have known how familiar this drive was to him, how many of his long runs began or ended or passed along this stretch of road, how many times he had ground up or sprinted down the canyon. And he did not tell her, not wanting to dilute in the slightest the excitement of her surprise. After twenty minutes, they passed the old, white country schoolhouse where he and his crew parked almost every Sunday, and from where they began their long out-and-backs on Flowers Road. Flowers was a dirt ranch track that turned into a rocky and rutted fire road extending some fifty miles into the mountains, and which was his favorite place to run.

After a rutted, bouncy quarter mile, she stopped, had him climb from the pickup and unhook an old wire and pole gate. A "SOLD" sticker was plastered to the red and white for sale sign that someone had nailed to a fencepost. After Sophie pulled through the gate, he looped the wire back to the post and trotted back to the truck, whereupon she accelerated away, laughing, leaving him quite literally in her dust. He coughed, shook his head—*so this is how it's going to be*—and trotted after her down the gravel drive to where she had parked in front of a weathered barn he had run past dozens of times. Surrounding the barn, once a traditional red, but now faded to a dusty rose, were piles of lumber and other building materials. A contractor's sign stood, newly planted next to the structure.

He let out a low whistle of appreciation.

"This is yours?"

"Lock, stock, and cattle trough," she said, arms wide. "Like it?"

He spun around in a slow circle, seeing in a new light a scene he had witnessed a hundred times before. "You've been here, what, two weeks, and already…wow."

"Yep, it's going to be my studio. C'mon in!"

She took out a key, unlocked a new padlock, rolled back the huge, wheeled barn door, watching the look on his face as they stepped into the shadowy, noticeably cooler air inside the old structure. Beams shone through the high windows, animating air dense with dust and nearly microscopic fragments of old hay. "I decided to spend some of the insurance money"—her breath caught, though she recovered quickly— "get set up to paint for real. I found an architect, and a contractor who can help me repurpose this place based on a description and some photos of de Kooning's studio in the Hamptons: lots of space and ventilation, skylights everywhere, with shades to maximize and control light, storage for materials; room to stretch canvasses...yahoo! And the hayloft is huge," she said, pointing toward an indeed gigantic loft, mostly shrouded in gloom, "so that will be living space. With a little luck, I'll have it plumbed and insulated and ready to inhabit before the snow flies."

She was smiling giddily, actually shaking a little with excitement. And she could see it beginning to dawn on him just how serious she was about her painting. She had not shown him any of her work yet, and they hadn't talked about it much during the few conversations they'd had in the few days since they had met. She didn't want to explain it to him, said he would just have to wait and see. She'd had some things shipped from Boston, and even as they spoke, the paintings were wending their way westward in climate-controlled comfort.

"Here," she said, "a little taste."

She grabbed an open sketchbook from atop a stack of lumber, handed it to him. He took it from her and stepped over to the doorway where there was enough light to see what was on the big, heavy pages. She knew she had given him no clue what to expect from her work, and knew that whatever it was he was imagining, it was probably not this. She could almost see the cogs in his mind turn as he wrestled the shapes on the page into something he could pin words to.

Finn

IT WAS A charcoal drawing, abstract, with a tall, reed-like shape soaring up the right side of the page, arrow-straight and growing slightly thinner as it approached the top. As the shape neared its zenith, the skinny monolith, whatever it was, without warning veered down and toward the eye of the viewer. Then it zig-zagged in uneven intervals back toward the top of the page, where it grew what looked to Finn like spines, and then—the only word he could think of was *exploded*—into fragments and shards that seemed an anarchy of motion in contrast to the stately and generally upward progress of the original slender structure. Some of these fragments were larger, akin to rocks and birds and whirligigs. Some were small and mote-like, and these bits swirled and cascaded, some of them up, like sparks on a gust, some floating down and away like dandelion fluff from the tall, misshapen wand. Of the bigger shapes, the flatter ones seemed to drift or glide away as if on an unseen breeze, while the denser ones appeared to plummet, if they were blocky or spherical, or hurl away like projectiles if they were thinner, more jagged, pointier. The objects became more diffuse as he followed them down the left-hand side of the page, the drawing leading his eye in a counterclockwise ellipse, until about halfway down the page the smaller bits became a sort of mist, then disappeared completely, leaving only empty space.

Near the very bottom, the page again became littered with shapes of all sizes, the objects covering what he could think of nothing else to call but the ground. The fragments, lying singularly or in little piles, were scattered from what his mind was now resolving to be the rear of the picture (smaller, less distinct shapes), to the foreground (bigger, more distinct, though still indecipherable abstractions). Though just a preliminary sketch, there was a lot going on, and clearly Sophie knew how to engage and occupy a viewer's eye. To render this vision in paint would be an ambitious project, but the drawing left little doubt that she was capable.

"I," he started, then stopped, trying to figure out exactly how to voice what he was thinking and feeling. He had expected her to be good—I mean, who plans an elaborate and expensive studio if they have no talent, right? But he hadn't expected *this.*

Finn had spent a lot of time in art museums growing up. His parents adored painting and sculpture, so no trip to New York ended without an excursion to MoMA or the Met, the Whitney or the Guggenheim, not to mention shows at the Tibor de Nagy, or any number of other galleries scattered throughout the city. He had visited the Tate Modern and the Louvre, while a couple of trips to Barcelona were orgies of art: the Picasso and Miro museums, El Museu Nacional d'Art de Catalunya with its sweeping collection of Catalan and Romanesque pieces, the Barcelona Museum of Contemporary Art, Arts Santa Monica in the Rambles. His mind was a blur still whenever he thought about it. He had visited museums and galleries on his own in cities as far-flung as Milwaukee, Minneapolis, Denver, and Santa Fe; the Getty in LA. The walls of the house he had grown up in were festooned with the works of his parents' accomplished friends, many of whom were Hamden College faculty. And Giz, of course, with one Ph.D. in art history and another in biochemistry, was a world-class art authenticator, and had browbeaten Finn toward even greater understanding. So the thing is, Finn knew from good, and he could see that the drawing he was looking at was the real deal.

She watched him patiently, plainly interested in what he was going to say, but very obviously needing no validation from him whatsoever. Her confidence caused a weird, involuntary shot of happy adrenaline to shoot through him. He shuddered, then finally, he spoke.

"Jesus, Sophie…I mean, wow." He exhaled, then shrugged.

Her expectant and serious gaze dissolved into a merry smile. Her eyes flashed. "My, my, my," she laughed. "The poet is at a loss for words. I will take that as a compliment."

"Oh, it is. It most definitely is." For a moment, a charged silence hung in the air, suspended with the dust motes and hay. "Can you…can you tell me about this?"

"Sure," she said, "but first, look at the back of the page, then go look out the window. That one there." She pointed to a large, paned window on one side of the barn to his right as he faced out the barn door, on a wall perpendicular to the front of the cavernous structure.

On the back of the drawing was written, *Lightning Strikes Twice; Study #3.* Finn nodded, walked to the window, and gazed out into the dazzling sunshine. As his eyes grew accustomed to the glare, he was greeted with a view of a late morning clearing, familiar from so many runs, all tawny in brown and gold, the various grasses looking brittle in the dry July heat. The clearing ended about a hundred meters from the barn, where the ground tilted sharply upward, rising to become the first of an endless series of rocky, conifer-covered ridges. He gazed out the window toward the ridge, and then his breath caught. He looked down at the sketch pad, then back out the window. Then he let out a low whistle.

"My God, Sophie, this is…it's…" he shrugged, once again without words. In the middle of the grassy expanse, about halfway between the barn and the ridge, stood a solitary lodgepole pine, a hundred years old and maybe a hundred feet tall. It rose, branchless as a telephone pole for nearly eighty of those feet, at which point there was a charred gash, which ran a few feet down the tree, before circling around behind and out of view. Sections of trunk denuded of bark were tattooed with Lichtenberg figures, and just above where the bolt had struck, the tree grew briefly down and toward the barn, then turned upward again, zig-zagging away and eventually resuming it's natural, straight-for-the-heavens pose. Just above the downward-jutting section, the tree began to send out branches in all angles, limbs thick with needles that carpeted the ground below and lying in piles among grasses, cactus, rocks, and desiccated horse droppings. Finn looked back at the drawing. The structure on the page was certainly the lodgepole, or some incarnation thereof, as seen from this very spot. He looked at the title and immediately grasped it: *Lightning Strikes Twice.* The tree had been struck by lightning, several years ago from the looks of it, the bottom three fourths losing its branches, the tree seemingly dead, but above the strike, the tree recoiled, grew downwards, then veered this way and that, but skyward, as full and alive as a lodgepole pine can get. *Lightning Strikes Twice*: one strike from above at the speed of light, the other rising in slow, green triumph from the ashes of the first.

"Wow," he said. "This is way beyond amazing. So you took this tree, and made it abstract, right? You're catching it simultaneously at the moment of being struck—I take it the air is full of stuff being blasted from the tree—and after the strike, after it has grown beyond the impact point. And the ground is littered with things that seem to have been there awhile. It's like the tree is in a perpetual state of being struck. Or something." He was only speculating, and since she was listening happily along, he sensed that this was what she wanted him to do.

"Wow, yourself," she said. "You have done this before. And you're close. This drawing, and it will be my first painting done in Colorado, is of what the tree is *thinking*. Or maybe dreaming." She stopped speaking for a moment, letting him take this in. "I try to imagine *things* as sentient beings, engaging with the world both intellectually and intuitively, but unable to communicate. I then use the basic shape of the thing as both door and roadmap into how this inanimate object might be reacting emotionally to the world, then try to capture that thought or emotion on canvas." She paused, shrugged. "And that, in a nutshell, is what I do." Then she added, "This tree, I think, would spend a lot of time pondering lightning. And lightning, my friend, can do some weird-ass shit. I've read about it." And then, with a purr, "Speaking of getting hit by lightning, what do you say we consecrate this joint?"

Which sounded like a fabulous idea.

Beannie

HE MAY BE a nut, but he's *my* nut. You fuck with Finn, I fuck with you...got that? Good. Anyway, let me tell you about Finn and Sophie.

So he's in Colorado, right? Been there for three or four years, and it's like he's some sort of fucking strawberry plant or something: sending off shoots and runners into every part of that town: the university, the writing community, the running community...hell, even the homeless transvestite wino community, for all I know. And obviously the soil's good, 'cuz he's bearing fruit like a motherfucker: finished the graduate degree, teaching a few courses at the U, publishing poems in journals left and right, running a hundred twenty fucking miles a week and making U.S. teams, flying off to races in Morocco, Belgium...fucking *Andorra,* for fuck's sake. He's making a little dough from teaching, a little better than that on the running circuit, still refusing to touch the trust fund money his dad left him, living the fucking life of Riley. He's got a million fucking friends, dames throwing themselves at his junk like always (more about that in a minute), three hundred-plus days of sunshine a year, a nice mountain bike, car that starts, soft trails to run on, an absolutely bitchin' record collection, more cheap, good restaurants than you can believe—real heaven on Earth shit, right?

But is our hero happy?

Fucking-A right, he's happy! Damn straight, he's happy; I mean, what do you think he is, fucking stupid?

But still. I mean hey, our boy's a bright one, right? He's read his Greeks, his Bible; he's read his Shakespeare. He knows that the lucky are the fuckpuppets of the gods—that you live the good life, get complacent, and...***BAM!***...they kill your flocks, maim your children, drop a plague in your pants, make your daughters conspire against you, sons steal your best pair of Nikes. The celestial Kick Me sign is super-glued to your back and you're taking it up the ass and the hits just keep on coming. Today's Ryan Gosling is tomorrow's Job, and who knows, maybe you're the next one the sadistic Motherfucker has His eye on. Finn is perfectly aware that neighbors are busy butchering one another in Rwanda and Bosnia, that moron is killing moron in defense of the One True Church all over the place, that *mere anarchy is loosed* on more of the world than not, and not for one fucking moment does he think it cannot happen here.

So let's just say he has made a shaky truce with his good fortune. As he begins every run, he says a big thank-you to whatever forces have mostly kept the bloody world from his doorstep. He writes checks almost every week to Greenpeace, the women's shelter, Save the Fucking Pomegranates, or some such. He gives change to every last panhandler, says what they do with the fucking money is outside the sphere of his responsibility. And he just plain fucking *talks* to people. I mean random fucking people on the street. I shit you not, he'll stop in the middle of a run, ask some exhausted, hung-over chick holding a STOP/SLOW sign for a road crew how drivers are treating her. He gets away with this shit. I'd get my ass kicked if I tried. He calls his mom every week, me and Giz more often than that. He's fucking Chauncey Gardener with grey matter, for fuck's sake, just walkin' around being nice and shit.

And he gives his poems to the world. Sure, he submits them to magazines, he builds a manuscript, suffers the slings and arrows of the career artist, but he also mails them to friends, reads them to dinner guests, hands them to students to illustrate some point he is making in class. He emails them to various and sundry, leaves them lying around rooms—his own and others'—like random flakes of skin. He's like the Johnny Appleseed or fucking Easter

Bunny of poetry, leaving at its feet the only gift he can present to the world. It's his own little stay against the creeping anarchy, the icky rewards of hubris, the horrible fate he believes is *this close* to being every person's destiny.

So yadda, fucking yadda... *What about Sophie?* you say. *What about this great, star-crossed American love story?* Cool your fucking jets, dude, I'm getting there.

Okay, let's backtrack a bit, follow the blazing arc of Finn's love life from point A to point Sophie. Dig, if you will, this picture: a sweet fifteen-year-old kid: kinda skinny, kinda rangy, nascent musculature, tanned from running around the countryside all summer. Give the kid wild, sun-streaked brown locks, piercing blue eyes and a shy, goofy smile. Make him smart; give him about a million books he's probably too young to read but have him read them anyway. Over-endow him with empathy; give him nearly endless patience for the stories of others; give him the hunch that maybe he's been blessed, that maybe he deserves this blessing no more than any other kid. And while you're at it, give him the terrifying new libido of any fifteen-year-old, the relentless sexual curiosity. Give him appetite, yes, but also—god help him—a sense of the soulmate, of some goddess who will bestow her gifts, physical and otherwise, upon him forever and always. And then, what the fuck, for parents, give this kid beloved professors at a remote liberal arts college whose student body is about eighty-percent female.

Thus is an innocent loosed among a veritable harem of bored, rich, city babes, all stranded in fucking *Benandjerryville*, and looking for distraction, and let me tell you, the daughters of privilege are kind to our boy.

* * *

THE FIRST TIME he gets laid it's in triplicate. I shit you not. Three young fugitives from the Upper East Side, students in

Mom's 20th Century European Writers class, beauties, one and all, hanging out at the homestead, yakking about Thomas Mann, eating mom's brownies and shit, and then, when Mom and Dad head into town, our *trois femmes riches* wander out to the barn and find—what have we here?—young Finnegan McGuinn, barefoot and clad in naught but cutoff Levi's, all tanned and leanly muscled, reading something by Updike on a blanket in the hayloft, played upon by late afternoon sunbeams, motes hovering about his tawny head. It's like something by Lawrence. The autumn air is warm and heady with the smell of hay and apples, and all at once, our young literature students have an epiphany: they feel all predatory and tender and shit; glances are exchanged, and things progress fast from, *Hiya, Finn, whatcha' reading,* to, *here, Finn, put your hand here, tongue here, dick here. Hey Finn, do you like it when I do this?*

Four hours later, the girls drive off, and Finn staggers into the darkened house, covered like a glazed donut in the drying juices of his tutors, sore and dazed, and yes, smiling that goofy smile. He's pretty sure this doesn't happen to all the boys. He hopes like hell it will happen to him again. He showers, falls quickly asleep, dreams of tigers and Teddy bears. He awakens a new man. And to this day, the merest mention of Rabbit Angstrom gives him wood. Go ahead, ask him.

* * *

AND THAT'S PRETTY much the story of his teenage life. The girls talk; interest is piqued; other lonely, horny college women come around, talk literature with his mom, ceramics or particle physics with his dad. They help his mom *put up preserves,* for fuck's sake. Eventually, inevitably, they lure Finn to the barn, their dorm room, a convenient car, somewhere to continue his education. He refuses their drugs, but almost never their sex, and under this careful tutelage he becomes quite proficient at *los Artes de Amor,* and by the time he's a junior in high school, the student has become the teacher. And then, the age-gap narrowed, Finn, given his proclivity for romance, his belief in true love, eventually tires of this smorgasbord and hungers for something a little more nutritious. Finn wants something a little deeper—wants love everlasting, greedy fucker—and senses it's not coming from the bevy of beauties temporarily shipwrecked on his shores. But he is a boy, after all, and continues to enjoy their largesse, happily fucking his way through the cream of the eastern seaboard's arty debutantes as he waits to set sail on his own post-graduation voyage toward eternal love.

As Finn's constant sidekick and gal-pal, some of this embarrassment of sexual riches eventually spills over onto me. I knew I liked girls pretty early on, and unlike my still blissfully ignorant classmates, Finn's worldly babes pretty much honed-in on this fact right away. Soon enough, I found myself being led by the, um, hand into a world of discovery way more exciting than the natural history museum. By the time these angels were done with me, I was pretty confident in my burgeoning sexuality, and more or less immune to the various reactions of my no longer oblivious peers. I was soon strutting my lesbo stuff and absolutely daring anyfuckingbody to say boo about it. Nobody did, not to my face, anyway. Anyhow, until we were seniors, although much more experienced than any of our peers, neither Finn nor I had ever slept with someone our own age.

Until I seduced him.

Sensitive twit that he was, convincing Finn to fuck me was harder than you might think. We were in his room after track practice, enjoying that post-run buzz, a spaced-out exhaustion at odds with our textbooks, more or less abandoned on the desk, a bunch of CDs (Cowboy Junkies, Peter Murphy, Sinead O'Connor, R.E.M.) soundtracking the moment nicely, when I just spit it out: "Finn, I think we should have sex, right here, right now."

He was clearly a bit stunned, though he hid it pretty well, retorting in his best queenly voice, "That sounds lovely darling, really, but one of us is homosexual, remember?"

"Only one of us?" I answered, eyebrows arching archly.

"Fuck you," says he.

"Now you're starting to get the idea."

My heart was a jackrabbit, fucking threatening to leap from my chest. I was scared shitless. The idea of sleeping with Finn had been fomenting for a while, but suddenly the time seemed nigh. I was at cliff's edge and wanted nothing more than to jump. I was very comfortable already with my sexuality, knew it was women for me, then and forever, but I did want to know, just once, what it felt like with a guy. And there was only one guy on the planet I could imagine doing the job.

Finn was my best friend. We'd been like milk and fucking cookies for thirteen years, seen each other sunburned, covered with measles, puking drunk, crying over sappy movies and sports losses. We'd run endless miles together, perpetuated minor acts of civil disobedience, memorized Monty Python skits, gorged on junk food—fought and made up and never questioned that the other's presence was permanent. In some ways, Finn was almost like a girl. He felt stuff; he listened; he cried…he was almost embarrassing sometimes, the fucking sap. He was a confidante and a collaborator, a rough and tumble outdoorsy guy to match my tomboy self, but as sensitive as any female I have known, before or since. So, not a real surprise that he could sort of turn me on sometimes. Plus a couple of our mutual playmates told me I simply had to do him before I embarked upon my life of lesbianism.

I'm not freaking kidding you, one of them said, coming up for air, *if you're going to screw one guy on the planet, it's got to be him. He's got skills that will make you scream. Plus, he already loves you, so what the hell?* Then (speaking of skills to make me scream), back down she went, and for the moment, Finn (not to mention all other life on the planet) ceased to exist. But the seed had been planted.

Finn though, was reticent. He was worried that sex would somehow hurt our relationship, alter the friendship in some fatal matter. He told me he didn't want to lose me. His lower lip actually started to quiver, the fucking baby. So I just took the bull by the balls, grabbed two fistfuls of that gorgeous hair, and pulled those trembling lips to my own, kissing that motherfucker as hard as I could. He responded just about like you'd expect. I pushed him away, took off my t-shirt and jeans while he gaped, and crawled into his bed. He'd seen me naked about a million times over the years, but never like this. I was hot and wet, and I told him so.

"This is your only chance, amigo. Get those clothes off and get over here."

And he did, pronto.

His parents were out of town for the weekend, and mine didn't give a shit what I did, so we spent the next two days in bed (not to mention on the floor, his dad's recliner, in the bathtub, the hammock in his backyard, and on the washing machine), and by Sunday night when his mom and dad came back from San Francisco, bearing gifts and none the wiser, Finn and I had pretty much done everything a man and a woman can do with—or to—one another. We found a sweet sexual rhythm to that Peter Murphy album, and to this day I get a little flushed when I hear Murphy sing "Sweetest Drop." We fucked like bunnies: hard and fast, slow and gentle, front, back, and sideways. It was wonderful, it was amazing, and it was a one-time thing. The first and last time I was with a man. And Finn was right, it did change us. It made us even closer than before. Turns out we knew each other in a new, more complete way. True, we were a bit weird around one another for a few days, but in the end, it became just one more thing we had experienced together, albeit a sweeter, more intimate thing, a thing we would carry inside us, never telling anyone.

And then it is off to college: me to Wesleyan, Finn to Middlebury. Giz, of course, goes to Harvard. We still see lots of one another, are inseparable over winter and summer breaks. Giz, our resident genius, discovers a bizarro-world of art history and biochemistry. I find Hunter S. Thompson, Joan Didion, and a girl with a used Fender Stratocaster and hankering for redheads. Finn falls for O'Hara, Baudelaire, and a moderately famous visiting poet with a ken for jogging and younger men. Music chases competitive running from my life, though I tend to get out most days to keep me from jumping out of my skin. Gizmo gives up track and cross country after high school, but Finn decimates college competition just as easily as he had in high school, wins DIII national championships in cross country, indoor and outdoor track alike. When home in Hamden, we go on long runs, play Risk like dorks, compare love lives, drink many beers, and breathlessly expound on our passions *du jour*. Our letters to one another are excited, chatty, and a bit pretentious. Still, we feel the world to be our oyster, and we partake like we were famished. With one another as safety net, the three of us become fearless. We believe we can do anything. And mostly, we are right.

So anyway, I met Sophie when my band, Skirtchaser, opened for Concrete Blonde at Red Rocks. I formed the band with some dames from college—dykes all—and we became pretty much a fixture in punk and gay clubs around New England. Our appeal apparently transcended our sexuality, our repertoire broadened, and soon, mostly thanks to the density of college campuses in the Northeast, we had all the work we could handle. We graduated, kept the band together, and gave it a go. It was a perfect fit for us: overeducated gals with no real taste for a day job, and we could make just enough scratch to keep body and soul together pursuing our sundry passions. I began to write music criticism and pop-culture features for alternative weeklies, and occasionally *Rolling Stone, Spin,* or *Utne Reader,* while Lisette painted (pictures *and* houses), and Evie was a freelance mechanic (Swedish and German, thank you very much). So anyway, *Johnette fucking Napolitano* catches us at a festival gig in Providence, and asks if maybe we could open for Concrete Blonde at a few shows out west, and *viola,* I'm hanging with Finn and his new love after sound check on this crystal Colorado September day, the eponymous rocks rising all around us just as pretty as you please.

Okay, okay, keep your fucking pants on, and I'll get to the point. . .Sophie. So she's standing there with Finn, and they're like the fucking Bobbsey Twins or something: shorts and tans and running shoes, sharing a beer and a water and finishing each other's sentences, the whole fucking deal. She was a total hottie, in an artsy, elite-athlete kind of way. She had a small tattoo of the Roadrunner on her ribcage, just below her left breast—now *that* must have hurt like hell—exactly like the one on Finn's right calf. If these two weren't so perfectly fucking wonderful, I would have puked. Sophie was smart, knew her fucking music, too. We talked about Patti Smith. She said her dad had played a little guitar. She had actually seen us play a couple times around Boston, even remembered a couple of our songs. Then Lisette found out Sophie was a painter, and they spent about forever talking about de Kooning and Frankenthaler and shit. Needless to say, we were all about as smitten with this broad as Finn was.

It was pretty obvious to me that this, finally, was *The One.* And about fucking time, too. As I have already discussed *ad nauseum,* Finn had no trouble with the general female population. He was an expert fisherman, but the world was a catch-and-release stream. Chick after lovely, talented chick wriggled her way onto his, um. . .rod: smart, artistic, athletic, rich. . .a Baskin-Robbins 31 Flavors of femininity; a sexual smorgasbord of epic grandeur, and could our hero find love? No, it would seem, he could not. And it was not, he said, because he didn't want to. Remember, his head had been full of romantic claptrap for as long as I could recall, and after each member of this endless troupe of auditionees came up somehow wanting, Giz and I began to suspect that Finn secretly wanted to spend his miserable fucking life alone, in love with an ideal that mere womanflesh could not match. He liked them all, these women, no problem there. And he fucked a good many of them, to everyone's satisfaction. But something, some ineffable, known-only-to-Finn quality was lacking. Pixie-dust, he called it. These were great girls, mostly, and it often broke Finn's heart more than theirs when he inevitably broke it off, or when they did, realizing early that it was never going to happen. I liked the few I met (especially that lovable fucking psycho, Nikki, who doesn't really count, and besides, that's a story for another time).

So when, a few weeks before I went to Colorado, Finn called, all breathless, to tell me he had met a woman, well, forgive me if I was less than jumping for joy. Ho-hum, you know? But then, the plot thickens. Seems this one had more or less moved in...*after a week!* Damn, just like lesbians! Sophie was building some kind of live-in studio, and she was staying with him, just until it was finished. Yeah, right. They were running together, doing their art...shit, they had taken up residence in one another's skins.

Standing in that stunning mountain amphitheater, the sun anointing us with its happy photons, it was obvious to all—the band, the sound guys, *Johnette fucking Napolitano,* hell, the hawks wheeling overhead—that this one was over, game, set, and match. You wanna talk pixie-dust? Ten thousand Tinker Bells have screaming multiples all over this pair. They actually shed light; their freaking running shoes leave no footprints. Fucking pixie-dust out the ass.

Allow me one digression. Two winters before, one of the great hordes of Finn's not-quite-loves, Wendy, had fallen completely head over fucking heels and had gone off her nut when Finn ended it. She slit her perfect white wrists one night, and only a roommate's unexpected return home for clean undies kept her story from ending right there in a bathtub full of rose-colored water. Finn swore off dating for a long time after that, and when he did go out, he was shy, tentative, a shadow of his former self. If he made people want to die, well, fuck it. This was the Finn Sophie had stumbled across that day at the track. Who knows, maybe the whole Wendy episode altered something in the universe, allowed Sophie to happen at all.

Just after the girl had attempted suicide, Finn wrote a tortured stream-of-consciousness poem about it. He never meant it for publication, but when I saw it, I realized it was a perfect fit for some music I had written. Now, whenever Skirtchaser had a gig and Finn was in the vicinity, we'd ask him onstage to sing *Am I your girlfriend?*

He had done the song three or four times, and given the touchy nature of the subject matter (I always wondered if he was paying a penance by singing the song publicly), was comfortable enough onstage. Our boy is a ham, and his readings are not to be missed. He is a poet with the soul of a rock star, or a rock star with the soul of a poet, but tonight Sophie is in the audience, it's a major venue, with the bored, semi-hostile crowd itchily awaiting the headliner, and he's fucking terrified. So, being the sensitive sort, I do my best to calm him down.

"You're a big, fucking baby," I tell him, "Hitch-up your skirt, bitch, and sing the fucking song."

We toast with a couple bottles of Fat Tire, chugging, then smashing the bottles against the wall (I'm not a churlish rock star, but I play one on TV), then walk onto the stage. Finn stands in the wings, shaking, as we play a few songs, getting the too-mellow, mountain-drunk audience into the swing of things, then bring out our boy to stand alone under a single spotlight. Laser-eyed and intense, he is not fucking shaking anymore.

The song begins with just drums and bass, a little atmospheric guitar noise from me, and then Finn reciting the first section of the poem, just as he wrote it. And as always, the poem takes him over, transforms him. The goofy, easygoing runner becomes something else—a gaunt figure filled with a quiet, desperate power, someone able to grab this crowd by the throat. He oozes both magnetism and despair: the despair of a lover driven to suicide, of the lover who did the driving. He has the mojo, our boy, and as the music swirls and grows around him, he begins to recite:

Am I your girlfriend? Why can't I
be your girlfriend? Why can't I be...

And the crowd is into it already, curious, hooting just like in the lesbian bars when some fucking *dude* asks that question, pulled in by their own curiosity and Finn's weird charisma. And maybe because Sophie is in the first row, maybe because he needs to spill his guts (though of course, she knows), who knows the fuck why, but Finn is fucking *on*. And everyone on that mountain knows it.

...your headshot, your Hottentot?
your flip-flop, your mountaintop,

tobogganing toward catastrophe,
heartbeaten, soulsucked, mindfucked
into some sweet sad surrender?

And then Lisette and I bust loose with a layered wail, a wall of guitar noise, and Finn stops reciting, begins to sing, to scream, actually, with a voice that sounds a little like Robert Plant, while cavorting like Mick in an antic dance, savage in its remorse and despair. The song is short, but wicked intense, and as it ends, Evie and Lisette construct a bridge of drums and base as I slide over to the piano, and we slow it down, segue into Joe Jackson's "It's

Different for Girls." I point at Finn, then the spot on stage where he stands—*you've got one more, buster*—grinning at the memory of him joining us on stage jaw agape, just as it is right now, when we played at Middlebury in those long-gone college days, staying on the theme, but lightening up on the tone, if only a little.

What the hell is wrong with you tonight?
I can't seem to do or say the right thing.
Wanted to be sure you're feeling right
Wanted to be sure we want the same thing.

She said, I can't believe it.
You can't possibly mean it.
Don't we all want the same thing?
Don't we?

Well, who said anything about love?

No, not love she said
Don't you know that it's different for girls?
(Don't give me love)
No, not love she said
Don't you know that it's different for girls?
You're all the same.

And when it's over, Finn waves to the crowd with a wan smile and walks offstage. And then the band and I crank it back up and blow those motherfuckers away. Top that, *Johnette fucking Napolitano.*

Sophie

SOPHIE SITS IN a puddle of yellow light, legs curled beneath her in the worn leather easy chair across the room from the bed where Finn lies sleeping. The chiaroscuro of him lying just beyond the halo's reach—his body expanding toward the light then retreating slightly as the bellows of his lungs do their work, his runner's heart drumming its slow tempo with a beat so strong it moves the curtains, the occasional tremor of a thigh muscle spasming beneath the sheet—all of this is just visible from where she sits sketching him. The slight scratch of her charcoal pencil plays a tune to accompany the beating of his heart, his barely audible breathing, theme music to the composition beginning to emerge from the page.

She soundtracks and recreates him in that not quite corporeal realm that exists between the glow of a lamp and a white wall's ability to catch and reflect the lamp's pale illumination. This play of light and shadow, these tiny breaths and twitches, these shudders that in such stillness grow to a sort of grandeur, give his figure an in-between quality. Both *this* and *that:* both of this world and yet lost in some hidden one. This hypnagogia is her kingdom, the country where she lives and works best. It is where the magic happens. Her medium is as much the viscous aspic of space as it is paint or canvas, pencil or paper. All is caught, like a fly in amber, in the hemisphere between waking and sleeping, darkness and light. Her job is simply to notice, then capture as best she can, given the tools at her disposal. She whistles a little as she works, a snippet of Skirtchaser's "Pincushion Heart."

She shifts a bit in her seat, uncoils her legs from beneath her and stretches them slowly into the air, pointing her toes at her sleeping lover. She holds the pose for a moment, and as her leg muscles begin to loosen, does a few scissors and spread-eagles, then stands, bends at the waist, and places her palms flat on the floor. She straightens—too swiftly; a head-rush engulfs her—sways as if a sea for just a moment, dizzied and breathing deeply, before rolling each shoulder slowly forwards and back, her neck clockwise then counterclockwise. She takes a long pull from her water bottle, yawns luxuriantly, and plops back into her seat, once again taking up pencil and pad. She has more or less colonized the big, beaten, and oh-so-comfy chair since her arrival a little more than a month ago. It delights her to no end when Finn refers to it as "her" chair.

The events of earlier that evening have crept in unbidden, begun to haunt the picture, to emerge like a palimpsest from beneath the sleeping figure on the page. How could they not? Watching the man with whom she is beginning to fall seriously in love perform on stage, seeing him turn into someone she does not recognize, if even for just a few moments, to watch him as he is claimed by—to share him with—10,000 people in one of the world's great concert venues, has seriously freaked her out. She is both thrilled and disconcerted at this glimpse of him she has not seen before, and she uses these feelings as fuel to tease what lies hidden out into the light. Entranced, inspired by her own burgeoning vision, she rides this night-breaking wave until the curtains begin to blush fuchsia, and she finds herself completely spent, on the beach of morning. Putting pencil and pad aside, she quietly crosses the room and slips beneath the sheet next to the sleeping Finn. Sleep claims her too, instantly, though her mind continues to make shapes and figures that whirl and dance in her dreams.

* * *

CAFFEINE MIRACLES SUBDUE the ghosts of cartoon dreams, drown headfuls of bees, allow uneasy truces with the sun. *This is not so bad,* Sophie convinces herself behind wraparound running shades, loping along in silence half a stride behind the annoyingly chipper Finn and Beannie, embalmed in a not completely unpleasant fog of fatigue. After a scant four hours of slumber subsequent to her midnight drawing marathon, she had prepared herself for all kinds of horrors as her body fought the relentless hills and lack of sleep. But happily, her fitness and generally sound sleep habits, along with a huge mug of strong coffee, seem to be sparing her the worst. The sun is hot against her skin, but the September air at this altitude has an undertone, a bite of cool autumn that invigorates, and soon her fatigue evaporates and wafts away, the heaviness in her legs fades, and she finds herself nimble as ever, dancing over the rocks of the more technical sections of Flowers Road as it climbs the ridges, burrowing deeper into the Colorado mountains. They run through the fragrant depths of groves of pine and aspen, graced with shadows that whisper swiftly over their moving bodies like a silent song. They crest a climb and are rewarded with a brief stretch of rockless, gentle downhill. The ground is mottled with leafshade and the shapes of swiftly scudding clouds, and a wisp of a favorite poem, Gerard Manley Hopkins' "Pied Beauty," moves just as swiftly through her head: *Glory be to God for dappled things—/ For skies as couple-colour as a brinded cow;/ For rose-moles all in stipple upon trout that swim;/ Fresh-firecoal chestnut-falls; finches' wings;/ Landscape plotted and pieced—fold, fallow and plough*...she smiles to herself, delighted that she and the long-dead priest and poet look at the world in the same way, that she can have these private conversations with him in verse or paint or dust.

Beannie calls out, breaking her reverie.

"Jesus, it's beautiful here," she gasps as the old logging road begins to grind its way up the next ridge, "but would a little oxygen be too fucking much to ask for?"

The thin air at altitude is always a challenge for those newly arrived from sea-level, and the rough terrain is no help either, but despite her protestations, Beannie is holding the pace just fine. In fact, she is setting it. Sophie is impressed. Yes, they might be moving a bit more slowly than usual, but Beannie is easily running as fast as the fleetest club runners do on this stretch, and those folks all have boxes full of age group hardware from local races. Finn had told her that Beannie was a star in high school and had turned down scholarship offers to run in college, choosing to pursue music instead. But she had continued to run, often hard, for the pure joy of it, had stayed fit and fast, and was training for the New York City Marathon later that fall.

"We could slow down, you know...if you *need to,*" Finn says, his voice dripping faux pity and condescension, goading her.

"Eat me," she answers, rising on her toes, leaning into the hill, and ratcheting the pace down ten seconds per mile. This was an old game for them, Sophie could tell, and she laughs along with Finn as they set off in chase of Beannie's tattooed form.

After another ten minutes, they have climbed to the turn-around, where they stop briefly, sucking wind, as well as water from bottles they carry in packs around their waists. They stand atop a steep ridge that tumbles away to their left, boulders the size of Buicks littering the creek that runs through the ravine below, watching breathlessly as hills painted in the varied greens of conifers, the yellow of quaking aspen, roll and climb toward the never-gets-old panorama of the high peaks, their summits already dusted with the silver of an early snow.

"Fuuuuuu..." says Beannie.

And then they are off, flying along the mostly downhill return-trip to the studio at breakneck speed, surprising both a colorful cadre of mountain bikers standing tall on their pedals, grinding inexorably upwards, and a sleepy porcupine trundling slowly across the path. A pair of speckled Appaloosa ponies from the neighboring property gallop next to them on the other side of a split-rail fence as they barrel down the now-smooth and dusty ranch road, across the final stretch of flat, valley floor and up to

Sophie's gate, just as Evie and Lisette emerge from the trail that winds up the hill behind the barn. Lisette totes a sketchpad, Evie a daypack Sophie would later find was loaded with pinecones and quartz crystals, and a pika's tiny skull. The group stands in the crystalline sunshine for a moment next to the lightning-struck lodgepole, catching their breath. Then Beannie says, "Anybody hungry? I could eat that fucking horse."

Sophie looks at Finn. "Silver Grill?" she asks.

He nods. "Silver Grill."

Skirtchaser have a day off before heading out the next morning to their next show in Albuquerque, and thus, shockingly early the morning after the Red Rocks gig, Beannie and the band had driven up to the studio to hike, or run with Finn and Sophie, check out some of her paintings and his new poems, relax, and catch up. They bring CDs and a stack of T-shirts with the band's logo on them. The design, created by Lisette, and gracing both black and white shirts, and which would soon adorn the backs of lucky members of the local running crowd, displays a bare derriere peeking from between a short, short red skirt and a pair of black stockings, and sporting a skull and crossbones tattoo on the right cheek. A single drop of crimson blood drips from the skull's eye socket like a tear, and falls toward the word Skirtchaser, which sweeps across the cartoon upper thigh in Varsity Script.

"I was the ass model, as you can probably guess. I mean, this be some fine shit, right? Check it out." Beannie drops *trou* and proudly displays the very tattoo—right down to the blood drop—so prominent on the shirt.

Evie and Lisette shake their heads as Sophie howls. *I love this woman,* she thinks. She loves the shirt, too, and proudly wears a black one to breakfast down in town. Her fatigue is once again held at bay, this time by laughter and a heaping plate of sweet cinnamon roll French toast and home fries with house-made salsa, not to mention much more coffee and multiple glasses of water.

She knows the sleepless night, long run, and high-carb breakfast will soon render her unconscious, but for now, caffeine, conversation and the general hubbub of a popular breakfast spot conspire to keep her relatively alert.

A few runners drop by the table to say hello, and a pair of college girls, obviously a new couple, take the opportunity to approach and shyly greet Beannie, Lisette, and Evie. They had attended the previous night's show, and are wearing the band's T-shirts, one black, one white, which Beannie offers to sign. A waitress proffers a Sharpie. The young woman with the black shirt instantly regrets choosing that color (the autographs won't show), and shrugs sadly, but Beannie, seeing the problem, pulls a copy of their latest CD from her bag, and the bandmates all sign the cover. After a moment or two of polite conversation, the women head for the door. The braver one (white shirt) turns, reapproaches the table, and holding the Sharpie out to Finn, asks, "Can you too, professor? You were awesome. I'm taking your class in the spring."

Sophie giggles as Finn blushes, stammers, "Me? Uh, yeah, sure," and scrawls his name next to those of his erstwhile bandmates. The young woman thanks him, smiles, and makes her escape, seizing her young lover's hand in delight, then marching off with her down the sidewalk, excitedly gesticulating at their swag.

"I'm the fifth Beatle," says Finn.

Beannie is beaming. "That never fucking happens. I love this place!" then, nudging Finn, "Fucking professor! Ha! How about that?"

* * *

AN HOUR LATER, the band are happily napping at Finn's bungalow, their tired, full, showered bodies supine and still in the guest bedroom and upon the living room couch. In Finn's bedroom, Sophie, smelling of lavender and wearing the trusty

Gaunt is Beautiful shirt, yawns prettily, straddles him, then says, her voice raised in a girlish lilt, "Gosh, I'm not sure I will be able to sleep. Is there anything you can do to help me…*professor?*"

* * *

FIFTY WEEKS, EIGHT paintings, and four thousand running miles later, Sophie finds herself happily awake, fully conscious in a dream that had never really been one of hers: a scene she had certainly never spent, like most of her friends, fantasizing about down to the minutest detail: waxing poetic over fabrics and cakes, flower and seating arrangements, petty acts of revenge and perfect underwear. No, she had never really given it any thought at all, but nevertheless, here she is on this breezy mountaintop, like a figure on a cake, all dressed up and standing next to this unexpected, tuxedoed man, gazing out at the faces of family and dear friends, the eponymous glacier of Mount of the Holy Cross glistening in the sun behind her. Maybe the self-help philosophers are right, she thinks, tucking a flyaway strand of hair behind her ear: when you are free from desire, that which pleases you the most comes to pass. Maybe she had won the karmic lottery, or possibly some god was rewarding her for always doing her math homework. Whatever. All she knew was that the cosmic dominoes had fallen into place, and much to her surprise, Sophie finds herself suddenly married.

Her dress is gossamer, and short, and she feels like some enchanted fairy wearing it, a horny Disney princess, anointed with and positively high on the pixie-dust Finn is always going

on about. A fancy, lacy, yet understated rag, the dress suits both her aesthetic and her athletic, elfin stature. And five minutes after the ceremony, it is folded and stuffed, along with Finn's tux, into someone's daypack, as she and her groom, along with a dozen guests—among them the Unitarian minister and mountain racer who had officiated the ceremony—now clad in shorts and T-shirts, speed along alpine trails, zig-zagging through stands of pine and pale green aspen, taking the long way to the lodge, some two thousand feet below, where the post-ceremony revelry would commence. The non-running guests pile into gondolas for a champagne-doused and scenic ride back down the mountain to the waiting food and drink, and where Lisette and Evie will be setting up their instruments, ready to peel some paint from the walls. Beannie, of course, is out running with the bride and groom. Everyone on the gondolas hoots and waves as the wedding party passes beneath them like a herd of happy antelope.

Sophie drifts along the rolling single-track, briefly alone and marveling at her good fortune. During this moment of contented introspection, a long shadow floats up and hovers alongside hers as it ripples across the faded grasses and stunted trees next to the trail, and silently, Gizmo appears at her elbow. He is tall and almost scarily handsome, with thick, black hair and a solid jawline. High cheekbones frame his bottomless indigo eyes, now hidden behind black running shades. She has often wondered if it is those eyes that the wealthy society-types and models Gizmo dates get lost in, drifting into an enchantment they emerge from only months later, a rude awakening usually recounted giddily by the London tabloids. Even she, as distasteful as she finds him sometimes, is not immune to the darkness of his eyes, the darkness that seethes behind them. Once or twice, she had caught him looking at her with an expression of undisguised hunger. At those moments, she had to tear her eyes from the tractor beam of his gaze, distract herself from the flushing of her cheeks, the electricity that stiffened her nipples, the heat that surged from her chest and settled, smoldering, between her legs. Those moments frightened and disgusted her, her uninvited lust quickly giving way to shame. She loathed this part of herself as much as she sometimes disliked him. She avoided him as much as politeness would allow.

His long strides gobble huge chunks of surface with apparent ease, the very portrait of effortless power. Though the narrow trail, with its tight switchbacks and sudden roller-coaster dips and climbs, better suits the compact, birdlike strides of she and Finn, Giz looks far from uncomfortable in his surroundings. Then again, Giz never seems uncomfortable anywhere. He moves through life, so far as she can tell, with a preternatural calm, an unflappability seemingly unaccompanied by warmth. She still has not figured out whether he is socially awkward or just a bastard. She looks ahead up the trail, to where Finn and Beannie zip along, chattering like jays, and tries to picture a younger version of the trio, running together in a fog of happy fatigue after a high school cross country meet, or on a long Sunday amble through the lilacs of a May morning.

It is hard to reconcile the tall drink of water, *GQ* model of a figure beside her with the awkward, nerdy, bespectacled young Gilbert Hornaplenty that Finn and Beannie describe, and whom Sophie has seen in slightly out of focus black and whites from Finn's high school yearbooks: a scrawny kid with a too-big head, piercing eyes somewhat magnified by the thick lenses of his glasses, and always uncombed hair. But in the rare photo that catches him smiling (young Gizmo had very little to smile about, she has been told, not that he smiles much now), a glimpse of the man who would emerge during his college years becomes startlingly clear. When he smiles, especially when absent his thick specs, as in the photo taken of the threesome after the state cross country meet their senior year, his straight, white teeth work in concert with his nearly black eyes. His sharp, high cheekbones, made even starker by the look of happy exhaustion on his face, complete the picture, show a glimpse into the future. The photo captures him at the exact moment everything had begun to change: the gangly puppy hinting at the wolf it was about to become.

"You looked beautiful up there," he says. Then, "I'm trying really hard to be less of an asshole."

Sophie laughs, a quick bark that echoes out over the mountainside like a birdcall. "Thank you. And it's about damn time!" With this, she playfully punches him in the arm.

"Ow! Yeah, between many thousands of dollars to my psychiatrist and Beannie threatening to kick my ass, I decided that maybe I could change my approach a bit." They run along in silence for a moment. "You see," he continues, weaving his words in between oxygen-gobbling breaths, Giz, like Sophie having long ago mastered the skill of high-speed conversation, "I tend to get jealous of other people's happiness. I tend to resent how easy it all seems for some people, when I actually have no idea how hard things are for them, which makes me even more envious: how can a person who has been through *that*—whatever it is—be so damn happy?" He continues with a seriousness that Sophie cannot quite tell is genuine or self-mocking, "See, I'm an even bigger asshole than you thought!"

"Not possible," Sophie says with a wink, then feels bad. Maybe she is enjoying this rare moment of discomfort just a tad too much.

He laughs, looks around, making sure nobody is within earshot, then continues. "And I have been jealous of your relationship with Finn. I know, that is crazy immature, not to mention selfish, but he and Beannie were the only people who gave a shit about me for so long, that it is hard to, you know, share. Hell, I have spent most of my life even being jealous of Finn and Beannie, of their closeness, as if my inability to be intimate is their fault. So I have decided to try to change that. I'm just not sure how, exactly. Anyway, this is not about me. I just wanted to say I'm sorry. And how happy I am that Finn found you."

Sophie's eyes flood. A nearly audible sob escapes her chest, her emotional cup running briefly over. It had been that kind of day. Then she smiles and—no mean feat, considering the difference in their height, the uneven surface over which they move, and the fact that they are traveling at about ten miles per hour—manages to give him a quick kiss on the cheek. "Thank you," Sophie says softly, then smiling hugely, "Now let's catch up to Finn and Beannie, see what sort of mischief they're up to."

Part Two: A Festival of Light

Just like the woman you lost, who will always be dark-haired
And flush-faced, running toward an electronic screen
That clocks the minutes, the miles left to go. Just like the life
In which I'm forever a child looking out my window at the
night sky
Thinking one day I'll touch the world with bare hands
Even if it burns.

—Tracy K. Smith, "Don't You Wonder, Sometimes?"

Sophie

SOPHIE PACES BEFORE the large, prepped canvas, which she has hung from two strands of thin cable attached to a track in the rafters and supported with a pair of adjustable sawhorses placed on the floor in the middle of her still too-pristine studio. She has covered the cement floor with ancient, threadbare Oriental rugs, salvaged from junk shops or charmed from rich old ladies renovating moldering mansions, and which she has, in turn, covered with a huge, splattered canvas tarp left behind by a contractor. The skylight has been adjusted to cast her workspace in a natural, yet unoppressive light, a perfect manipulation of the mountain morning's irrepressible radiance, such that she works inside a glowing orb, which pulses and ebbs and flows as clouds wander overhead and the sun trundles towards evening. The barn's crepuscular shadows are pushed into corners, where they will murmur and plot doomed insurrections against the light, nonetheless insinuating themselves whisperingly into the painting's nooks and crannies. The studio smells of new sawdust and old timbers; wet earth; the pleasant pungency of ancient horse manure. Closer by, and knitted to the fragrance of the barn, is what she calls *art smell:* the combined exhalations of her oil paints, brushes, pencil shavings, the faint animal scent of gesso from the canvas itself, the occasional obliterating whiff of turpentine, all with a delicate topnote of fresh linseed oil.

Tacked to a large corkboard on her left are several charcoal and pastel studies she has done for the piece, mostly late at night from her chair in the bedroom, Finn aslumber and unaware of his role as artist's model, of his essences being distilled from the ethers and scratched onto paper. In her mind, these essences move about in their own dreamspace, where they rustle and sigh, then, when translated to paper, go blessedly still. When she looks at these pictures, she sees him as clearly as if he were in the room with her. She can hear his soft nightsounds, smell the earth and musk of him. How can she translate the synesthetic cornucopia of her mind onto the two dimensions and into the single physical sense engaged by a canvas hung upon a wall? How can she draw a viewer through this flat plane and into the cacophonous thrumming of her many-dimensional world? She couldn't tell you, but on an almost cellular level, she knows exactly how it will be done.

The canvas is covered with nearly invisible pencil marks, a sort of blueprint—or more apt, considering her style, a choreography—for what is about to transpire. Dressed in grey Tufts sweatpants, a ratty race T-shirt, and retired running shoes, her hair tucked into a beaten orange Denver Broncos cap—stolen from Finn for luck and worn backwards—she paces before the canvas with a lithe, but itchy grace. She has just finished an easy five-mile run, down and back up the Young's Gulch trail (no rattlesnakes today, thank God), and, like after warming up for a race, she is flushed with light fatigue, her limbs and brain awash in blood and oxygen, ready for more strenuous exertion. She rolls her neck, bends forward from the waist, places her hands flat on the floor, holds the pose for a moment, feeling the tension bleed from her lower back and hamstrings. She then straightens, stares at the blank canvas, shifts her weight from foot to foot, shakes out her hands. She inhales deeply through her nose, exhales noisily through her mouth. She bends at the knees, lowering herself nearly to a full squat, and pops into the air from both feet, like a sprinter burning off adrenaline before easing into the blocks. Finally, she stretches her fingers and wrists, bending the fingers of each hand backwards with the opposite palm, and pushes the play button on the CD player. From the professionally arrayed speakers spill the almost unbearably exquisite first notes of Max Bruch's violin concerto, Joshua Bell's violin sending geysers of involuntary adrenaline shooting through her veins, an aurora borealis of pulsating color across her field of vision. *Whoa, steady there, little buckaroo,* she tells herself, then takes a slow, deep breath, ingesting the music like it is oxygen, letting it fill and fuel her.

Sophie closes her eyes, shakes out her arms one last time as the music sizzles along her neurons, then turns to the worktable at her right, selecting a fattish brush from the waiting array. She picks up the small square of sheetrock upon which she has mixed small puddles of pigment. Satisfied that all is in order, she takes another deep breath and addresses the canvas, then settles into a rapt moment of calm. Underneath the music, which is orchestra-pit loud, the world hums with a steady buzz, a heady, electric current. She breathes deeply one final time—in, out—and harnesses that energy, plugs in, and becomes one with it. Then, in a single, fluid motion, she dips her brush into a blob of deep purple paint and pounces upon the canvas like a wildcat.

* * *

IT WAS CHAIM, back at Tufts, who had opened the door to what would become her trademark style of painting. He suggested she marry her natural athleticism, a physicality honed from years of daily training, to her love of music and an innate sense of rhythm, then apply this gymnastic approach to her burgeoning skill with paint and brush. It was he who suggested that she look at painting as an athletic enterprise, convinced her that by moving across the canvas like a runner across a field or a dancer across a floor, she would imbue each gesture she made with a brush, no matter how large or small, with a kinetic resonance that would make it leap from the canvas as if alive. He had suggested that she paint to music, having heard her describe how certain songs made her see colors that moved and whirled like living things in her mind. This was where her art lived, he told her, and if she could capture these chimeras these synesthetic holograms, and set them dancing across the canvas, their movement would be visible for all to see. Chaim showed her video of "action painters" like Jackson Pollack and

Willem de Kooning in their studios, and she saw how they used the canvas as a field across which they moved, and from which masterpieces erupted. By the time Chaim finished his lecture—his sermon, his tirade—he was almost shouting, gesticulating excitedly, his bald head wrinkling, unkempt eyebrows furrily punctuating his every expression, spinning into existence a world, that though brand-new, Sophie recognized as home.

* * *

HER FIRST BRUSHSTROKE is a long, wide, floorward swoop. It begins from a point to her right, high over her head, and plummets steeply in a shallow curve toward her left foot. She starts on tiptoe, then spins downward on a swivel as her arm moves leftward across her body. She ends this stroke in nearly a crouch, brush hand at her right hip, her spin having taken her to her left, leaving her shoulders perpendicular to the canvas. From this crouch, she erupts into another swoop, painting backhand, upward, and to the right, creating an arc inverse to the first: shorter this time, and much less steep. Then a switch of hands and a fast, near vertical stroke that, at its peak, sends a fine spray of paint nearly to the top of the canvas. Another downward arc, another jab, then a swift backhand, a deep-purple semicircle. A drip, slowing and stalling as it dries. A swipe of the wrist across the forehead to wipe away sweat, a quick tuck of hair behind the ear, then a lazy horizontal, right-to-left, near the top of the canvas. A slow retreat to ponder; a little epiphany and a quick smear across a drying sweep. Another step away, a glance, a nod of satisfaction, then a three-step lunge, like a fencer, back into the fray.

Sophie bobs and weaves, wheels and pirouettes, jabs and feints, moving laterally, vertically, and at every conceivable angle to the plane of the canvas, gliding and spinning like a bullfighter or a flamenco dancer in graceful arcs and curves punctuated by staccato stabs at the canvas or backwards flicks of the wrist that pepper the sweeping broad ribbons of color with emphatic splatters of purple pigment. Long, sweeping strokes are interrupted by sudden jabs and little salute-like wristflicks from eyebrow-level as the sleeping figure begins to emerge from the white background and sprawl into life. Sophie dances inside the music pulsing in her ears, moves like an Olympic figure skater, performing complex choreography with seeming ease, the shapeshifting kaleidoscopic palette in her head fueling this athletic, unseen performance, her virtuosity underpinned by a technical proficiency borne of years of obsessive study and labor. That and weeks of preparation for the piece have made possible this dance, established the boundaries of her playing field, set the stage for this seemingly spontaneous eruption of paint. She knows what she is doing; her preparation is complete. Now it is time to play.

And play it is, making a picture. Though the process of painting is serious business to her, and though the result will be the product of years of diligent groundwork before so much as applying a single brushstroke to canvas, the making of the picture itself is a moonshot explosion of joy and wonder, an adrenaline-soaked and gleeful adventure into the unknown. Full of technical problems requiring seat-of-the-pants solutions, to be sure, entire days spent in brow-furrowed, gut-churning indecision before hurtling again forward on Saturn-Five rockets of inspiration, absolutely. But how is this any different than a kid trying to build a world from Legos, Tinkertoys, and spare Barbie parts? In her sweats and Broncos cap, she is happy as a preschooler with a big sheet of paper and tubs of fingerpaint, and, like a child, she plays with reckless abandon, happily lost in a world she makes up as she goes along. But as with a child at play, it is not all just fun and games. Just like that of a child, the world she builds is *real.*

The hours pass in a blur, at least when she tries to recollect them afterwards, but while she is painting, time halts and she lives inside a single elongated moment. She is nature's perfect antenna, a single multisensory receiver, in fine-tuned to every signal the universe is broadcasting her. And she responds in turn, broadcasting her own club mix of everything she has taken in, weaving a three-dimensional whirling moodscape of shape, color, and texture with paint and brush, creating a sculpture of pigment and canvas that one can almost dance to. She draws from the deep well of her experience and inspiration, conjures a magic bestiary of new life-forms from empty space, setting the studio alight with this synesthetic interpretive dance, until hours later, the spell breaks and she staggers away from the canvas exhausted, famished, and desperate for a pee.

* * *

HER NEXT SIX months are consumed by making the painting—three steps forward, two steps back—a daily ballet and boxing match with the canvas that would leave her simultaneously drained and energized, exhausted, yet too wired to sleep. Some days are slower, more contemplative: Corelli's *Concerto Grossi* on the stereo; long moments spent staring at the canvas before darting in for a single, fine dab of the brush, then stepping away to ponder her next move. Some days are electric: a charge into the studio full of piss and vinegar to hurl paint like Zeus with his thunderbolts, a boom-crash opera soundtracked by The Clash or AC/DC or Nirvana. Whatever she is feeling finds its way onto the canvas, different areas of the picture becoming repositories for whirlaway emotions to simmer and develop selves, personalities subsumed over the months into the whole. And of course, the months of feelings, the tenderness and wild eroticism that fuel the painting cannot always be completely contained within the confines of the canvas. On these nights (as with this first one, and which Finn later tells her he can always immediately recognize from the look in her eyes as she comes through the door) she finds him, her breath coming quickly and shallowly, almost a pant, and wherever in the house he happens to be, simply takes him, lets the creature of pure appetite with whom she has been dancing all day have its way, giving Finn no quarter as she wordlessly fucks him senseless.

Other nights, exhausted beyond the ability even to drive down the canyon, it is all she can do to force herself to eat some soup and bread or a salad, then drag herself up the coil of staircase to her loft, scarcely possessing the energy to shrug off her paint-splattered clothes and collapse into bed, pulling a blanket over her head just as sleep comes crashing down.

* * *

THEY HAD FALLEN into a way of living well-suited to them both, their days spent dancing to a melody and a rhythm that came naturally, a series of solos and harmonies with which they painted the easy early days of the relationship. They ran, together, alone or with an ever-changing cast of training partners, most weeks accumulating more than a hundred miles on the track or the roads and trails above town. They worked, Finn on his poems at home in a sunny nook off the kitchen or in his campus office, Sophie painting or drawing in her studio or her chair next to the bed, roaming the surrounding hills and plains, sketching or taking photographs that would evolve into paintings or mixed media pieces. She loved the sweet yearning and loneliness that would fill her during the hours they spent apart, the "squishy feeling" that would swell within her when she would come home at the end of the day to find him washing vegetables in the sink, grading papers, or folding laundry, or hear him come through the door whistling, as she stretched or set the table for dinner.

Casual acquaintances would remark upon how easygoing they both were, how seemingly unassailable by petty bullshit and everyday strife. Everybody agreed; Finn and Sophie were totally chill. Which was true enough after the day's labors were over, but such appearances belied the hours they spent focused single-mindedly upon their sport and upon their art, the many everyday pleasures that most took for granted—a movie or a night out at the bars, a weekend ski trip—that were near impossibilities. They lived the lives of genial obsessive-compulsives, happily surrendering the quotidian pleasures enjoyed by most citizens to pursue wholeheartedly the gifts of speed and endurance, the shared second sight, the ability to translate that sight into a piece of art they could give to the world. If anyone were to point out the sacrifices they were making for their artistic and athletic careers, they would have laughed. Even in the down moments—a sore hamstring, an illness that kept one or both of them off the roads and out of the studio, a passing dose of creative malaise—they would consider their situation for a moment, then find themselves simply stupefied with gratitude at the life they were allowed to lead.

* * *

EIGHTEEN MONTHS EARLIER. Her big, new travel bag (provided by her big, new shoe company sponsor) lay open on the bed, and Sophie danced from dresser to closet to bed, bopping her head, shaking her slender shoulders and hips, singing along loudly to The Cars' "Good Times Roll." Happily, she stuffed the bag with socks and underwear, with the clothing she had decided on after much deliberation earlier that morning: a hoody, a pair of jeans and a pair of Madras shorts, a couple of tees and tanks. Also, a new sundress; a sexy little number she couldn't wait to unleash on Finn the evening after the race. Also, three pairs of shoes (retired, comfy trainers, beaten, black Doc Martens, strappy sandals), underwear (both practical and not so much), toiletries, the bare minimum of cosmetics. Vitamins; sunscreen; a box of Clif Bars—everything she needed for the four-day trip neatly packed into the brightly-colored, mid-size duffel. She felt almost giddy filling all the clever little pockets and zip compartments, all of the bag's numerous virgin nooks and crannies with her stuff, delighted and stunned that someone was giving her shoes and clothes and bags, not to mention a small salary, to function as a five-foot, two-inch, swiftly moving billboard, happily plastered, cap-to-sneakers with their company's name and logo.

It was a little disconcerting to think that running was now her *job*, that this activity she had pursued almost daily since she was fourteen was something she would actually be paid to do. Sure, she guessed, there was a bit more pressure to perform—people actually expected her to win races now—but really, nothing had changed. She ran because she loved it. She ran because, when she laced up her shoes and stepped onto a red-dirt trail on a hot Colorado evening, or into the teeth of a February blizzard, with nothing but her eyes exposed to the chill, or when she raced over some beaten patch of turf, hell-bent for leather on a leaf-strewn New England autumn afternoon, she was doing so for the unfettered joy of it, for the visceral thrill of a self-made wind on her face, the scenery sliding by in a crystal blur, for the pounding of blood in her ears, blood that carried the oxygen she gulped in greedy breaths from the atmosphere to every far-flung cell in her moving body.

She ran to appease, to delight the animal living in her brain and under her skin, the lithe and hungry creature that purred and paced and pounced inside the hard elasticity of her calves and biceps and hamstrings, the bobcat howling from deep within the hungry muscle of her heart. Sure, it hurt sometimes, uncaging the beast, setting it free to pursue its demons, satisfy its ancient hungers, slake its primal thirsts. Sometimes it hurt like hell. Letting the animal hold sway sent her to places no normal human would willingly go: down avenues of unspeakable weariness and unnamable woe, to mudcrusted muscles cramped and screaming, lungs reduced to a death rattle with miles yet to go through a dreary March drizzle or mirage-filled August glare, her eyes glued shut with the salty gum of summer or the ice of frozen tears.

Worst of all was when the animal inevitably fell silent at some dark-night-of-the-soul moment in the interminable, stupid middle of some long race, and she would find herself running on empty, nothing but suffering spread before her from her next footstep to the horizon and beyond, the beast suddenly sated and napping in some lost corner of her mind, like a pussycat in a patch of sun as she looks over at the competitor running next to her, all sleek and nonchalant, and she is filled with the profoundest self-pity, wanting nothing more than to step from the racecourse, grab herself a Big Gulp and a ticket on the first bus home. But teetering there on the precipice of the abyss, she had always, at least up until now, managed to goad the beast awake, bring forth the nastiest version of herself, snarling and snapping and full of menace, managed to replace the dull emptiness in her gut with a bloodlust that drove her forward with new purpose, and if it did not get her to the finish line first, it certainly gave her competitors a sense of what it felt like to be prey.

But such thoughts were a mere buzz in the background as she grooved and shimmied to the music, zipped her bag and carried it to the front door, setting it next to Finn's, then returned to the bedroom to pack the *important* stuff. Into a smaller shoulder bag—this one also emblazoned with the shoe company logo—went the things she could not entrust to gate agents and baggage handlers, items that, if they were lost, would render the weekend moot. Into this bag she slipped her racing kit: new racing flats, worked out in once; the matching bun-huggers and racing bra, a set of new, blue and white warmups and a long-sleeve T-shirt, two pair of tight, thin socks, extra elastics to secure her hair into the single braid in which she wore it for races, a breathable white cap (again with the logo) in case of a bright sun, and her new, bright yellow running shades.

Into an inner pocket she tucked the Ziploc bag containing her charms: bangles with strong juju, talismanic powers that gave her strength during those unbearably tense last moments on the starting line, when every fiber of her being would be yearning to bolt for the dim, silent sanctuary of the hotel room. First was the magic safety-pin with which she would fasten the upper-right corner of her bib number to her top. This was the pin which had secured her number during her first national championship in college, and which she had used to fasten a number in every subsequent victory. This pin had been there before. It knew how to win. Also nestled in the plastic bag was her elephant cloisonné pin, which she would fasten to her hat or bra before the race. The elephant was named Jumbo, its namesake long-dead by fire, and which was the Tufts University mascot. Jumbo, too, had been through many races, and she could always count on him when the chips were down. A matching—and quite permanent—likeness of Jumbo adorned the skin atop her left hipbone.

And finally, the shiniest, most powerful bauble of all. This one however, did not reside in a Ziploc bag tucked into the dark recesses of an athletic bag. This one occupied pride of place around the fourth finger of her left hand, where it still felt strange. Tingly, new, and oddly heavy considering its negligible weight, she had only been wearing the ring since the previous afternoon, when, pausing briefly amid the swirling snowflakes at the turnaround of their run up and back down Redstone Canyon, stopping for a moment before racing darkness downhill to the blessed warmth of the car, Finn had taken a knee amid the frozen red dirt and asked her to marry him.

She spun the ring twice around her finger, a new habit she was going to have to break herself of pretty soon, and let out a shuddering sigh: part disbelief, part fear, and mostly a nearly overpowering joy. She shook off the feeling, returning to the task at hand. She added a new pair of lightweight training shoes to the bag, and a paperback copy of Nabokov's *Pale Fire,* along with a couple of running magazines and the latest issue of *ARTnews,* and of course, a sketchpad and tin of pencils, zipped the bag closed, and slung it over her shoulder. She looked at herself in the mirror over the dresser, amazed at how young the person staring back at her appeared. She hadn't felt particularly young in quite a while, and it felt good to momentarily recapture the giddy sense of youth that had fled on that May morning three years before. *I'm doing good, Ma,* she whispered. She tucked a loose strand of hair behind her ear and shook her head in wonder. She gave her ring one last twirl, gave her reflected self a wicked grin. *Let the good times roll, indeed!*

* * *

TRAVELING TOGETHER TO races was the best. Just when the grind of paint/run/sleep would begin to seem a little oppressive, a race would appear on the horizon, the level of happy anticipation and motivation would build, and then one morning she would find herself on a jetliner winging her way toward Buffalo or Portland (either of them) or Hartford, sometimes alone, sometimes sitting next to Finn, who hated flying and would hold her hand in a death-grip, chanting, "I'm on a bus, I'm on a bus, I'm on a bus," to which she responded, gently mocking him, "You're a wuss, you're a wuss, you're a wuss," until the bell dinged and the fasten seat belt sign blinked off. This time, they were flying south and east, where they would trade the frigid winds and horizontal snows of a Colorado February for the moist and temperate breezes of Florida. January and February were racing season in the Sunshine State, and big-money races like the Jacksonville River Run and Tampa's Gasparilla Classic—named after legendary pirate José Gaspar—dotted the calendar, and droves of pale-skinned northerners of all abilities descended on the state for a midwinter amble over distances from fifteen kilometers to the half-marathon on streets blessedly free of ice or slush or terrifying transplants from California who couldn't drive in the snow.

The Naples Half Marathon was a chance for Sophie to run the longer distance—more than twice as far as she had ever raced—for the first time, on a flat, fast course against a slightly less intimidating professional field than the ones at Jacksonville or Gasparilla. Still, the starting line would be peppered with seasoned, Olympic Trials qualifiers in the Marathon and a few (as Finn called them) "not ready for prime-time" Kenyans. She would have her hands full, but she was going there with every intention of winning.

* * *

THE GREY-GREEN WATERS of the Gulf were cool, and lapped soothingly at her race-sore legs as she waded in, enjoying the slight wobble in her equilibrium that entering the ocean always caused her until, taking a deep breath, she would extend her arms, tuck her head between her shoulders and dive under a breaking wave, the world righting itself as she surfaced and began an easy freestyle away from shore. She hummed tunelessly to herself, exorcising the ghost of whatever song had last played on the rental car radio, and absently watched the slow progress of a sailboat moving across the horizon, her hands trailing through the water as it crept to her knees, and then her waist. The sun on her bare shoulders was nearly as intoxicating as the single, strong Mojito she had enjoyed at the hotel bar before they departed for the beach. Finn had gallantly volunteered to be the designated driver, as that lone drink married itself to the lingering effects of the previous day's exertions and left her with a pleasant buzz, a delightful outlook as to her general prospects, and no ability whatsoever to drive. She was relatively sure she could still swim, however, and slipping barefoot into the calm green water under the hot midwinter sun (hot to her, anyway, though there seemed to be a lot of locals walking around in fleece), felt positively decadent after spending large chunks of every day outside, beating feet through the coldest Colorado winter in a decade, swaddled in high-tech layers, her breath clouds freezing any hairs that had managed to escape from her stocking cap, making frosty sculptures of her eyebrows.

Even more decadent had been shopping for a bikini the previous day, when, after the race, breakfast, a shower, and a long nap, they had limped hand-in-hand to the skate and surf shop down the street from their hotel for a little shopping spree. It had been a long time since Sophie had bought a swimsuit with other than strictly functional criteria in mind. Or since she had done any recreational shopping at all, for that matter. She spent nearly twenty minutes looking through a truly mind-boggling array of candy-colored possibilities, holding what seemed like dozens up to her body (she had worn shorts and a running bra to get a better idea what the suits would look like next to her skin), Finn nodding yes or shaking his head no, or shrugging noncommittally, his imagination running in overdrive—she could tell. She finally decided on a periwinkle two-piece with tiny green polka-dots, tie-up spaghetti straps, and racily high-cut bottoms.

"I may need a little help," she told Finn, blinking innocently, "tying and...*un*tying this. Is that something you could, um...*handle*?" The clerk, still in high school, a tiny peroxide-blonde skate punk with a tan, a barracuda tattoo on her ankle, and a nearly microscopic diamond stud on the side of her nose, snorted as Sophie handed her the suit with a wink.

Finn blushed as the girl took the bikini and walked past him to the register, leering at him without an iota of self-consciousness or professional decorum, but he grinned, and in his best white-hatted cowboy voice replied to Sophie, "Well, ma'am, I reckon I could give it a shot."

Sophie smiled at the recollection, not to mention the recollection of the modeling session that took place in the hotel room later, and the X-rated activities that followed. She looked back over her shoulder to where Finn lay relaxing on a towel on the nearly deserted beach, wearing bright-yellow board shorts festooned with black skulls—suggested by barracuda-girl from the surf shop, who, charmingly, scared him just a little—his eyes momentarily closed behind his sunglasses, as she moved farther from shore, relishing the delicious feeling of saltwater lapping at flesh, licking at the whirling legs of the Roadrunner tattooed on the taut skin just below her left breast, which, small though it may have been, the new bikini top just barely covered.

Though the new suit was probably, per square-inch of fabric, the most expensive item of clothing she had ever bought, she felt not the least bit guilty about the purchase. The prize money from her second-place finish the day before seemed to warrant a small splurge, plus, it was a bit hard to play in the ocean without a swimsuit, now, wasn't it? And besides, she had an engagement to celebrate!

So she waded into the warm water of the Gulf until it was nearly to her chest, then dove in and swam lazy quarter-mile laps parallel to shore for about thirty minutes, feeling deliciously naked as she moved through the warm green swells in her tiny new suit, the soreness from the previous day's race slowly melting from her limbs. While she was swimming, Finn, who had run an easy ten miles earlier that morning, had joined her in the water, alternately swimming and treading water a few yards farther out, not wanting to interrupt her solitude.

* * *

AND THEN, A fifty-mile drive north up Highway 41, top down on the Volkswagen Cabriolet they had rented, Third World's "Now That We Found Love" blasting from the car stereo. They flew through gardenia-scented breezes toward new, luxurious digs on Sanibel Island, where on high thread-count sheets and white sand beaches littered with shells, the pressure and pain of the race behind them, they could begin celebrating their pending nuptials in earnest. Under the syncopated spell of the reggae pulsing from the speakers, the aromatic and slightly sultry air rushing over her skin, and Finn singing from the driver's seat next to her, she felt in danger of floating away, of drifting like a happy balloon into the brilliant blue sky that hung over the water of the Gulf, and disappearing into the oblivion of her own sweet bliss. She roller-coastered her hand through the wind rushing past the window, and her long, brown hair, set free from its usual braid or hat, billowed behind her like a riotously waving flag, one that signaled to passing motorists that some happy hell was about to be raised.

At first, she had been pissed-off with her race, losing in a kick to a fierce and diminutive 1992 Ecuadorian Olympian, Martha Ordoñez. But by the time she staggered from the finish chute to be embraced, congratulated, and smiled blindingly at by the victorious South American, she had begun to reconsider. She had, after all, run over two minutes faster than she had realistically expected she could run, and when she found out she had been beaten by someone who had finished 27th in the marathon at the Sydney games, she felt pretty silly about kicking herself. And while cooling down with Finn, Martha, and her coach, former world record holder, Steve Jones, Sophie learned that Martha spent most of her year living and training in Boulder, less than an hour away from she and Finn. Delighted, the two women ran ahead, plotting future lunches and training runs, while Finn trotted along with Jones, learning all about the new Harley Davidson the amiable Welshman (one of his heroes) had just purchased, his plans to ride it to all his favorite Western fly-fishing spots the next summer.

The last of Sophie's chagrin over her race evaporated later that afternoon, when she admitted to herself, wrapped around Finn in their hotel bed in a fog of post-race, post-bikini shopping, post-coital tristesse, that there was not a single thing she could have done to reclaim the two-seconds of territory that had bloomed between she and her new friend over the race's final meters. "Not a damn thing," she mumbled sleepily to herself, shaking her head in resignation. Her disappointment melted away, replaced by a bone-weary kind of contentment, a little well-earned pride. And at the thought of Finn pulling away from an impossibly baby-faced 18-year-old Kenyan named Josphat Kiptoo at eleven miles for the win, her delight was doubled. She wished she could have seen it.

"Finn?" she murmured as their post-mortems of the race wound down and they drifted toward sleep.

"Hmmmm?"

"But that is really a long fucking way to race."

He wrapped her in his arms from behind, gently nipped at the nape of her neck, and answered, "You'll get no argument from me."

* * *

TOOLING TOWARD SANIBEL the next day, Finn added a little more perspective.

"Look at it this way," he said over the thumping reggae. "You are fairly fresh out of college, running your first half marathon, and still, you just barely lost to a thirty-year-old Olympian. Time is on your side; chances are you will never lose to her again. And while I may have won," he continued, "I am at the point where personal bests are beginning to be fewer and farther between. The odds of me beating a prodigy like Kiptoo ever again are probably worse than getting struck by lightning. So what I'm saying, my love, is that your future's so bright you need shades."

"Got 'em right here, baby," Sophie said, tapping her new Oakleys. "And so lucky for you," she added, "that you have me to look after you, here in your dotage."

Finn

HE AWOKE TO sore shoulders and a stiff neck, to a symphony of pins and needles playing some overwrought Tchaikovsky number in his hands and wrists, which were still immobilized above his head, where three hours before, Sophie had used the strappy new bikini to tie them securely to the headboard of their four-poster hotel bed.

They had driven straight from the beach in Naples to the waterfront hotel on Sanibel (the room was an engagement gift from the Rock Runners crew), and as soon as they had deposited their bags on the floor in a stunning room, replete with fresh cut flowers, fruit basket (are those *guavas?*), and ocean view, they made straight for the shower, intent on using soaps imbedded with ground apricot pits, maybe the dust of locally harvested pearls—hell, for all he knew, the crushed molars of mermaids—to exfoliate their tired bodies, to scour away the sweat and sand and brine that had dried to their skins during the drive. Finn knew Sophie loved being scrubbed and gently sandblasted by him, knew it took her back to that first night, the previous summer. And he loved it too: the memory, the slow exploration and debridement of every hollow and curve, the scrape, then slick of lather on skin, the radiance and opening of a body being made clean, made ready.

And of course, there was *the spot*, the place at the front of the hip that always made her suck in her breath with a quick hiss of pleasure as he scrubbed then kissed it, a spot that after washing, he touched lightly with his tongue, kissed and nibbled upon softly. This ministration made her buck and shudder, a place so tender, so nearly unbearably dense with nerve endings that it almost scared her to think that it was merely the gateway to someplace even more sensitive, a spot that when touched would explode every pleasure center in her brain, send her body into spasm, bring on a thundering flash of oblivion that rolled over her and lit her up for long shuddering minutes, an erasure as complete as it was temporary. And so, he had lingered there, his lips and tongue and teeth dawdling for a bit in the hollow, the wee indentation below her left pelvic bone, exactly opposite the elephant tattooed above the one on the right.

He led her on, gently tortured her, letting her quiver and moan and try unsuccessfully to push his probing mouth lower. He let her try to pull his hands upwards, to make him—*please, dear God*—skip the last inches of inner thigh, which he had scrubbed from knee to just short of the engorged and glistening place toward which he had been moving ever since he had turned on the water, and make him just *fuck her already!* But he made her wait. From the moment he had taken the bar of fragrant soap from its recycled cardboard box, he made her wait. Through the sweet torture of him slowly shampooing and rinsing her hair, combing out its wet length, he made her wait. He made her wait as he washed every inch of her, from the nape of her neck, all the way down to the callused soles of her feet. Yes, he made her wait, refrained from triggering the detonator at her desperate center until the rest of the touching was done. He could see by the look in her eyes that her mind was empty save for an increasing wave of static: the deafening sound of her every fiber calling out for consummation.

She shook and panted, each breath finishing with a whimper or the ghost of a moan. She clutched his hair with the trembling fingers of her right hand, trying to force his head to where she so badly needed it to be, tried to pull his fingers upwards and into her with her other hand. *Please,* she begged, her eyes closed, her voice barely a whisper, *now.*

And then he relented, helped her from the tub, dried her carefully, himself less so, before leading her from the bathroom and to the big, high bed. As they walked across the room, though it was just a few short steps, she regained a measure of composure, and by the time they reached the bed and he had turned down the comforter, she was breathing more slowly, shaking less visibly, was still looking at him with the same hunger, but now with an almost predatory cast to her eyes.

"Lie down," she said, bringing her breath under control, "I will be right there."

It was more command than suggestion, and he did as she asked, easing onto his back atop the exquisitely soft sheets, watching her as she walked to the mesh beach bag she had dropped by the door, reached inside, and withdrew the still damp bathing suit. This puzzled him, but *no worries*, he thought as she attended to this brief errand. He loved watching her muscles work as she walked away from him, the flex and release of high, sculpted calf, the sinuous coiling and uncoiling of hamstring, the way a dimple formed on either side of her small, rounded ass as she crossed the carpeted floor. He adored the neatly trimmed vee of pubic hair like an oasis below the gentle ripple of her taut belly, the visible xylophone of her ribs, the small, slightly upward pointing breasts, the hard nipples, like raspberries yearning from tiny, henna-colored aureoles as she approached. She walked back to the bed, the look on her face hard to read; a combination of mirth, desire, and some hidden purpose. She was a woman with a plan, a woman, suddenly, *in charge*.

She crawled onto the bed from the foot and moved up his supine body until she was straddling his chest. "Give me your hand," she said.

He did as he was told. She moved higher, her crotch directly over his mouth now, then pinned his shoulders to the mattress with her knees. She quickly tied his right hand to one tall bedpost with the bikini top, did likewise to his left hand with the strings of the suit's bottom. She had sailed off the Cape as a girl; she knew her knots. She looked straight into his eyes as she bound him, holding him rapt in the power of that gaze. There was something new in her eyes—desire, yes, but of a whole new magnitude, and something else as well, something wicked—and as she tested her handiwork with obvious satisfaction, seeing that she had just the amount of slack she required, she leaned over him, kissed him on the ear and whispered, "You really shouldn't have teased me like that," before beginning the torture of her own slow tease.

He tugged with one arm, then the other. His bonds were secure. She whispered their safe word, "pickles" into his ear, then laughed—a short, triumphant bark—and pinned his wrists to the pillow above his head. *You are mine*, her gestures said, *to do with as I please.* And so, she claimed him, took possession of him slowly over nearly two hours of slow kissing and meandering caresses, of itinerant forays of lips and fingers and tongue. After many long minutes, she pulled away slightly, repositioned herself athwart his chest and masturbated slowly, touching herself unselfconsciously, bringing herself to the place he had refused to take her, coming hard with a single, yelped *oh!* as he watched, ravenous, awestruck, and utterly helpless. Afterward, she put her fingers to his mouth, parting his lips and slipping them inside, so that he could taste her, lick and suck the wetness from her fingers. She began, then, to once again kiss and caress him, crawling along his body to taste and touch as she saw fit, eventually repositioning herself astride him, adjusting the rigging, knees pinning his shoulders, demanding that he drink of her, telling him exactly what she wanted as she eased herself down toward his yearning tongue.

* * *

SHE LEFT NO stone unturned, ignored no part of his body as she explored at her leisure. Yes, she took her time, as he had with her, working with an exquisite and exasperating patience, touching and licking and sucking at places that would ratchet up the tension, the sweet suffering, bring gasps and moans from deep in his chest, make him arch his back in a reflexive, doomed attempt to bury himself in her. She bit his nipples, plunged her tongue into his ears and his belly button, kissed him behind his knees, a secret erogenous zone that delighted her. She lingered at the crack of his ass, spread him and slid slick fingers over the pucker of his anus, darted a small wet fingertip inside as he gasped. She caressed and licked every inch of him, from head to toe, as he wriggled and moaned with increasing desperation.

Every inch...except where he wanted to be touched the most. She ventured ever nearer to his cock, spent long moments licking the very spot above his hip where he had so tormented her, stroking his thighs, occasionally cupping his balls, which made him groan loudly, but she did not touch the trembling, slender, and slightly curved bulk of his erection, no matter how he arched or writhed. It was torture, delicious and terrible anguish, and then—*sweet Jesus!*—finally she touched him, took him in hand, stroked and licked and sucked him, almost instantly bringing him to the brink of release before retreating, returning him to a just-bearable baseline of unfulfilled desire. Three times she left him stranded at the brink of the abyss, her fingers circled tightly around his throbbing balls to keep him from ejaculating, three times left him panting and moaning and muttering, *Please. Oh, Sophie...please.*

She too had moved once again to the precipice. Even in his delirium he could see that. She had brought herself to orgasm, over an hour ago now, then had come once again riding Finn's probing tongue, and now here she was, at the exact place, and at the exact moment where she had so slowly and expertly taken him. They would leap into the abyss together.

She kissed him deeply, then positioned herself above his quivering penis, taking it in her hand and guiding it to her vagina and slipping him inside. She slowly eased her full weight down onto him, taking him fully inside her with a long, involuntary gasp. He moaned loudly as she settled onto him with a tiny yelp. She raised up slowly, feeling him withdraw until only the tip of him was within her. This time, however, she slammed her hips down hard burying him to the hilt, and placing both hands on his chest, rode him as hard and fast as she could—no more waiting, not for either of them—their cries drowning out the sound of the waves and seabirds outside the window, until they came, quickly, cacophonously and together, and collapsed in an exhausted, conjoined heap.

* * *

SOPHIE, HE THOUGHT as he awoke an hour later, relishing her name on his lips, his arms all a-tingle. Endlessly surprising Sophie. Sweet, kinky Sophie. Sophie, who lay sprawled across him, snoring ever so slightly, her naked body warm and slightly sunburned, her back, rising and falling gently with her every breath, striped with the shadows of whispering curtains in the dying winter light. Sophie, his one true love, his alpha and omega, Sophie who needed to wake and untie him pretty darn quick, because, oh my goodness, he really had to pee.

* * *

THEY HAD DRIVEN straight from the beach in Naples to the tony Sanibel hotel where they would be spending the next two nights, their days spent shell hunting, running slowly on the beach and nearby bicycle paths, swimming, and making love, before flying home just in time for another Colorado blizzard. The first night, after he had awakened her and she had unbound him that he might hobble to the bathroom (where he had to piss sitting down; his hands were still not working, not even well enough to handle the relatively simple task of urinating), they showered again, this time quickly—no funny business—as they handled their own ablutions, dressed in the nicest clothes they had brought, Finn in linen trousers, a blue Oxford and navy blazer, Sophie in a whisper of a cornflower-patterned sundress he had not seen before, and walked hand-in-hand to the elegant hotel restaurant, arriving with five minutes to spare before their dinner reservation.

They had known they would not want dinner until late, and by the time the hostess had shown them to their table at a window overlooking the marina, most of the other diners had left, those who remained lingering over dessert or an aperitif. Finn looked out at the marina, the dock closest to them clustered with a host of gently bobbing dinghies, Zodiacs, and other small craft. A rack of parti-colored rental kayaks stood at the near end of the pier, while out beyond the dinghies were tied some more impressive playboats, including a sleek and gleaming classic wooden Chris-Craft, which Finn found to be as erotic and intoxicating an object as a finely-made and polished cello. And beyond these small crafts, a short distance out into the harbor, were moored a pair of large yachts, one dark, save for lights pulsing fore and aft, a green glow emanating from the instruments on the bridge, the other alive and strung with more lights than a Christmas tree, a dozen or two people drinking, dancing, or leaning at the railing, looking out to sea.

He looked out at the yacht, its happy display of conspicuous consumption, and let out a low whistle, felt an odd combination of disgust, condescension, and awe. Envy he did not feel; his life was perfect. He looked at Sophie and shook his head.

She took his hand across the table, the diamond on her finger sending out little shooting stars of reflected candlelight. "Toto," she said, "I don't think we're in Kansas anymore."

Two days later, they clicked their heels three times, boarded a 747, and left the sunny climes of Oz, happy they had come, but eager to get back to their home, their work, even the deepening snows of a Colorado winter.

Sophie

THE DAYS WERE beginning to lengthen, so it was now possible to run safely on the snowpacked area trails until just after five, but Finn had mysteriously insisted they wait until perilously close to sunset before setting out, so they wore lightweight LED headlamps over their stocking caps just in case. They took the rocky, steeply switchbacked trail that began behind the football stadium, an area already deep in shadow, and climbed past the huge capital A whitewashed onto rocks by generations of university students. The metal coils of the Yaktrax they had strapped to their trail shoes dug into the ice and packed snow, making their footsteps midsummer secure. This was not her favorite way to reach the top of the ridge, which lay between town and the reservoir around which so many of their runs took place, either on the long, hilly road high above both lake and town, which offered spectacular views in all directions, or spidery single-track trails that meandered to the water's edge. By stitching in a few scattered stretches of road, one could—in theory—circumnavigate the entire reservoir, something neither she nor Finn had ever attempted, though they talked of maybe giving it a try the following summer. The steep climb commenced a little too close to their house (*our house!*), for her taste, as she was never quite warmed-up enough when she reached the sudden climb, her heart, lungs, and legs not yet quite working in harmony, so the grind to the top always seemed harder than it should. She much preferred the meandering trail which skirted the large pond farther down the ridge, then crossed through a large prairie-dog town before beginning to snake its way up the conifer-flecked hogback. But the cryptic Finn had told her that way would be too long, and besides, he wanted to show her something. Sophie was mystified. They had gone on maybe a hundred runs together, and she thought she knew every permutation of road, path, and trail open to her in the patchwork of open space and mountain parks west of town. Apparently, she was mistaken.

Finn kept alluding to something special, saying things like, "I think conditions should be right," or, "This looks like a good day for it, yep," so by the time they pulled on tights and toques and the precautionary headlamps, she was completely baffled, and more than a little curious as to what was about to transpire.

The late afternoon light was mesmerizing: bright, yet at such a low angle that on such a dazzling, cloudless day (and frigid: the thermometer in their kitchen read nine degrees), it made the whole world a patchwork quilt of sunlight and shade. Spotlit areas of stunning clarity crisscrossed areas of deep shadow, a chiaroscuro that foretold the coming of a bitter night, droplets of which had already spilled, pooling in the lee of every hill, rock, and tree, a crepuscularity that would grow and deepen, shadow pooling into shadow, until everything between the stars in the sky and the lights of town was consumed by a ravenous and inky black.

For now, however, the clouds of their breath ascended into a deep and singular blue, a tract of sky unmarred, save for the vapor trail of a single high jet, already being pulled apart by the winds aloft. They leaned into the hill's steep last meters, and were rewarded at the summit with a patch of smooth, flat single-track, illuminated by the blinding disc of the sun, a white winter orb that set the red cliffs across the lake aflame and painted both the snow-tipped trees they ran between and the distant, snowy mountains in silver splendor. As they wound along the flat trail through the yucca, sagebrush, and dead winter grasses that led to the lake, Sophie detected movement to their left, and looked over to spy a small herd of deer—no more than ten or twelve—grazing on tufts that protruded from the snow, cleverly camouflaged to blend in with the small pine trees and clumps of sagebrush that dotted the snowy ridgetop. The one closest to the trail raised her head, watched the runners move silently past, and, sensing no danger, returned to her grazing.

Sophie smiled at Finn, who had seen them too. He gave a quick bob of eyebrows, as if to say, *That was cool,* then returned his attention to the winding single-track. A minute later, they had crossed the road and were now descending, following the trail down to the lake, which shone beneath them, an icy blue mirror in the final glory of a heatless sun. The trail wound its way around small, fossil-laden outcroppings and clumps of bushes, some still bearing hard, red berries that the birds refused to touch, until it reached the lake's edge, to which it clung, running for a few hundred yards along a tiny cove where flat-topped chunks of sandstone were licked at by the icy water. The snowpacked single-track then switchbacked up and away from the lake, climbing above the short cliff that emerged vertically from the water, before dipping again lakeward on the cliff's opposite end. The usually gabby Finn was being oddly circumspect as they approached the lake, so she followed his lead, padding wordlessly behind, until, as they reached a spot about fifty meters from the water's edge, she heard it. Indistinct at first, but slowly growing loud enough to be audible over the slight breeze whispering through the old yucca pods and dry winter grasses, here it came: a faint tinkling sound, the volume of which seemed to grow until, when they rounded the shoulder of a final hill and arrived at the rocky little beach, they were greeted with a small, yet majestic symphony. Finn stopped, waited in the rock-peppered, frozen sand at the water's edge, and held out his gloved hand. She took it and stood silently, enraptured by the sound, thrilled to witness what was causing it.

They stood in a spot where the lake had carved out a shallow u, and where the wind, blowing into their faces from across the lake, made little waves that blew into the concavity, sheering off the millimeters-thin layer of ice that had formed during the still hours of morning and afternoon, and which had covered an area that reached from shore to maybe a dozen feet out into the lake.

The breeze was negligible, but enough to push the feather-light ice up onto the narrow, rocky beach. The ice, as it cracked, sheered away and was driven onto the backs of other thin sheets, and began to pile up in crazily tilted angles along the rocks and sand, making the most remarkable music she had ever heard. The orchestral pile-up extended maybe five feet out into the lake and for at least fifty yards in either direction up the shore. It sang out a melody of shattering: a quiet cacophony made of a million tiny bells.

Sophie squeezed Finn's hand tightly as a balloon of pure wonder and delight inflated within her. This was something rare, completely new, without a doubt the very best thing ever. They stood silently together for a moment, Finn releasing her hand, moving behind her and wrapping her in his arms, keeping her warm as the steam rose from their bodies into the last of the light.

"Now look," he whispered, pointing to where the windblown plates of ice continued to pile musically atop one another.

She looked at where he was pointing, confused for a moment, but then it began to happen. Swift rivers of light began to zig-zag among the shattered platters of ice in all directions, sinuous rills of lightning that swam through and under the ice then shot off in beams and beacons into the air. Depending on how deeply the ice was buried among other layers, and at what angle, the veins of light running through the ice were either the fiery reddish orange of the sunset, the palest, iciest blue she could imagine, or a blinding, brilliant white. Though completely rapt in wonder, her experienced painter's eye swiftly sussed out the situation, and she put together exactly how this phenomenon occurred.

The sun was setting behind the low cliffs across the lake, a pale orb burning cold and bright in the deepening blue, and it set the low clouds atop the ridgeline afire with a deep red flame. Its light came in low and flat across the water, hitting the million mirrors of ice that lay piled along the shore at a shallow angle, setting their edges alight like a planet of shattered prisms. The sunlight reflected and refracted, bounced along and through the myriad hallways of this most complex of funhouse halls of mirrors, setting it athrob with bright blue veins, molten orange rivers, spotlight-white beams of dancing light. The light came from multiple angles, from multiple depths, making a mosaic that confused the eyes with the minutiae of its dancing fractals. Sophie stood a moment, transfixed by these tessellations, then extricated herself from Finn's embrace and squatted at the edge of this singing ice field set aflame, and stared unblinkingly until the sun slipped below the horizon and the lightshow winked out.

"Whoooaa," was all she said when it was over, the single word coming in a long, clouded exhalation. They had not spoken in nearly fifteen minutes, and now, in the new darkness, the chiming of the ice seemed even louder, the wind adding its voice in a low lonely harmony. "The groaning gusts grew to a slow moan," she orated with an insincere solemnity, breaking the spell. She clicked on her headlamp, then turned and began to run up the trail in the direction from which they had come.

"Joined by a twee tintinnabulation of tiny tinkles," Finn recited back in an uppercrust English accent, turning on his lamp as well.

"Wow," she said. "You should be a poet or something."

She stopped at the top of the first little rise, turning off the headlamp once more. Finn did likewise. They took a moment to reacquaint themselves to the darkness, which was now total, save for a lavender glow on the western horizon.

"Look," she said, pointing upwards, where the sky was now an inky dome dotted with a million bright pinpricks, "and listen." Behind them, the ice continued to collide and shatter and tinkle in the darkness. "It's almost like the stars are singing."

* * *

THAT NIGHT, SOPHIE found it impossible to sleep. She was a synesthete, and the experience at the lake almost blew her wiring.

Music, and sometimes even voices, sent an aurora dancing across her field of vision, waves of pulsating color that changed according to the tone and the volume of the sound. These nimbi brought with them strong, yet often capricious, surges of feeling, strange magiks and energies that fueled her as she wheeled, darted and spun before a canvas, wielding her brushes like a toreador. The experience at the lake had exponentially enhanced the effect. It was like trying to sleep through a supernova, a sensation she found unnerving, though not entirely unpleasant.

She lay there, waiting for sleep, the colors, with their attendant music (and even fleeting smells: haba-neros, jasmine and lime) dancing behind her lids. She opened her eyes and watched Finn as he slumbered blissfully on, as untroubled as a child. Being an artist himself, he understood her gift; that, he had made perfectly clear. She knew he was secretly a little jealous of it, too, though he was a dear and never let on. It touched her how he knew that this was exactly the thing she was always looking for, an example of nature turning figure into an abstraction that would fuse her senses, worm its way into her mind, and demand to be satisfied, to be lived in, obsessed over, and recreated in masterful explosions of paint. He had only experienced the phenomenon with the ice four or five times himself, he said—always at dawn or dusk—and had waited anxiously for a day when conditions were right: a cold, calm afternoon with a light westerly breeze kicking up just before a cloudless, or at least mostly cloudless sunset. He said that waiting to show her this was worse than being a child and waiting for the dawning of a Christmas morning.

As was almost always the case after such a dose of sensory overstimulation, Sophie more or less attacked Finn as soon as they arrived home from the run, not even waiting to shower, and when she commanded him to bend her over a living room chair and take her from behind, he was

more than happy to oblige. As he fucked her, her vision pulsed with oranges and yellows; sugar burned and caramelized on her tongue and in her nose. Their running clothes were scattered in haphazard piles, discarded just inside the front door, which had barely closed behind them before they began desperately kissing and disrobing, happily ransacking one another just over the threshold, both still wearing their stocking hats and socks, fucking like bunnies before the open and forgotten curtains of the window for the whole world to see.

Afterwards, they had showered, eaten a salad and the chili that Finn had made, which had been simmering in the slow cooker all day, sopping up the broth with big chunks of hearty homemade bread. Then she retreated to her chair to sketch for a bit, to figure out the base mechanics of what she had seen, as Finn graded student essays in his nook. They talked in bed for a bit and Finn drifted off to sleep. Sleep came more slowly to Sophie, however, as the wild display of light through ice, the crazy percussion of frozen bells played in thunderous IMAX inside her head, tormenting her thoughts until, at last, her thoughts turned into dreams.

* * *

IT FELT GOOD to be back in the studio, with its smell of new art supplies and old horseshit, good to have a brush in hand and a series of sketches tacked to the corkboard, to feel the rush of excitement and fear as she stood before the empty sweep of by far the largest canvas she had yet attempted. It was good to feel the technicolor thump of adrenaline, rocket fuel for another journey into the unknown. She adjusted the lighting, turned on the music which would soundtrack this first foray into the creation of the painting. She eased through the stretching routine that would chase the last of the post-run stiffness from her muscles, ease any tightness that had not bled away during her shower after the run, which had elevated her heartrate, enhanced her alertness, made every sense more aware, sharper, and ready to paint.

Fourteen more inches of snow had fallen in the three days since the brittle sunset symphony, and Sophie had been relieved to find the road up the canyon, across the ranch, and to her doorstep finally plowed, to be at the wheel of her Subaru wagon, which, with its four-wheel drive, easily managed the snowpacked roads from town to her studio. The drifts of plowed snow on either side of the drive from the ranch road to the barn were now more than six feet high, and the rancher she paid to plow had left a curved semicircle in front of the barn, a cleared apron more than big enough for their two cars. The thermometer on the outside of the barn read minus-seventeen degrees. Finn had followed her up in his truck, and they had run a workout on the mostly flat dirt roads that ran through the long, ranch-studded valley.

The roads were snowpacked, but not icy, and the compacted snow squeaked beneath their feet like Styrofoam, a perfect surface on which to run, and in studded trail shoes they were able to hammer out ten miles of fartlek (Swedish for "speed play," steady hard tempo, dotted with bursts of a half or three quarters of a mile at faster than race pace) without worry of falling or being hit by a sliding car. It took a long time to warm up in such deep cold, and wearing tights and two upper-body layers underneath Gore-Tex suits was not exactly conducive to fast running, but they knew these were exactly the workouts their competitors from more temperate climes were not doing, and which would make them very tough to beat when the snows melted and the roads cleared.

They ran an out-and-back course from one end of the valley to the other, through a sun-drenched and frosted winter landscape. Finn gradually pulled away until he was a brilliant blue speck on the white road in the distance, a speck that swiftly grew larger after he reached the turnaround (a gnarled, lightning-struck old cypress) and began to run back toward her. He had warmed up enough to pull the polypropylene facemask from over his mouth, and his breath had made vast iceworks out of his eyelashes, brows, and the few locks that escaped from his jauntily tasseled ski cap. His face was a frozen crimson, save for a pure white circle on each cheekbone, and a sweat-sicle had grown from his chin to his chest. Seeing him, she was glad she had kept her mask pulled up, even if she had to tug it down occasionally for a quick spit. The clouds of breath escaping the mask froze her eyelashes shut, and every few minutes she had to pry them quickly apart with thumb and forefinger, not an easy task with fingers encased in bulky gloves. Sunlight reflected crazily from every angle, and the cold air burned the small strip of exposed skin between her balaclava and shades. Each breath soon became an act of will, and every stride, as she accelerated into yet another hard half-mile surge, seemed to cost her a little more dearly. She was fried. She was hurting. She was having a blast.

Finn, too, was in the middle of one of the fast bits as he came flying past, and also obviously suffering, but still, he reached out to return her high-five, panting out, "Lovely. Weather..." between laborious and cloudy breaths, before disappearing down the road behind her in the direction of the barn, wherein he will have made a pot of tea for himself and one of coffee for her by the time she sprinted through the door some six minutes later.

After the run, they warmed up in front of the woodstove in her loft in the barn, Finn shedding his jacket and the two layers underneath, toweling off, then donning a T-Shirt and heavy wool sweater before inhaling a mug of tea, slipping into a puffy down parka and huge, floppy-eared hat, and returning to town, where he would grab a quick shower, then head to campus for class. Sophie drank her coffee, taking the full travel mug with her into the shower, where she stayed for ages, head under the blessed torrent of hot water until every bit of post-run chill had melted from her bones, gathering the resources to dress and descend the spiral staircase to her studio.

* * *

SOPHIE PAINTS *A Festival of Light* to Messiaen's *Des Canyons aux etoiles...*, spends the next five months inside the infinite dome depicted by the music, inside the bubble of light that illuminates the twelve panels of the canvas, which she moves over like an indefatigable spider, weaving a shattered and shimmering web made of nothing but color and light. The individual canvasses—one for each movement of Messiaen's piece—come together in a gentle crescent that mimics the shallow u of the cove where the laser-concert of shards and bells had taken place. The 95-minute long chamber piece, whose title translates to *From the Canyons to the stars...*, and which attempts in turn to translate Utah's stunning desert and skyscapes into music, creates a perfect sonic space within which she could move, a vast playground of the mind, awash in aurorae borealis that pulse and throb through the wide and empty interstices between bursts of song. The atmospherics created by the music, by Sophie's memory of the light show, by all the tools at her disposal—the paint and brushes and canvas, her muscles, bones, and ligaments, the blood thrumming through her veins, each oxygen molecule bringing life to every cell in her body—this synesthetic blender of color and music and emotion, of nerve and synapse and electrical impulse run amok, all of it explodes within and around her like a supernova. And though, in a tiny control room in her mind, there sits a ruthless technician who approaches the canvas with a cold and technical eye, the rest of her surrenders completely to this cosmological dissolution and reformation, this violent and perfectly choreographed apocalypse. In a very real sense, she works in a space that contains far more than three dimensions. The boundary between brush and canvas, paint and painter, sight and sound disappears. She is elemental. She is music. She is light itself.

Sometimes frenetic, sometimes gentle, plunging from the bombast of brass into a silence sprinkled with tiny glissandi and broken piano phrases, the music paints its own picture on the canvas of her ear. At a level beyond thought, she weaves strands from these auditory images to filaments from the visual extravaganza of that night at the lake. The colors that had flashed through tiny fissures in the shards, the bell-chorus as they shattered, have somehow married themselves to the hues of Messiaen's music somewhere deep within the radiant cathedral of Sophie's brain. Lightning flashes; thunder rolls; epic silences pulse with bands of blazing color, like synapses firing in the mind of God. *Cool,* she thinks, *now all I have to do is paint it.*

She is excited and intimidated by the challenges this piece presents, spends endless hours thinking through the immense technical problems the painting demands she solve. How to deal with the complexity of multiple amplitudes of finely nuanced light, the way it zipped and sizzled between layers of ice? She spends hours on the phone with Chaim, discussing technical minutiae. How to recreate the single ice sheet, wind-shattered and blown into a palace of panes, a chiming crazy-quilt of mirrors that occupied every gradient on a continuum between transparent and translucent, between translucent and opaque? And the sheer scope of it! Twelve four-by-four foot squares must be made to flow together and work as a single unit. The necessity and challenge of the slow, shallow curve, and again—and always! —the dozen colors of light, each with its own particular volume and hue. How to capture both the vastness of the scene, the sunset horizon and the encroaching emptiness of space, the creeping indigo, the wind whispering along the lake and cliffs, the stars beginning to pop on in the heavens behind them—while remaining focused on the tiny, immense grandeur of the myriad cracks, the movement as the shards splintered, the nearly infinite capillaries of light bursting to life along a million planes and edges—all of this weighs on her during every waking moment. Over and over, she plays the Messiaen. In its music, weird and spare and holy, lurks the code which will unlock her painting. Its singing will help her to see.

* * *

SHE BECOME SILENT and distant on runs. Still able to focus her physical energies on the task at hand, she becomes nevertheless lost in the canyons and stars and ten thousand tiny lightning bolts of the painting. During these runs, she is lost also to Finn—who kind of misses her, though there she is, just inches away—matching him stride-for-stride, but still light-years gone. He accepts her need for space, uses the new silence of their time on the roads together to work through whatever poem he is writing at the moment. He tells her later that when she is deep into a painting, when she becomes kind of a benign ghost that haunts his life, it helps him to cope if he imagines that she is simply away on a business trip. Or maybe an astronaut orbiting the Earth a few miles above him, the light of her craft visible through a nighttime telescope. And thus, though he goes about his days as always, dealing with the quotidian banalities of real life, his every moment is now saddened by her distance, yet sweetened by the anticipation of her eventual return.

"There's a hole in my life," he tells her on a run one afternoon, "but hey, abscess makes the heart grow fonder."

She does not laugh; she does not even hear. She's gone again, off into her painting, lost somewhere in the hunks and colors singing from deep inside her own head.

And he takes care of her physical needs, for which she is more grateful than she could say. He cooks and servs her meals, does the shopping and the laundry, makes sure she eats and drinks and brushes her teeth before bed. He tells her he is nervous she might cross a street without looking or stopping while on a run, will, as he puts it, become a "pretty hood ornament," which she assures him will not happen, though in truth, she isn't so sure. This is kind of new, this becoming so lost in her work, these extremes of obsession and detachment, the swings between insatiable sexual desire and a disinterest bordering on depression. Finn attempts to put it in perspective, to comfort her. He tells her how he suffers from the same affliction when deep inside the belly of the beast, wrestles with his own art-induced bipolar disorder while lost in a poem.

He reassures her that all geniuses go through this, which gats the intended laugh, but really, she is freaking herself out a little. Sure, she had always had great focus, both in her art and in her running, and she is good at disappearing inside a piece while she is working on it. Chaim and Jimmy had become good friends through keeping one another informed of her whereabouts, as she started coming habitually late to the track or the studio, lost in the depths of a training cycle or art project. They both knew a great talent when they saw one; they understood the demands such gifts placed upon her. But never had she attempted something so daunting as this, something that not only demanded all of her abilities and resources, but in fact demanded exponentially more than she knew how to do, forcing her to climb a learning curve that looked a little like Everest. She spends every waking (and dreaming) moment lost, deep in the belly of her own beast, doing everything she can think of to paint her way out.

⁂

SIX MONTHS LATER, the gigantic painting, around which an obsessive Sophie still flutters, swooping in to apply last dabs of pigment or make miniscule alterations even as the panels are being assembled, is installed in the main gallery of the university's sparkling new arts building, just in time for the building's grand opening and the beginning of a new school year. Sophie blames Finn for this development. She had allowed him onto her barn's studio floor from time to time during the making of the painting (not her usual practice—she superstitiously refrained from showing a painting to anyone until she was finished—but since he had been there at the genesis of the work, exceptions were made), and Finn was so stunned by what he saw that he begged her to let Gizmo come take a look. An impressed and clearly surprised Gizmo quickly summoned up some art world clout. Meetings were held, other expert opinions were solicited, arms were twisted in the administration building, and suddenly, *A Festival of Light* was the jewel set in the dazzling heart of the glittering new building, the centerpiece for the high-profile opening gala. The governor would be in attendance, Big Head Todd and the Monsters and the Samples would be playing, champagne would flow, and Sophie and her painting would be center stage at the event of the year in this thriving college town.

When Finn had presented the idea to her just two months before, over dinner of fruit and chilled pasta salad at the picnic table outside the barn, the painting was only three-fourths complete, though she had to admit it had gained terminal velocity. She could close her eyes and envision nearly every brush stroke from that point on. They had just finished an easy run down Young's Gulch, their feet wet from its dozens of stream crossings, and Sophie had given him a rare glimpse of her progress on the painting, the effect of which necessitated he sit down or risk falling over. After he was finished gaping at the nearly finished work in mute stupefaction, Finn made the observation that the piece would fit spectacularly in the new art building's main gallery, that maybe they should talk to somebody. She had shrugged, said "Sure," and forgotten about it, chalking it up to idle chit-chat born of post-run stupor. Three weeks later, as she sits stunned in the office of the university president, discussing particulars with Gizmo, curators, and nice enough, but slightly condescending university officials, she makes a note to never, ever underestimate Finn again when he starts championing her work and making crazy suggestions. *Jesus. Next time he comes up with an idea like this, I am going to punch him.*

The painting's twelve panels fit seamlessly together in a gradual u-shape about as deep as a bird bath or a spaghetti bowl. Its shallow arc is backed against a temporary wall just shy of the center of the large room, from where it swoops into the gallery's main space, its arms enveloping viewers in an electric embrace. It stands in its own island of lucent energy at the center of the room, which in general is more dimly illuminated, mood lighting that suggests an intimate cocktail party, while paintings on the walls are lit by bulbs hidden in discrete sconces. A long, slatted wooden bench had been placed in front of the painting, nearly between the opposing faces of the canvas. The bench had been occupied by an uninterrupted series of dazzled and hypnotized viewers for the duration of the evening.

"It turned out okay, I guess. . .didn't it?" Sophie says to Finn between sips of champagne, two hours in, feeling more relieved than exhilarated. She is only just beginning to get used to the glances from tuxedoed and gowned attendees, the nudges and nods in her direction from four generations of people clad in formal wear. (New to the West, she wasn't sure she cared much for the combination of tuxedo and cowboy boots sported by a surprising number of men, though she thought the occasional tux/Chuck Taylors combo to be quite dashing). She wishes she had a dollar for every time she had overheard someone whispering, *That's the artist.* She shakes off an adrenaline shudder and grabs another flute of champagne from a passing server, downs it in a single, furtive gulp.

Finn laughs, wraps an arm around her bare shoulders, and beams. "Yeah, you could say that."

Puddles of impressed party-goers had coalesced and dissipated before the painting all night long, cooing and nodding and whispering excitedly to one another. Perhaps the highlight of Sophie's entire evening was overhearing an enraptured graduate student, decked out in piercings and thrift store finery, and standing transfixed between the painting's wings, say to her mohawked companion, resplendent in jeans and velvet waistcoat, *I can actually hear it! Can you hear it?*

* * *

"EXCUSE ME?" SOPHIE stands in a puddle of late afternoon sun, drinking iced tea and stretching her calves, holding the phone to her ear with one hand, as she pulls out a kitchen chair with the other. The person on the other end of the line has just said something that knocked her in the knees; she needs to sit down. "I'm not sure I heard you correctly, could you say that again?" She eases into the chair as her caller repeats what she had said. "Okay," says Sophie, trying to remain calm, "Uh-huh, yes, that would be fine." The other person speaks again briefly, then Sophie, running her fingers through her hair in disbelief, answers, "I understand. Yes, I think that will work. You too, goodbye."

Sophie stands up, extricates herself from the phone cord, which she has wrapped around herself three times during the short conversation, then slumps back at the dining room table. *This can't be happening,* she says to herself, maybe silently, maybe aloud. *This cannot be real.* She takes a long drink from her sweating glass of tea, idly runs a finger through the ring of condensation it has left behind on the table, then picks up the business card that had been sitting next to the glass. She looks at the card, returns it to the table, stands, and starts to pace. Back and forth across the sunny kitchen she goes, five steps to and five steps fro. She stops, gazes out the window, disinterestedly notices the patina of red dust, the crusted white spatters of bird shit on her Subaru, begins again to pace. She picks up the business card, puts it down. She is dressed to run. Finn will be home in twenty minutes, and then they will be heading to the track. She is not at all sure she will last that long before her head explodes.

* * *

"ONE HUNDRED SEVENTEEN thousand dollars."

She couldn't believe how calm Finn had looked when she said it, the look he gave her that said, *Sounds about right.* He was just as raving mad as the rest of them! She had waited until they had begun their warmup run to the track before she told him. She was nearly jumping out of her skin by the time he got home, but she kept her cool while he changed and grabbed his spikes, waiting until they had gotten a couple of blocks from home before she told him about the phone call from Anais Fleischer in New York.

The previous Friday night, after the opening of the university art building, as Sophie and Finn had stood on a second-floor balcony, enjoying a final glass of champagne and looking out over the now-quiet campus, Sophie trying to decompress after the unexpected splash her painting had made at the gala, Gizmo walked over to them smiling, and handed her a business card. Despite Sophie's contentious relationship with Giz, she had to admit that he was gorgeous. Tall, dark, and buff in Armani, all evening long he had been cause for women (and some men) of all ages to stare and stop conversations in the middle of a sentence—a couple had even spilled their drinks—as he worked the room. Noticing that he stopped often to talk with Sophie, a few women who Sophie had never met asked her to make introductions, which she did, and gladly. It was a nice diversion from the general nerve-wrackingness of the whole affair, not to mention an effective diversion of her own vexing attraction. He smiled and spoke graciously with the women, though when their backs were turned, he rolled his eyes at Sophie and slashed his hand across his throat—*Stop it!*—before returning his polite attention to his new admirer. Sophie simply shrugged and discretely stuck out her tongue.

Between schmoozing and fending off besotted women, Giz had directed a pair of photographers who had begun taking photos of her painting in the last empty moments before the party had begun, and had continued to do so, from all possible distances and angles, until the evening was through. She had no idea what he was up to, and in the crush of the evening had had no chance to ask him, but here he was at last, walking toward them while deftly juggling several plastic film cannisters and grinning like the Cheshire cat dressed for a wedding.

"There you two are! I've been looking for you everywhere!" He started tucking film cans into various trouser and jacket pockets, before, from the inside pocket of his jacket, removing a business card and handing it to Sophie. "I am pretty sure," he said, joining she and Finn on the balcony and taking a deep breath of the fragrant late-summer air, "that you will be getting a call from this person sometime in the next week or so."

She looked at the card, heavy and beautifully embossed in burgundy and cream. It said simply, The Anais Fleischer Gallery, with an address and phone number in Manhattan. Sophie was not sure what was going on. "Okaaaay..." she said.

"An associate of mine. I am sending her some pictures of your painting, if you don't mind. Who knows, maybe she will want to come to Colorado herself, have a little look-see." He looked at Sophie's uncomprehending face, smiled sweetly, then continued. "This is a college town, right? There must be someplace we can dig up a pizza. Do you know how hard it is to find good pizza in London?" The building was empty, save for Sophie, Finn, Giz, and the cleaning crew. Giz looked at them, eyebrows raised, hands extended, palms up, all about the pizza. She was pretty sure she was going to punch him. He laughed at her consternation. "Okay, okay, take me to your favorite pizza place. I will tell you what I'm thinking on the way."

* * *

TEN DAYS LATER, she found herself represented by the Anais Fleischer Gallery, a relatively new, but well-financed outfit with spaces in New York and Santa Fe. Anais Fleischer herself, accompanied by a terrifyingly hip and efficient assistant ("I am Enrique," was all he said to Sophie the entire afternoon), arrived five days after the gala. Fleischer was professional, but warm, her

Donna Karan made slightly bohemian by scarves and bangles. Enrique, sleek as a knife blade in all black, offered nothing but his name as he gave her an air-kiss and a mildly disapproving once-over. Then it was all conspiratorial whispers to "Ms. Fleischer," who spent thirty minutes inspecting *A Festival of Light* from all angles, gesturing and whispering to Enrique, who followed her around, taking notes on a yellow legal pad inside a leather folder as Sophie wandered the gallery, looking at the art hung on the walls and sweating bullets.

Then it was a half-hour ride up the canyon to the studio, over which Fleischer effused, asking many questions about its construction. She asked as well about the small, but growing number of works Sophie had created there, all of them tiny and jewel-like, save for the large *Lightning Strikes Twice* and the much larger *A Festival of Light*. Even the hipster sphinx showed signs of being impressed. After an hour, Fleischer had seen enough, Enrique put his legal pad back into his thin Coach messenger bag, and they were quickly back in the Subaru, heading toward town. Sophie had no clue what would happen next.

* * *

"ONE HUNDRED SEVENTEEN thousand dollars! Finn, that is insane! Nobody will pay that for my painting."

They were meandering through the streets between the park and campus in the aftermath of the phone call, taking the long way to the track, where they were meeting Rachel and Rex for a workout, followed by a weight session at the college fitness center before dinner at Gonzalo's, their favorite Mexican restaurant. Sophie was aware of how manic she was about this, but her mind was completely blown. It had to be a joke. This kind of shit simply didn't happen to people like her!

"Gizmo told you this might happen, remember?" Finn was obviously doing his best to keep her calm, though he was looking a little stunned himself. She was glad they had the good, hard track workout to focus on, something exhausting to deflect the weight of the news from New York, its possible implications. "He said your work belonged out in the world, that Fleischer could make it happen."

"Yeah, but he had pizza sauce on his nose at the time, for God's sake. Finn, a piece of fucking cheese was hanging from his chin!"

* * *

EZEKIEL TALKED WITH his hands. Beautiful, with long lashes and long, delicate fingers, he wove tapestries in the air, even as his melodic, Arabic-inflected English wove a spellbinding mosaic of words. Anais insisted the four artists, whose group show was set to open at the gallery the next day, tell their stories, one by one, and in as great detail as possible. She also insisted they do so at a sleepover at her Upper West-Side co-op the night before the show's early November opening. It was a fabulous way for them all to get to know one another, she said, to kill the preshow butterflies and nip any sibling rivalries in the bud.

"She's a fucking loony," whispered Ophelia Essex, a greyhound-like sculptor from Liverpool, in Sophie's ear when Fleischer had delivered the edict two days before, as the show was being hung, "but I adore her!"

So Sophie instructed Finn to make alternate plans for the evening, while she and her new friends had a slumber party. She came back from the gallery to pack a bag and found that Finn had already thought to do so, filling a paper shopping bag from Whole Foods with a pillow, a pair of child's footy pajamas, a stuffed bunny, a sippy cup, and a coloring book. *He cracks himself up,* she said to herself and laughed at the sweet silliness of the gesture. Finn had already left to meet Giz and Beannie at an old college haunt of theirs in the Village (both Finn and Beannie had gone to grad school at NYU). Sophie had planned on hanging with them, but this was a business trip, after all, so sleepover it was.

It had been a long time since she had felt lonely or apprehensive, but this was an unforeseen and overwhelming experience for her and having no Finn to talk to when she got back to the hotel to gather her things filled her with a low-grade anxious melancholy. Being the youngest and least worldly of Anais Fleischer's crew, she was nervous and just a bit shy, an exact sensation she had not experienced since the first day of cross country practice her freshman year at Tufts. But, as on that occasion, her apprehension quickly evaporated. The doorman's greeting of "Ms. Ringrose! We're so happy you're here," was wonderful, and the gin and tonic handed to her by a beaming Anais Fleischer as she walked through the front door didn't hurt either.

Ezekiel Ali, who at thirty-eight was the senior member of the group, had gone first. An Israeli national, with a Jewish mother and Palestinian father, Ali had emigrated from Khan Yunis, in Gaza, to New York with his French wife and two sons after the failure of the Oslo Accords. He was in the middle of a telling the assemblage about his oldest son Claude's nascent career as a pubescent hip-hop artist and was illuminating his tale with elaborate hand gestures and some impressive dance moves. Sophie knew a little of Ali's story from an *Art in America* profile: the life lived on a razor's edge as the child of two cultures whose relations see-sawed between armed standoff and outright war. His parents were doctors who had worked side by side during one patch of bloodshed or another, and as is often the case in such stressful situations, formed a bond that deepened into love. Disowned by both of their families and harassed by both Israeli and Palestinian officials at the outbreak of the First Intifada, they sent their son to France, where he attended college, married, and began to paint seriously. Shortly after the peace—which everyone had hoped would take root with the Israel/Palestine agreement in Oslo—

began to quickly unravel, his father was killed in an Israeli air raid on his way to a Gaza hospital. Ali returned to the territories with his young family to care for his mother, who died of a heart attack the following year. Heartbroken and full of rage, he took a teaching appointment in New York, buried himself in painting and his students who worshipped him. His painting career had subsequently taken off, Anais had presciently snapped him up, seen to it the art press noticed that he was both different and good, and... *viola,* sleepover! In two months, he would take the U.S. Oath of Allegiance.

Sophie was a little in awe of Ali, due both to his life story and his remarkable work: Rothko-sized canvasses painted in a neo-expressionist, sort of post-Basquiat style, mixing abstraction and figuration in roughly equal doses, and depicting the clash and sometimes remarkable marriage of cultures, two sides of a coin of he knew all too well. Though like Sophie's, Ali's paintings lived in a bordertown on the frontier of figure and abstraction, his were full to bursting with man-made detritus and warped cross-cultural iconography, while hers depicted intricate scenes from the natural world, boiled-down like stock for jambalaya to a basic DNA of shape and color, then through a sort of alchemy that was her singular gift, cooked into complex stew of synesthetic imagery, abstract, though still strongly seasoned by the ghost of the original figure. Despite the differences in their work, Sophie had felt an instant kinship with Ali, and was stunned not only by his painting, but also his ability to transcend the violence of his past and bust hip-hop moves in flannel jammies in the chic living room of an Upper West Side townhouse.

Next up was Elroy "Rocket" Hedberg, a blond giant of a former Nordic ski racer from Duluth, Minnesota, whose series of nude portraits of aging mothers and their grown daughters managed to scandalize some viewers in an age where everyone felt themselves above such banalities. The paintings were not particularly graphic—Sophie found them hypnotically beautiful—and broke no obvious taboo, still, some (mostly male) critics cringed at the idea behind the work, while certain feminist critics screamed exploitation. And he had attracted the ire of vocal and annoying evangelical groups, which, according to Hedberg, "sprouted like toadstools from the shit-smelling petri dish of right-wing Stearns County," which he explained was an exurban conservative enclave just to the west of liberal Minneapolis. Being caught in the crossfire of the arbiters of political correctness, while simultaneously being the whipping-boy of the religious right seemed to delight him to no end.

The son of Minneapolis lawyers who had abandoned lucrative partnerships to become coffee shop and brewpub owners, "Rocket" was as laconic as a young hero in an old western, and impressive in the manner of a minor Norse god, maybe a playful cousin to Thor. He seemed as comfortable in his skin as any young person Sophie had ever met, with a smile straight from a toothpaste ad and a small constellation of freckles dawning across his cheeks and nose. She imagined he had no trouble finding someone to keep him warm during those long Minnesota winter nights. Speaking of those critical of his work, he said, "If my stuff embarrasses them, they can avert their tender eyes. Plus," nodding at Anais, "a little controversy is good for business, am I right?"

"Quite right indeed, my boy," responded their tipsy Svengali, resplendent in a pair of vintage canary yellow men's silk pajamas that contrasted nicely with the lime in her drink. "Quite right indeed."

"Wankpuffins, the lot of them" added Ophelia, before launching into the *Reader's Digest* condensed version of her own story. She grew up the daughter of Thatcherites, her father a banker and minor Tory pol in a workingman's stronghold, mother a housewife, and chafed in tweeds and crinolines until, at eighteen, she escaped to art school, socialist politics, and the rave scene.

"I was a pretty good draftsman, and focused on still life, not to mention party drugs, for a time, but boredom set in, even as my combinations got odder. You know: *Still Life with Carburetor, Persimmon, and Han Solo Action Figure.* That sort of thing. From there it was a pretty short and slippery slope to becoming Betty Bricolage. I began assembling junk into sculptures for my own amusement, and pretty soon that was my thing."

She says that after her father died of cancer, for which her mother blamed her, she escaped to the Continent, where she followed her tumbledown Muse while living as the lover and assistant to French installation artist, filmmaker, and musician, Patrice LaLonde, whom she soon eclipsed as a sculptor, much to his Gallic male consternation. Visionary and obsessive, she quickly transcended mere bricolage, developing an uncanny ability to visualize relationships between seemingly disparate objects, using found materials, both man-made and natural, to weave a narrative that most often commented on consumerism's swift and methodical immolation of the Earth. Her installation *We Eat our Own* had been a smash hit at the previous Biennial, and her piece for the current show, *Desert/Dessert,* was a trippy masterpiece of frosting and sand. Essex is sleek and dangerous, tall and shorebird-like in organic black cotton p.j.s, with spiky, prematurely grey hair and an aquiline nose. Spellbound, Sophie is thrilled when the sculptress turns out to be quick with a cackling laugh and wit caustic enough to peel paint. Ten years Sophie's senior, she could easily pass as her more cosmopolitan older cousin. Everything about her is an invitation to mischief, and Sophie made a mental note to keep her wits about her when Ophelia Essex was nearby.

After an hour and two more gin-tonics, Sophie is comfortable enough to tell her own story with little trepidation. Everyone leans in, laughs, or shakes their heads in sadness where appropriate. The others find it curious and delightful that she actually *runs for a living,* former athlete Hedberg even offering to accompany her on her morning run, before noting the earliness of her planned departure and—yikes!—just how lean and fit she actually is, and politely demurring. Much like on that first Sunday run with Finn,

Rex, and Rachel, she finds her new mates welcoming, which surprises her, given the little she has heard of the art world. She is beginning to see a method in Anais' madness. When she is finished telling her story, everyone claps, as they all had at the others'. She has to admit she feels a lot better, a little less like a total fraud.

During the companionable silence that follows her dissertation, Sophie gazes out the window, watches little tornadoes of desiccated leaves blow along the damp street below, their skittering shadows racing one another through puddles of pale light cast by streetlamps upon the wet pavement as they frolic among the elegant old buildings reflected from the asphalt, before finally stitching themselves into the tapestry of darkness that hangs at the lightpool's far shore. She wishes she had pad and pencil. She closes her eyes and lets the muted shapes and colors, the ghosts of movement, etch themselves into her memory. The scene reminds her just how much she loves late fall in New York: the sharp chill of a blue-sky afternoon, the fleeting smells of woods and sea that dart among the infinite aromas of human habitation, the cacophonous and strangely harmonic barrage of a hundred languages and dialects, the myriad honks and screeches and bangs. Though she still tends to associate the season in the city with hardscrabble cross country races over the famed and brutal hills of the Bronx's Van Cortland Park, with the bloody triumvirate of spike gashes that marked one such race and which still ghosted her left shin with faint parallel scars—those memories, pain and all, are now just one thread in the cocoon of contentment and happy wonder she wraps herself in as, for this one weekend anyway, she finds herself immersed in the New York of novels and popular cinema: the New York of art openings and men in sleek suits, of bohemian artists who feel like interlopers, like saboteurs, even though it is their work everyone is coming to see—the New York of good food and ample drink, of friendship, laughter, and new love. Everything would turn to shit eventually, of that she has little doubt, but for now she is just going to enjoy every fucking second.

Even so, she declines Anais' offer of one last drink; she has to be up early for a workout in the park before final preparations at the gallery, and then (Holy Shit!) the opening itself.

* * *

GIZMO AND ANAIS are lovers. That much becomes quickly apparent to Sophie early the next afternoon, when she wanders into Anais' office looking for a pen, and finds them in the throes of passionate coupling, Anais on her back atop her cluttered desk, skirt above her waist, legs athwart the hips of a standing Gizmo. The air is afire with articulate preverbals. Papers and office supplies fly. Sophie makes a hasty retreat before she can be seen, shaking her head in an emphatic "no" at Enrique, the assistant, who also has business in the office and is about to walk through the door. He obviously has been around this block before, and after rolling his eyes and quickly consulting his watch, turns on his heel and returns to the gallery floor, there to deter anyone from venturing officewards until the reunion has been consummated. Sophie wanders the floor, studying the works of her gallery mates intently, sincerely hoping the vivid details of their work will chase away the image of Anais grasping the edge of the desk, her knuckles white, as she arched her back to meet her younger lover's thrusts, her head back on the desk, mouth open, eyes closed tightly in ecstasy.

Later that evening, Giz and Anais were the picture of decorum, though quite obviously together. They stood in the center of the room, an atoll about which swam a shifting school of sharks and parrotfish: finely dressed patrons of the arts. They stood, arms loosely draped around one another's waists, laughing and benignly gesturing here and there with flutes of champagne. Sophie, standing with Finn and Beannie, was the island at the center of her own little archipelago, as were the other artists, each ringed by admirers all their own. The artists were occasionally called over by Anais to meet the mucky-mucks. Introductions were made, compliments were bandied about, technical questions were asked and answered. The scent of the filthy lucre that lubricated the art world perfumed the proverbial breeze. As Sophie spoke with power brokers, curators and collectors, she was pleasantly surprised at how much she instantly liked most of them, how easily she was able to overcome her shyness and hold up her end of a dozen small conversations, trying not to giggle as Gizmo stood behind her interlocutors making the "yackety-yak" sign with his hands behind their backs.

And then it was over, guests gone home, Enrique plowing napkins and dropped business cards and shards of glass from broken flutes into a pile with a wide push-broom. Anais huddled her artists together for a quick post-mortem.

"As you could probably tell," she said, her eyes tired, but still crackling with intensity, "things were humming here tonight. I think that over the next couple of weeks things are going to get quite interesting. People are impressed; purse strings are loosening." Already, many pieces, including three smaller studies of Sophie's, had been affixed with a sticky red dot, signifying it had been purchased. "I am going to work the phones and do my magic. Fingers crossed, I will have happy tidings for you all quite soon. Now go! Kiss your kids goodnight, canoodle with your partners, start pondering your next masterpieces. Do whatever it is you do, but do it somewhere else. I have things to discuss with Mr. Hornaplenty."

Sophie discretely rolled her eyes. Finn caught Gizmo's eye, quickly inserted the index finger of his right hand into the ring he had made with the thumb and index finger of his left, doing a couple of quick in-and-outs, while Beannie, grinning, showed unusual restraint. Ophelia Essex, a Londoner who knew plenty about Gizmo from the tabloids, simply snorted.

Grow up! Gizmo silently mouthed at them over the shoulder of his lover.

* * *

ANAIS WAS A gift from above, a guardian angel, a fairy-godmother. Sophie's biggest fear, as it began to be apparent that she might be embarking upon an actual *career* as an artist, was that the business and social aspects of that career would take over her life. She wasn't ignorant of the fact that if she wanted to get paid for her work, she would have to do something to promote herself, but just as she ran for the love of running, and raced because she loved to go fast, she painted because she loved to paint, because the dervish of sound and color within her demanded release, not because she wanted to be particularly rich or famous. She wanted to spend as much time as possible out roaming the hills or in her studio making pictures, and as little as possible schmoozing and glad-handing.

"I don't want to be Garbo or Salinger," she told Anais tentatively. "I'm not a fucking recluse. I just don't want to be distracted. I like my life. I have my running, I have Finn. I have a great studio and the time I need to spend there. It has resulted in some good work. I just don't want to mess it all up by spreading myself too thin." She took a deep breath as Anais considered this, a bit nervous as to what her mentor's reaction might be. When she broke into a wide smile, Sophie almost fainted from relief.

"Well my dear, making sure you have time to crank out those wonderful paintings is what I get paid so handsomely for, now isn't it?" She took Sophie's right hand in both of hers. "You are such a lovely girl, and I think you are going to be making marvelous art for many, many years. It behooves me to do everything I can to see to it that happens. So, I tell you what, let me woo and coddle, kiss ass and take names. You keep painting, do the occasional magazine profile, be your adorable self at openings. Otherwise, retreat to your mountain stronghold, be as mysterious and inaccessible as you like. Make your pictures, run your legs off, and love the stuffing out of that darling poet of yours. I'll take care of the rest."

At which point Sophie burst into tears.

* * *

FOR THE FIRST time in her life, Sophie found herself surrounded by women. What with Anais waving her magic wand and sprinkling pixie-dust all over the art world, not to mention leaving sundry messages on her answering machine, dispensing gossip, good wishes, and advice on everything from fashion to finances to her relationship with Finn (some of which made her blush), it was as if she had been united with an eccentric, long-lost, and slightly overweening aunt, pulled close to the ample and comfortable bosom of true family. And then, there were Rachel and Martha, who met at her studio or Martha's house outside of Boulder for a run and breakfast at least once a week, and with whom the miles passed in a colorful blur of talk and laughter and Colorado gorgeousness. Unexpectedly, her life was flush with the heady sensation of sisterhood. This unanticipated and wondrous development filled her with such honey-colored joy that she wondered how she had lived this long without it. In high school and college, she had friends, sure, but she was so gifted an artist and athlete, so single-minded in the pursuit of her talents, that there was always a gulf between her and the girls in her classes and on the team. She spent a lot of time alone in the studio, or running with the men's team, and while her female relationships were friendly enough, she had little time for or interest in a social life circumscribed by boys, bars, and shopping. Looking back, she saw how superior and aloof she must have seemed, wondering why they were even nice to her.

She never knew how badly she needed this. Sitting with friends at her kitchen table, or at a sunny window booth at Donatella's, indulging in post-run brioche and Americano, or zipping along the Mesa Trail at the foot of Boulder's spectacular Flatirons, she would find herself flabbergasted, filled with a feeling that made her mourn for the version of herself who had somehow blundered along not knowing this richness was possible. Her mother was dead, her grandmothers on opposite coasts, and she had never had friends who understood her commitment to painting or running, so she had carried on, mostly alone, mostly unaware of this void, until she met Anais, Rachel, Martha, and most unexpectedly of all, Donatella Mitumba.

* * *

"JESUS, 'TELLA, IT looks like Betty Crocker exploded in here."

Sophie stood agape in the spacious kitchen of Donatella's Delectables, amid a mess of such epic grandeur that it seemed impossible for one person to have made it all. It was like a war zone, if wars were fought with cocoa and raspberries and butter. Pots, pans, and sundry utensils lay scattered about like the debris of exploded tanks, while the sole victor strutted and danced amid the wreckage like a conquering field general. Donatella baked like Sophie painted: athletically. She flung flour and sugar and fruit like a rampaging four-year-old or Jackson Pollock on angel dust. She wheeled and spun, blended, whipped, and puréed, danced and sang and had passionate, circuitous conversations with herself. She had a method and it was madness. Things got delicious and sometimes the walls got covered in goo.

Donatella Mitumba was a genius, and geniuses do things their own way. A former 400-meter All-American for the University, with a masters in bioethics and a gift for turning dough into art, she had stayed in town to do a Ph.D. and work in a local bakery. Linzers and layer-cakes intervened, however, a dissertation was abandoned, and before she knew it, she was the proprietress of the town's hottest coffee and pastry shop, the biggest patron of the local women's shelter, and high priestess of Donatella's Distance

Dames (or, if they happened to be drinking, Donatella's Delicious Bitches), an unofficial tribe of women runners united by a hankering for dessert and social justice.

Sophie grabbed a stray macadamia nut, slid it through a glob of jam adorning the stainless-steel table that ran the length of the kitchen's back wall, popped it into her mouth, then stood aside to watch the mad scientist at work. When Sophie tried to describe Donatella to Finn she had trouble finding the right words. Statuesque was certainly an understatement. Six-feet tall and leanly muscled, Donatella possessed the classic physique of an elite quarter-miler: long and lithe, with endless, sinuous legs and a rippled midriff. She had inherited the finest features of both her father, an exiled Nigerian journalist and 1968 track Olympian, and her mother, an Italian diplomat. Her skin was the color of a polished nut, a shade somewhere between her mother's Mediterranean olive and the midnight black of her father, and seemed to smolder with a banked inner radiance. When she moved, it was as if a finely carved, supple tree had been kissed to life by a magic wind, making a ballet of the most ordinary movements. Her ample dreadlocks had a slightly reddish tint, and she often wore them tucked into a bright traditional gele, though on this morning she had stuffed them into a flour-covered Denver Nuggets cap, turned backwards and tilted low. Most striking of all were her eyes, one green, one blue, courtesy of an Irish great uncle, and which glittered with mirth and mischief, or flared with anger when confronted with injustice. Her flat nose was dusted with a small constellation of Gaelic freckles, which stood out even more than usual this morning on a face encrusted in flour crisscrossed by rivulets of dried sweat. Sophie had not yet been able to convince Donatella to let her paint her, nude, in her kitchen habitat.

Donatella wore her usual kitchen uniform of battered Nike trainers, flower-print running bra, and cargo shorts, covered by a white industrial apron, which by this point in the morning's festivities resembled nothing more than the paint-stained tarp on the floor of Sophie's studio. She reached into a small burlap bag with one hand, extracted a fistful of something that Sophie did not recognize, and tossed it into a large, bubbling saucepan she stirred with her other hand. Racks of delicate layers of buttery crust awaited this filling on the workbench beside her. Jimmy Cliff blasted from the stereo.

"Girl, you're making me nervous, eyeballing me like that," Donatella said. "Grab yourself a scone from the warmer, get out front, and have Nicole fix you a latte. I'll be out soon as I get these tarts in the oven."

* * *

SOPHIE HAD AWAKENED earlier than usual, run an easy seven with Finn on the forgiving turf of the golf course. They had made sweet, efficient love standing up in the shower afterwards, then he had made a pot of tea, four slices of cinnamon toast, and retreated to his nook to write. Sophie had thrown on shorts and a T-shirt and lit out for the studio, where she was putting the finishing touches on *Finn, Sleeping*, stopping in Old Town at Donatella's for a nosh and maybe a quick chat before heading up the canyon.

She and Donatella had business to discuss: the upcoming Dames' Distance Derby, a women's-only running festival, comprised of evening five and ten-kilometer road races for citizen runners (of which they were expecting nearly two-thousand) and an elite 5,000 meters on the track, in which Sophie, Martha, and Rachel would be competing. The races would be followed by a concert under the stars on the infield of the track, featuring three local all-female bands: Throe Rug, Lumberjax, and the Debutau nts. Skirtchaser would headline, finishing the evening under a dazzle of fireworks.

The running parts of the festival, taking place only two weeks hence, were being handled by a professional race-management company, but the music, the post-race food and drink, the fireworks, the volunteers, and coordination with the women's shelter, for which the derby was a benefit—the million myriad non-running details were left to the Distance Dames, a diverse and talented crew to be sure, but most of the work would be done by Sophie, Rachel, and especially Donatella, who was beginning to get a little frayed around the edges. All of that would have to wait, however, until after a dissertation on the state of Donatella's complicated and always colorful love life.

Her current entanglements were the French-Congolese backup shooting guard for the Nuggets ("How is a girl supposed to resist a fine brother named Jean-Jacques? And that accent! Girl, you know what I'm talking about, you've heard him!"), and a woman named Sue: the petite, blonde owner of an organic wholesaling firm that supplied the shop with fruit, nuts, coffee, and tea ("I swear to God, Soph, it's like she's the gymnast and I'm the apparatus. She may be tiny, but *damn,* the woman is *flexible!*"). She pouted, stuck out her lower lip and puffed out an extended breath, ruffling the front of her dreads, which hung loose, encapsulating her face in a ragged frame and highlighting her perfect cheekbones.

"I know I should be happy," said Donatella, who had emerged from the kitchen wearing a Donatella's Delectables hoody and a pair of track pants, "and I am, really, but damn, this romance shit is wearing me out."

"Well, it *is* possible to have too much of a good thing."

"Tell me about it." She slid into the booth and sprawled in a puddle of sun across the table from Sophie, sipped from her cup of chai, shaking her head. "Why do I keep getting myself into these things?"

"I have no idea, but it must be glorious being queen of the pan-global, pantheist, pan-sexuals." Sophie lifted her mug in a toast.

"Not to mention queen of out of the frying pan and into the fire." She frowned, then burst into a radiant smile, returning the toast. "Here's to a full and interesting life."

"You certainly have that."

"Damn, don't I know it. And what about you? Still avoiding your Dark Lord, all those nasty thoughts he stirs up?"

Sophie rolled her eyes. "I knew I should have kept my mouth shut about that."

"Nah, girl, it's good for an old married lady to have a twisted fantasy or two, especially if it stays a fantasy. Something to keep your mind—and your hands—busy on those long winter nights alone at the studio. And since you don't much like the man anyway, I really can't see the harm."

Sophie groaned. "Why him? Of all the fucking people in the world, why Gizmo?"

"'Cuz opposites attract, baby, that's why. Because you are a good girl, and he is most definitely NOT a good boy. Because he has those cheekbones, those full motherfuckin' lips, those teeth that are better to eat you with, my dear. *Mmm-mm.* And those bottomless eyes that look at your paintings and see the molten stuff at your very core."

Sophie pantomimes pounding her head on the table. Donatella continues. "Because he knows all that churning magma is for Finn, and it pisses him off. Hell, he told you as much at your wedding. But he also knows there's a secret Sophie that goes all weak in the knees when he looks at you a certain way. Motherfucker diddles that part every time he gets the chance. It's his revenge on the whole damn world for not giving him what you and Finn have. I'd turn the shit back on him, tease the man nonstop with the glory of what he shall never possess. But yo, that's just me."

* * *

DONATELLA HAD SAID something similar when Sophie unloaded a bit of erotically weighted baggage one morning late that spring. She and Finn had just returned from London, where a few of her pieces had been part of a show called "New American Painters" at the Tate Modern. Finn and Gizmo had been working on a glossy coffee table book, Finn writing ekphrastic poems inspired by paintings chosen by Giz, who would also provide a brief essay on each. They were in discussions with Tate officials about partially underwriting the book's publication. Finn had gone off to Bruges for the weekend for a cross country meet, while Sophie stayed behind in London to catch up with Ophelia Essex and get to know the city a bit. Thus, late one afternoon Sophie found herself alone with Giz in a tragically hip and otherworldly expensive London bar, talking about painting and waiting for Ophelia to arrive. The room was wall-to-wall financiers, all wearing bespoke suits in subtly radiant fabrics Sophie wanted badly to touch. They laughed with supermodel-types sporting never-ending legs and laser cut cheekbones, everyone hobnobbing with the kind of ease that only real money or stratospheric beauty can bring.

"Wankers," Gizmo snorted in the direction of a cluster of laughing pretty people. "So nice to be able to let one's hair down after a long week of raping and pillaging." He spoke and carried himself with the insouciance and easy scorn of one who moved effortlessly in such circles, yet felt himself to be quite above their sort of fray.

One of the group, a forty-something wearing a 31-flavors-of-grey suit and an aristocratic nose, looked in their direction, raising a glass to Giz. Gizmo hoisted his glass in return, flashed a smile only a professional could tell was counterfeit.

"Quentin Entwhistle *the Fifth,*" Gizmo said through his smile. "Returned his family to financial prominence by legally robbing every pensioner in Yorkshire. Lovely chap. I quieted his fears about the authenticity and provenance of a lesser, though truly astounding Rembrandt he had basically stolen from an addled old friend of the family. For which he remunerated me quite handsomely, by the way."

Sophie looked at him with a cocked eyebrow, trying and failing to be droll.

"Oh yes, sweet Sophie, beloved of my bestie, ambrosia and albatross of my afternoon, your buddy Gizmo is a whore. Every bit the prostitute as those lovely young ladies over there, and every bit as well educated, though not, alas, as well-compensated." He paused for effect, drained his Monkey 47 and tonic. "Well, at least I don't have to blow the bastards. Or marry them." He looked into his empty glass, its shards of ice, its wreckage of cucumber and lime. "I think I might be a little drunk."

"You think?" She was a little stunned at the ferocity of his tirade, more stunned to find he possessed a conscience.

Ophelia had rung to say she was running late, so Sophie and Gizmo settled in for some more quality people-watching and truly breathtaking gin.

He looked again in the direction of Entwhistle's table and shook his head, then let it go with a sigh. He returned his attention to Sophie. "God, it must be wonderful to be so real," he said, looking at her with a gaze of such intensity she had trouble meeting it.

"What? I'm sorry, I don't know what you mean." The sudden change of direction had pulled the carpet from beneath her feet. And she really didn't like the way he was looking at her, like she wasn't wearing any clothes.

He answered her with another question. "You really have no idea how good you are, do you?"

She started to stutter a response, he cut her off. "For the past hundred years people have been proclaiming painting dead—the pompous fucking assholes—and every time they do," raising his voice now, earning the nervous glances of some new money at the next table, "somebody comes along and turns the whole thing on its head, proves the motherfuckers wrong. Picasso, Pollock, Basquiat," he dropped his voice nearly to a whisper, "and maybe you, Sophie, maybe fucking you."

She opened her mouth to speak but could not; he pinned her to her chair with an expression somehow bereft and exultant at once, inhaled deeply, and continued. "Sure, you are young, you're not quite there yet, but if what I've seen is merely your juvenilia?" He signaled a passing waiter for another drink. "My God, Sophie, you might be the one they are still writing about two hundred years from now."

She finally found her voice. "Giz, that's crazy."

Then he did something she never would have expected. He reached over, gently put an index finger to her lips, said simply, "No, Sophie, it isn't."

A few minutes later, as she emerged from the ladies' room, he pulled her into the recessed doorway of a broom closet and kissed her deeply. She did not resist, giving herself over for a moment to the heady atmosphere, her slight drunkenness and his weird erotic power, before breaking free and hurrying back to their table, heart pounding, head a hurricane of confused emotions. She felt as though she had been struck by lightning. When Ophelia Essex arrived a few moments later, it was like being rescued from a burning building.

* * *

TWO HOURS LATER, with Donatella's laughter still echoing in her mind, Sophie stands before the nearly finished *Finn, Sleeping*. The picture hangs in a beacon of vertical sunlight, awaiting a plethora of final flourishes and finishing touches, tiny details that for her could make or break the painting. She might stare at the section of painting to be revised for as much as an hour, her knees slightly bent, shoulders relaxed, swaying slightly as if in a gentle breeze, her attention gone below the surface of the painting, where she moves about like a spelunker, seeing its three dimensions from within, the painting an almost subterranean landscape through which she moves, taking in the sights, humming as the bats and glow-worms sing.

After a brief eternity of this concentration, Sophie darts in, makes a quick, decisive brushstroke or dab with a thumb, and moves on to the next decision. This long deliberation, these moments lost in contemplation are really, though, just a means of putting off the inevitable. If she were to be honest with herself, she would admit that she knows every remaining brush stroke, each remaining dribble and dab by heart. In truth, every remaining move is as clear to her as that of a chess master commencing with an endgame. It is just that she has lived with—and in—this painting every day since she and Finn were married, and in truth, since their very first night together, when she watched him sleep, imagining how she might translate what she was feeling onto paper and canvas. And even as she put the finishing touches on *Lightning Strikes Twice,* began and completed *A Festival of Light,* and worked on all the other drawings and smaller paintings, she had always been at work on *Finn, Sleeping,* sketching him as he slept, drawing and painting small studies, spending entire weeks down the rabbit hole of thought about the painting and the man. And then there was the all-consuming act of making the picture itself, the attempt to make something tangible from her joy and gratitude, to build an altar to this very particular love, using only paint and brush and canvas, muscle, sinew, and breath. Letting go was proving much harder than she had ever anticipated, so this last week or so with the painting was really a long goodbye, a chance to wrap it around her like a blanket, wear it one last time like second skin.

And so, it is with a feeling of accomplishment colored by profoundest loss that three days later, under the final sunbeams of a dying day, she applies the final stroke, a three-inch crescent the grey of the mottled pony to whom she feeds a carrot every morning upon arriving at the studio. She steps back to look at a work that is no longer in progress, sets down her brush, takes a slow, raspy breath, and breaks into sobs that continue unabated until well after the sun sinks behind the mountains.

* * *

THE DAMES' DISTANCE Derby had gone better than Donatella, Rachel, and Sophie could ever have hoped. Finn, Rex, and their army of male volunteers, along with their non-running children, had done everything in their power to see to it that the women who flooded the streets had everything they needed. Water tables were stocked with cups filled with just the right amount of water or Gatorade, the course was well-marked, and there was someone clearly reading out splits at every mile. Many husbands, boyfriends, and other local runners wore cheerleading skirts and shook pom-poms, cheering on the runners, sometimes doing elaborate routines. More men and kids worked the finish line, helping both jubilant and wobbly women through the chutes, making sure they had a friendly shoulder to lean on, a bottle of water, and a goody bag filled with food, samples of organic cosmetics, a pair of breathable running socks with the phrase "Women Run the World" embroidered on them, a ticket to the concert, and a glowstick. The evening was clear and hot, as was to be expected, but as the final runners straggled through the chutes, the shadows were lengthening and the temperature had begun to drop a bit. No serious heat injuries had been reported, the medical tent was only moderately busy, and Donatella and her crew could breathe a big sigh of relief.

Sophie warmed up for the elite race with Martha and Rachel, who, along with a couple of other sponsored area athletes, including Nikki Desmond (like Sophie needed more motivation) and a half-dozen college runners, would battle it out on the track for twelve and a half laps under the lights, encouraged by the very runners who streamed by them now, as they ran the racecourse backwards, preparing for their own event while clapping for and encouraging the citizen racers. Sophie went nuts, doing a little dance and wolf-howl number when Beannie sprinted by, nearly a hundred yards ahead of the second-place woman, less than a mile from the finish of the 10K. Beannie responded with a grimace and a quick thumbs-up. Then it was back to the nearly wordless warmup, the tango with pre-race tension, her nerves taut as violin strings. She really, really hated this part.

But an hour later, it was all fun and games as she sprinted down the final straightaway, waving, pumping her fists and smiling like a madwoman as a large crowd of tired, happy runners cheered her wildly home. She had let Martha and Rachel battle for the lead early, the two marathon runners attempting to get away from Sophie, as well as the wily and talented Nikki, or at the very least, take the sting out of their kicks. But Sophie's training had been solid, and she had no trouble with the early pace, even as the other competitors dropped back one by one. She never ceased to be surprised that, even though her weekly mileage had almost doubled in the four years since graduating from college, her top-end sprint speed had actually gotten *better.* By eight laps in the four of them were well clear of the field, nearly ready to lap the slowest of the college athletes. Sophie tucked in behind Martha and Rachel, running on the rail, tired, but completely untroubled by the pace. She was running faster than she ever had for the distance, yet the pace felt easy, nearly a stumble. Nikki Desmond lurked, a stride back.

Sophie was pretty sure she could stay right where she was for another four laps, then sprint away, dueling only Nikki (who she knew possessed both good finishing speed and a rather sizeable mean streak) for the win off the final curve, but she was feeling a bit bored, a bit antsy, and besides, by the looks of her competitors' deteriorating form, the way they were beginning to fight for breath, she was pretty sure they were red-lining. She was not in that state of extremis yet, not even close, so just before they caught a couple of stragglers, which would have made passing a little more dangerous, she moved out to lane two, accelerated smoothly, and just like that, the race was over. She dispatched her friends, who were much more suited for longer distances, with surprising ease, running each of the final three laps faster than the previous one, finally dropping a game and tenacious Nikki with a lap remaining, then sprinting the spotlit final homestraight grinning and waving madly, chasing her own shadow to the line.

* * *

LATER, SOPHIE SNUGGLED with Finn on a blanket on the infield of the track, watching happily as children chased each other around with multicolored glowsticks or draped sound-asleep across their fathers' shoulders, and as Beannie, looking no worse for wear, stalked and pogoed and played her heart out on stage. Sophie daydreamed for a moment about the day when she and Finn would be carting their own children to events like this, watching them cavort like little animals until they crumpled into sleep in their parents' welcoming arms. It was something she and Finn talked about often, something they both wanted. But there would be plenty of time for that when Finn was tenured and Sophie was ready to take a break from competitive running. For now, this was enough: husband and friends, good health, days spent at speed in the clean mountain air or hard at work in her studio, nights wrapped in Finn's arms or in a puddle of lamplight, sketching him as he slept.

This was heaven. The stars were out, the air was warm enough that shorts and a light fleece kept at bay any post-race chill. She had won a race in her adopted hometown, then run and laughed through a cooldown with her new friends (including Nikki, who come to find out, was a fucking *riot*). And here she was on a blanket on the grass, her back against her still-new husband's chest, his arms wrapped around her as they watched their friends shred on stage (giving a grateful Finn the night off), much to the delight of the thousand or so runners and their families who had stayed up late, prolonging the magic of the evening as long as city ordinances or cranky kids would allow. She had finished two or three bottles of Fat Tire, which, along with the music, a pleasant post-race fatigue, and Finn's arms encircling her, cosseted her in something akin to bubble wrap, and she allowed herself to drift away, cocooned in a puffy, psychic shawl, each little pocket a balloon filled with helium and bliss. *And hey, wasn't that Nikki, dancing with Beannie up on stage?*

* * *

IT WAS THE night before the party, the moondrenched, creaking-house hours of her first wedding anniversary. Sophie lay beside Finn, watching him sleep. Even though the painting was finished, shrouded in darkness and mystery fifteen miles up the canyon, waiting until evening to be unveiled, she still watched Finn sleeping, as she did almost every night, an action which had become as habitual to her as breathing. As familiar as he had become to her over the year of their courtship and during the first year of their marriage, still, every night brought some fresh revelation, some new gift. Maybe it would be a tremor in the muscle beneath a shoulder blade or newly grown curl of hair, or a mysterious muttering: a few syllables of gobbledygook, then a quick chuckle devolving into a sigh, perhaps a view of some by-now infinitely familiar body part seen from a new angle, in a new slant of light, perhaps accompanied by a new soundtrack of birdsong or train whistle or rain on the roof. Each night brought some new insight into this man: her lover, husband, and friend, something fresh to catalogue and add to the database, a file she was pretty sure she would still be adding to on the day she died.

This night did not disappoint. He lay sprawled on his back next to her, very close to the edge of the bed, one leg dangling slightly over, a spot at which he always ended up eventually, though they began most nights loosely entwined. His breathing was slow and deep, as always, and she could feel his heart vibrating the bed between them. An oscillating fan in the corner of the bedroom rustled his hair as it swept its breeze across the room. Sophie could feel herself succumbing to a happily creeping languor, sinking slowly into the welcome quicksand of sleep, when Finn cried out.

"Bullshit!" he shouted, kicking out with one leg and sitting bolt upright. His face, though his eyes were still closed, was a mask of indignation bordering on rage.

Sophie, ripped from her slow descent into slumber, shot up, mirroring his posture, her own spine straightened by surprise and concern. But whatever psychic storm had assailed him, it was already past, and had moved on harmlessly into the empires of night. He shuddered, sighing slowly and with what appeared to Sophie to be great sadness. His features dissolved once more into sleep. She reached out, stroked his back through the sheet, whispering vague assurances, at which he murmured contentedly.

From Finn, he of relentless good cheer, such a display of anger, even so briefly and in sleep, was shocking. She and Finn had been together for two years, and they had never even fought, not once, not really. Oh, she would gently chide him for leaving teabags in the sink or empty Dr. Pepper bottles on the counter, and he would become momentarily irritated at her habitual, slight lateness, but these irritants were trivial in the face of their overall happiness, small imperfections on the skin of a luscious and seemingly infinite fruit. She had known him to rant and rave over cruelties both large and small, the vastness of human ignorance played out on the pages of their newspaper every morning, Finn becoming a small cloud that delivered thunder and lightning for a few moments over toast and tea, the storm petering out by the time he reached the comics page, dissipating as he chuckled over *Doonesbury* or *Pearls Before Swine*. And not once had he shown any real anger towards her. In fact, Sophie had seen Finn truly angry only once, and from that incident she learned a great deal about how he dealt with things that truly bothered him. The funny thing was that in that particular case, she was the first to get mad. At the moment in question, Sophie was ready to throw down, make the fur fly, but it was Finn who stepped into the breach, looking capable of actual violence. He was, she thought, lying next to him as he slept, really quite something.

* * *

AS THEIR WEDDING day had approached, plans had gone more than smoothly. They had the same idea about what they wanted from the day, as they did about most days. They both wanted a simple ceremony, outdoors in a lovely spot. And short: just brief vows they had written themselves, a quick poem from Finn, a song from Beannie, before Joseph, their friend and Unitarian minister, sealed the deal. And that was just hunky-dory with all the invitees as well, as then everyone could get down to the serious business of running and drinking and dancing, of seeing to it that Finn and Sophie's immersion in married life began as seamlessly (and as raucously) as humanly possible.

And then into this little glade of bliss blundered Uncle Leonard with his ideas about marriage.

* * *

LEONARD WAS HER mother's brother, a pompous, pompadoured blowhard who had made a medium-sized fortune in real estate, and who had at a young age established a very close relationship with his Lord and Savior, understanding it to be his mission to bring everyone in his life the good news, whether they wanted to hear it or not. Leonard wore moderately good suits with dark ties, or pressed golf slacks and polo shirts, and ingratiated himself into conversations with an oily enthusiasm and a reptile charm. Much like Sophie's father before him, Finn hated the self-righteous asshat, waving hello and quickly exiting any room he had the misfortune to share with the man. Sophie, like her mother, smiled, nodded her head, and imagined her uncle devoured by rats, or dreamed herself to be miles away, engaged in something more pleasant, like maybe a body cavity search at some banana republic airport.

Finn, whom everyone agreed was patient to a fault, had always had a low threshold for being pressured to conform to the faith of another. He firmly believed that *no* meant *no,* and that,

just as he would not generally foist his own theism off on anyone else, he would brook no proselytizing from any fuel-injected true believer, in-law or no. More than one Jehovah's Witness

or Mormon missionary would rue the day they knocked on Finn's door, only to be invited inside, given food and beverage, and then met with a Ph.D.-level inquisition. Finn would bring out his heavily annotated *Book of Mormon* or *Oxford Study Bible* and launch into a genuinely curious, passionate, and thoroughly unexpected interrogation of his bewildered guests. Finn would be friendly, but relentless, and after a few minutes and a couple of Oreos, these poor servants of the Lord would be casting furtive glances at the door, muttering something about having more pamphlets to deliver or kids to pick up from school, and Finn, like a benevolent judge, would release them from their testimony, ushering them to the door with a smile, a hearty handshake, and genuine wishes for success in their endeavors. This passive-aggressiveness was a bit out of character, but missionaries of all sorts tended to push his buttons.

Uncle Leonard, who moved in a protective bubble of affluence, and whose sense of privilege he had steeped in like tea for most of his life, was a different breed of cat. So highly advanced was his piety that it had become as leathery and impregnable as rhinoceros skin. He had, alas, proven quite immune to Finn's technique. Such was his arrogance that he merely looked upon Finn with pity, shook his head sadly, and refused to answer a single one of his questions.

"Son," Leonard had said the first time Finn had rebuffed his attempt to save Finn's soul, "your pride in your intellect makes me sad, as it makes our Lord, Jesus Christ, sad. Such pride is

a sin, a heavy weight that will drop away like a stone when you stop *thinking* and accept Him into your heart. All your false knowledge only keeps you from seeing the *Truth.*"

Finn, to whom the very idea of a compassionate God had seemed ridiculous since he was a four-year-old watching his beloved big sister be eaten away by cancer, and whose beliefs had been forged in response to the righteous onslaught of his own uncles and aunts, had zero patience for this arrogant son of a bitch. He took a deep breath, unclenched his right hand—which had curled into a fist and yearned to lay waste to some very pricey dentistry—and replied calmly, "Well, Leo,"—Sophie's uncle *hated* being called Leo—"I am really glad that being unable to, you know, *read,* has not interfered with your faith, I really am, but next time, you can just keep your sanctimonious horseshit packed in your suitcase, because we have no interest in buying what you are peddling." Finn smiled as he said this, the very image of beneficence, though he used the word *peddling* quite deliberately, a barb sure to rankle the upper-middle class ego of this perfectly coifed salesman and future in-law.

Well, that shut him up, at least for a moment. Sophie looked on, wide-eyed, an expression she saw mirrored on the face of her Aunt Patsy, whom she liked a great deal more than the uncle with whom she shared some actual DNA. She had never seen her mild-mannered fiancé go after someone like this, and Aunt Patsy had certainly never seen her husband, revered Sonoma businessman and fawned-over church deacon, bested, or even tested before. Uncle Leonard looked at Finn as if he had been slapped, his jaw working, looking for something to say. From somewhere he dredged up a look of shopworn pity, plastered it like a cheap

Halloween mask across his tanned and blandly handsome face, and turned back to Finn. "Son," he said again (inside, Finn, the boy who had lost a father, was screaming, *I'm not your fucking SON!* Sophie could see it, could see Finn's hand curling once more into a fist), "I feel sorry for you, I truly do." He turned to Sophie, shook his head with exaggerated pity, then grabbed Aunt Patsy by the hand. "Patricia,"—his voice was firm now, having convinced himself he had won this battle— "let's get going, let these two think about what has happened here." He then shoved Finn out of the way and made for the door.

Sophie tensed and began to reach for Finn, whom she was sure would now finally take a swing. She was a heartbeat too late. Finn had taken two fistfuls of her uncle's pressed polo, and most likely some of the flesh where his pecs had become incipient man-boobs, planted his feet, and used his powerful legs to lift her uncle off the floor and slam him against the wall, where he held him, saying nothing, impaling him with a glare. Sophie gasped, moved to step in, but Finn had already regained control of his temper. He was smiling broadly and, she could tell, doing everything he could to keep from laughing out loud at the bizarre turn this had all taken. He lowered Leonard slowly to the floor, smoothed out the front of his shirt. He walked over, gave Patsy a genuine hug and a kiss on the cheek, then patted Uncle Leonard heartily (and considerably less genuinely) on the back. "Yes, yes, we will think about what happened here. In fact, we will think about nothing else for the next week, isn't that right Sophie? With breaks for *The Simpsons,* of course." He continued to pound the older man on the back, guiding him none too subtly toward the door. "Okay, buh-bye, have a nice flight." He shut the door behind them almost before they had passed through it, not bothering to watch them walk to their rented BMW and drive off.

Sophie was both nonplussed by Finn's behavior, and a little impressed. Finn never got mad. *Never.* But then again, she had never seen anyone physically accost him before. So, watching him stand and listen to her uncle's tired bullshit, clenching and unclenching his fist, enduring everything up until the shove with real restraint, but then finally lifting and slamming him to the wall, had surprised her a little. But more than anything she was happy to see it. His relentless good cheer, his almost meticulously constructed passivity, sometimes concerned her. At times, it seemed to her like a slightly dangerous sort of denial, a trait she had come to recognize in herself. So, to see him almost come uncorked at her idiot uncle and his marriage advice filled her with an odd little cocktail of pride and relief. And then to see him laugh at the pious fucking peacock was even more rewarding. But poor Aunt Patsy.

* * *

THE PERSON WHO suffered from the altercation the most, though, was not even present for it. An hour or so after Leonard and Patsy departed, Sophie and Finn met Rachel and Rex at the track for a set of intervals. Finn was full of good cheer as they dressed for the workout and ran to campus, but Sophie could tell that the incident with Uncle Leonard was eating at him. The workout was twenty times four hundred meters, with a two hundred jog between each, and from the first repetition, Sophie could tell that Finn was still pissed. Usually, when Finn and Rex ran the same workout, they took turns leading each rep. It took less energy to follow than lead, to break the wind, so Rex and Finn, and anyone else who joined them, would switch off leading, sharing the work. It was also good practice for track races, learning both to lead and run from behind comfortably. The unwritten rule, however, was that once a runner could no longer hold the pace—be he having a bad day, a little under the weather, whatever the reason—once he could no longer hit the agreed upon splits, then it was every man for himself. The same rule held true for Sophie and Rachel, as well as Martha and whomever else had the temerity to join them.

It became apparent right away, to Sophie at least, that Finn's anger at Uncle Leonard was going to blow the usual game plan right out of the water. Finn and Rex's plan was to run each 400 in 62 seconds, just over a four-minute mile pace, with a slow 200-meter jog between each 400. It was a moderately ambitious workout, not terribly long, not terribly fast, but the pace and the volume together meant the session would be no walk in the park, and all four runners (the women were doing an equivalent workout, same number of reps, just a few seconds slower) had been steeped in apprehension by the time they toed the line.

Finn led the first rep, and even though Sophie was concentrating on her own workout, she could tell by the rapidly increasing distance between them that Finn was flying, running faster than the proscribed pace. He finished the lap nearly a full straightaway ahead of Sophie and Rachel—unheard of—and nearly ten meters ahead of Rex, who had still run faster than planned. As she finished her own 400, Sophie could hear Rex call out to Finn between heaving breaths: "Fifty-eight…way…fast."

Finn, breathing hard, his hands clasped behind his head, just nodded, and then all of them were jogging the silent, delicious, and way too short 200 recovery. At the line, Rex moved into lane one, accelerating smoothly into the lead. He was about three inches taller than Finn, and slightly more muscular, a miler's build to that of Finn's birdlike, marathoner's physique. This particular workout was where their skills and body types met. Twenty quarters was exactly the workout that required both the speed of a miler and the strength of a marathoner. So Rex led while Finn followed, in his slipstream and hugging the rail, just as planned.

At least at first. At three hundred meters, however, Finn was clearly impatient, running at Rex's shoulder, and by the time they got to the line, he was at the taller runner's side. Again, Sophie could tell the pace was too fast, and again, Rex, who was, if anything, more laid-back than Finn, said something to him, trying to calm him down, ease him off the throttle. The third and fifth intervals were repeats of the first, with Finn exploding off the front and Rex struggling to stay on his heels, while the next two that Rex led found him going faster than written, pushed by Finn from off his shoulder, and who nonetheless finished abreast of Rex each time.

By the sixth repeat, all bets were off. Finn simply went to the front without a word, parting the modest headwind that blew down the backstraight and letting Rex do his best to stay in his slipstream. It was a killing pace, three or four seconds per lap too fast, and soon the men were more than half a lap ahead of Sophie and Rachel, who were sticking to their own plan like clockwork. By the workout's midpoint, the 200 recovery was ridiculously inadequate. Nobody was talking, as every breath was hoarded, storing oxygen for the next repeat. Lap after excruciating lap it went on, the eighth to sixteenth repetitions taking on a terrible sameness. Depression crept in. The pain would go on forever; the workout would never end. But then, after the sixteenth interval—one mile to go—the runners allowed themselves a little hope, allowed themselves to think about the end of the workout. The last four would be awful, as the accumulated fatigue, the rising pools of waste gathering in their muscles, would leave them heaving and staggering after each one, but now each lap they completed was also a greater and greater percentage of what remained, so finishing each was a cause for greater celebration.

They had yet another unwritten rule—one of many—and that was that the penultimate rep had to be the fastest, with the final one not even timed, thus taking the pressure off, making the last lap almost not count, so worried were they about the one that preceded it. Unbelievably, Finn had kept up the insane pace, grinding out 56s and 57s, while Rex gamely hung on, finishing two or three seconds back. On the nineteenth rep, however, Finn simply ascended to a different plane, exploding from the line, rising up on his spiked toes, driving his arms and running away from Rex like he was a Sunday jogger, lapping a shocked Sophie as he did so. Two years they had been together. They had run together hundreds of times, but never had she seen anything like this. He was covered in a thick sheen of sweat, his breath exploding from his chest loudly with each exhalation, to be sucked in at nearly the same volume. Despite the effort of his breathing, his face was calm, his eyes vacant, his lips and cheeks almost flapping they were so loose. He went by without even acknowledging her presence, his back visibly expanding and contracting, such were the bellows of his lungs. At that moment, he was an oxygen machine, mining the atmosphere of that most necessary of gasses, awesome and otherworldly. He was *gone*.

Rex was gone too; completely destroyed. He never quite caught up to Rachel and Sophie, finishing his penultimate quarter a step behind them, and nearly ten seconds behind Finn. He looked at his watch, shook his head in disbelief, rattled out a sputtering and wheezy "fuuuuck" on the exhale. He held out his wrist to Sophie, showed her the time on his watch. 61, exactly the time he was supposed to run. Just how fast, then, had Finn gone? Scary fast, was all she knew. Sophie and Rachel were blown out, exactly as tired as they were supposed to be, when they began their own next-to-last interval. But Finn and Rex, now on their last one, were simply wrecked. The first eighteen 400s, run much too fast, had taken their toll, surely, but the nineteenth had simply ripped out their hearts.

Their final 400 was a death march. Their limbs refused to track correctly; their breath came in ragged, phlegmy moans. The women tucked in behind, let the broken marionettes they loved pull them through their own, fastest-by-decree penultimate lap, which the four of them finished together, Sophie and Rachel jogging onward, feeling almost celebratory, to run their final repeat, while Finn and Rex leaned on one another like drunken soldiers after the wake of a comrade who had died horribly and much too young, staggering, gasping, and yes, crying as they moved to the infield and collapsed in a heap.

So yeah, Sophie learned, Finn did get mad. Fanatical uncles and training partners beware.

By the time they had recovered enough to ease into a slow four-mile cooldown, Finn, whose rage at Uncle Leonard had been more than burned off by the workout, was feeling sheepish. He apologized repeatedly for ruining everyone's workout, until Rex broke in.

"Ruined? My God, Finn, that was the best work out of my life! I should be thanking you." He paused, grimacing a little. "And I will thank you in a week or so, as soon as I am walking normally again."

Finn laughed. "You and me both." And just like that, Finn's rage was extinguished. Everything was back to normal.

Aunt Patsy attended the wedding alone.

* * *

SOPHIE SMILED AT the memory, stroking her husband's now untroubled head, brushing a few strands of hair away from his eyes. Finn was once again sleeping sweetly, whatever terror had gripped his dreams now wandering off like a swift summer squall. The tenderness of her feelings for him, the lateness of the hour, the sound of his leisurely, rhythmic breathing, all conspired to slow her own heart, act on her like hypnosis, and soon she too had surrendered to the pull of sleep.

* * *

COULD THERE POSSIBLY be a more ridiculous song to wake up to? Sophie lay with her eyes still closed, luxuriating in the smells of coffee and toasting bread, and giggled at Finn crooning along to "My Sharona" as it played on the radio. She stretched, laughing at the realization that this was her first thought of the day.

Da-da-da-da-duh-DA, my scuh-rotum. He sang out the guitar riff, as well as the modified lyrics, playing percussion by way of the plates and mugs and silverware he clunked onto the table, the cupboard doors he clicked open and happily banged shut. It could have been just about any morning, as Finn, who went to sleep earlier and woke marginally easier, made the two of them their usual pre-run repast of toast, coffee or tea, and fruit, and Sophie yawned happily as the day began in its usual, comfortable fashion. But when she finally opened her eyes, blinking the morning into focus, her breath caught in her throat. She gaped at the transformation the bedroom had undergone as she had lain sleeping, and was reminded in the most glorious way that there was nothing whatsoever ordinary about this particular day.

For starters, there were flowers. *Everywhere.* It looked like an FTD delivery van had crashed through the wall at some point in the night and exploded, leaving bouquets in every imaginable combination of colors crowded upon every available surface. Bundles of red, yellow, and white roses occupied the slight indentation Finn had left in the mattress; individual cosmos and daisies were littered artfully about, and a spray of late-blooming lilacs from the bush in their back-yard burst from a pint glass on the nightstand. To her surprise and delight, when she swung her feet over the edge of the bed to stand, they found purchase on a carpet of pink rose petals, which led out the door and toward the kitchen, where Finn continued to charmingly mangle The Knack.

The air in the bedroom held the perfume of a thousand blooms, and the olfactory and visual stimulation set off a small symphony in her synesthetic brain: glissandi and eruptions of tonal fireworks going off in her ears as a menagerie of shivers chased one another over her skin. She sneezed twice, stood, spun in a slow circle, arms spread wide, swaying to the music in her head, which had almost drowned out the comic New Wave drifting in from the kitchen, and, a little reluctant to leave her floral wonderland, followed the trail of petals to the kitchen where Finn, and the first breakfast of their second year as husband and wife, awaited.

She surprised him, caught him mid-shimmy, now dancing around the kitchen to Bananarama's "Venus," hands overhead, drumming the air with a pair of butter knives, and he started, blushed, and burst into that goofy-ass smile she loved so dearly. "You," she said, pointing at him and grinning. "Get over here."

She pulled him into an embrace and kissed him deeply, then pulled her face away, shaking her head in wonder. "Finn...the flowers...wow."

He grinned again. "Yeah, I'm awesome like that."

"You wanna see awesome, sailor?" she intoned lasciviously. "Just follow me." She turned and walked casually back toward the bedroom, adding a little boom-shacka to her narrow runner's hips and high, round ass, and slowly pulled her R.E.M. T-shirt, which was all she had been wearing, over her head, letting it dangle for a moment on an outstretched fingertip before allowing it fall to the floor.

"Yes, ma'am!" Finn let the piece of toast he had been preparing drop half-buttered to a small plate and followed in her petal-strewn footsteps to the bedroom.

Half an hour later, they were happily pulling rose petals from places where rose petals are not usually found. Their breakfast had grown quite cold.

Another four hours and the flowers were still having a hootenanny in the olfactory centers of her brain. The air was a little trippy, a little cartoon-like, stuttered with streaks of primary colors, and she was still sore from the earlier lovemaking, which, as was their norm when they had little time, but lots of inspiration, was intense, animalistic, almost brutal. Thus, she was still tender, could feel her heart throbbing between her legs, still feel him inside her as they ran together along the ribbon of red single-track that unspooled along the edge of the shallow pond that lay at the base of the long, pine-flecked ridge to the west. Her awareness of her post-coital soreness began to make her hot once again; she could feel herself becoming wet. *Jesus, you little trollop*, she said to herself. *Eye on the prize, baby, eye on the prize.* But yeah, later tonight, Finn was *definitely* going to get what he had coming to him.

So she focused on her breathing, her footing, the scenery through which the trail wound, at that moment bisecting a large prairie dog town that covered nearly a square-mile of yucca, sagebrush, and cactus-littered high-desert open space. They ran in companionable silence, happy to be easing together into this most momentous of runs, moving wide to accommodate the occasional horseback rider or mountain biker coming from the other direction. A lesser ridge rose to their left, hiding the cyclocross course, with its steep little hills and hairpin chicanes, that lay on the other side. The hardpack trail they ran on hugged the smaller ridge for a time before curving away and cutting diagonally across the narrow valley toward the high hogback on their right. Among the cactus, yucca, and prairie grasses, small patches of short-stemmed flowers, whose name she had not yet learned, grew in splashes of periwinkle, pink, and white, while fiery barbs of Indian paintbrush and feisty yellow primrose added their voices to the chorus. Her limbs were flush with love and blood and oxygen, and she loped along the trail with an easy animal grace, feeling sleek and supple and ready for whatever came down the pike next. The day's glories, it seemed, would be unceasing.

* * *

EARLIER, AFTER SPENDING a few minutes entwined and breathing hard, decompressing after the aggressiveness of their lovemaking, they had made more toast, warmed up their coffee and tea in the microwave, and wolfed down some strawberries and cantaloupe before reluctantly parting, heading off in opposite directions to run last minute errands in preparation for the evening's festivities. Finn drove the thirty miles to the airport, corralled Beannie and his mother, and a couple of Sophie's cousins, while Sophie made a quick run up the canyon to supervise the last-minute decorating, helping Donatella unload supplies. They met back at the house at two, changed quickly into their running gear, and threw back a final glass of water. Then, they put on white caps and sunglasses and moved together into the hot middle of the day.

That they would get the scheduled workout in was never a question. To them, running, even on a day as full and important as this one, was as essential as breathing. It never occurred to them to take the day off, to put the hilly tempo run they had scheduled aside until tomorrow. Their one concession to the party was to run but once, condensing the morning's easy jaunt and the hard evening workout into one brutal midday effort, timing the run so as to beat the thunderstorms that were forecast for late in the afternoon, with heavy rain, damaging hail, and frequent lightning that promised to wreak brief, but serious havoc on the surrounding areas. But if the National Weather Service was correct, the storm would arrive safely after they had completed their run, and would have passed through town and out onto Colorado's eastern plains well before the revelers began showing up at the studio for the party.

Their engagement celebration and the unveiling of *Finn, Sleeping* would happen in the rain-washed and sweet-smelling aftermath, among the foothills of the Rockies, under a panoply of almost touchable stars. As they laughed and ate, drank and danced, they would be whispered over by cool, pine-scented breezes and dazzled by a blinding sliver of new moon. So if they had to endure a brutal run in the sunblasted heat of day, well, bring it on.

* * *

THE WEATHER HERE was *HUGE*, and though it sometimes terrified her, Sophie thrilled to it. She loved how the varied stimuli of wind, precipitation, light, and barometric pressure would have a field day with the miswired circuitry in her head, leaving her prone to polyrhythmic barrages of visual, auditory, and olfactory psychedelia. And though they could definitely cramp her style running-wise, she adored the blizzards that could bring feet of snow in a matter of hours, driven by howling westerlies that would leave some areas of ground scraped free, some buried in drifts that could reach to the rooftops. She loved the frigid, brilliant-blue and white days that would follow, the air aglitter with crystals that blew free from the drifts and winked like miniature animated prisms as they caught the heatless yet dazzling morning sun. To Sophie, these individual flakes floated with a whispery buzz that ended with a sharp *ping* and a brief whiff of ammonia as they were immolated by rays of light that sang in her mind like mezzos practicing scales.

And the thunderstorms! The previous summer Finn had driven her east, to the vast emptiness of the Pawnee National Grasslands, which awed her nearly as much as the peaks of Rocky Mountain National Park, the San Juan's to the south, or Wyoming's Tetons. In the grasslands, there was nothing to interrupt the eye save the Pawnee Buttes, bluffs that rose from the high prairie like what she told Finn looked like the weathered bones of long-dead sentinels.

"Died of boredom, probably," Finn responded, working a long blade of grass in one corner of his mouth, the scenery bringing out his laconic cowpoke side.

So much for waxing poetic.

Waves of green and tan and brown undulated in the breeze, an ocean of mixed grasses stretching to the horizon, which seemed both close enough to touch and impossibly far away. The landscape was dotted here and there with sagebrush or the well-camouflaged bodies of pronghorn, who emerged from the monochrome only when they moved. About a quarter-mile off, a small herd had been startled by something—a rattlesnake, Finn ventured; they had seen several already—and burst into motion, running toward them at a speed that took her breath away, then turning en-masse at an abrupt ninety-degree angle, synchronous as a school of fish, and slowing easily to an amble, stopping and beginning once again to graze. Sophie watched them, absolutely rapt, following the herd and, as they drifted nearer, individual antelope, with a painter's eye.

Working fast, she made numerous small sketches in her pad. Finn, who was amazed at how quickly and accurately she could draw, had his trusty Moleskine, which by day's end would be filled with gnomic written images, descriptive phrases and bits of syllabic music which, to the untrained eye, would look like merely inscrutable calligraphy, weird runes, or renderings of unintelligible hieroglyphics—absolute gobbledygook—but would later be nurtured to bloom into any number of poems, most having very little to do with grass or antelope. He also manned the camera with its telescopic lens, pointing and firing away at whatever Sophie told him to. Sometimes, he got a shot that was fit for framing, but the goal was merely to provide something suitable for Sophie to borrow upon later, something that through an alchemy known only to her and her kind would turn the slightly out of focus realism of his photo into an explosion of wildly expressionistic pigment on canvas.

As they watched the antics of the antelope, so too did they watch as a storm budded and began to grow to the northeast. Innocent-looking white clouds billowed and grew darker, eating away almost imperceptibly at the sky's blue expanse, until, almost before they knew it, thunderheads had climbed to impossible heights, the air around them turning a murderous green. To Sophie, the clouds looked like gigantic kernels of popcorn. *Means hail,* Finn said, meaning the green sky. It got very quiet, the birdsong and insect chorus that had volleyed around them all day suddenly silenced as if by a switch. Lightning flashed through the clouds in forks and curtains, and the intermittent, light zephyrs that had rustled the grasses stiffened into a hard wind, with gusts that tore at their clothing and audibly shook the truck, parked just up the hill from where they stood. The cloudwall, now pitch-black and solid looking, bore down upon them, covering ground with terrifying speed.

The pronghorn drifted closer to the shelter of the nearest bluff. Meanwhile, minor chords tortured from the keys of mis-tuned pianos erupted in Sophie's ears, like a barcarolle played by some demon from the mind of Tim Burton. Little electric fish darted from her limbic system and blazed though her arteries. From her fingertips burst butterflies and a lavender mist. She spun slowly as the clouds finally engulfed them and the first fat drops began to fall. At some point, she realized the whole sky was spinning at just about exactly the tempo she was, and that this was not a product of her synesthesia. Adrenaline bolted through her then; real fear. And then Finn's hand was on her elbow, turning her toward the truck. "Come on, Soph, we need to get away from here. Right now."

She nodded her head and tried to hurry back to the relative safety of the battered black Toyota, but her heart seemed to be pumping molasses. Despite the adrenaline, sensory overload was making her sluggish. To Sophie's mind, the wind was purple and filled with slithering veins of yellow and black. Demonic choirs sang in dissonant bursts of competing harmonies, dueling loops of vowels that swooped and pirouetted around her head like oddly beautiful vultures. When the rain began in earnest, vast arpeggios from a thousand pianos cascaded down from on high. It was like Franz Liszt had declared himself God.

What the thunder did to her was beyond explanation.

And then they were in the truck, racing down the dirt road that would take them a few miles south to the two-lane state highway that made a beeline to the west and home. Finn drove as fast as he safely could on the partially washboarded gravel, the rain coming now in blinding gouts that pushed the windshield wipers to their limit. Though only four in the afternoon, it was serious dark.

Sophie, now fully back to herself and shaking with fear, buckled her seatbelt, noting the tension in Finn's jaw, the way the muscles in his arms bulged as he fought the wind, working to keep the pickup on the road. He looked quickly over at her, gave her a surprisingly reassuring smile. "We're having some fun now, huh?"

She grinned back at him. Despite the very real risk of bodily harm, it was true. Terrified as she was, she was having the time of her life. Jackrabbits and tumbleweeds dashed through their headlights. The air was full of small debris. The Toyota shook and shuddered. To Sophie's nose, the air was redolent of sulfur and fresh peaches.

The dirt road actually took them the wrong way for a time, deeper into the heart of the storm, but if he could get them to the highway and headed toward the mountains, he told her, they should be out of it fairly quickly, rocketing westward as the storm slid away to the southeast, bringing the possibility of disaster to any number of the small farming communities that dotted Colorado's eastern plains, but leaving them well out of danger.

And sure enough, after a frightening ten minutes of hurtling nearly blind down a rutted dirt road, and a few miles of hydroplaning along the patched and weather-beaten asphalt of Highway 14, they emerged, as if through a suddenly-opened door, into a sunsplashed summer afternoon. They pulled off onto a dirt apron at the crest of a long prairie swell and got out of the pickup to look at the storm behind them. Now that they had left it behind, what they witnessed sent a chill like a frozen icepick spiking through both of their chests. A supercell was suspended in the sky like an inverted fortress, a slowly spinning green-black mass many miles across, reaching altitudes of more than thirty thousand feet, and in places hanging down nearly to the beet, corn, and wheat fields, the lonely farmhouses and irrigation machinery looking ridiculously fragile against a backdrop that could turn them instantly to scrap metal and kindling. Three separate tornadoes, each a terrifying white, detached themselves like spindrift from the body of the storm and reached towards the Earth like the arms of some gargantuan octopus. Two groped blindly through the air for a moment before receding back into the cell, while a third touched down in an empty field, immediately thickening and turning a violent brownish-black, before it too changed its mind, disappearing back into the belly of the beast.

Finn let out a long, low whistle, but neither he nor Sophie spoke as they walked back to the truck. As always, he opened her door for her, but this time, the gesture, after such a harrowing experience, filled her with the sweetest tenderness, a sensation quickly followed (this being Sophie and Finn, after all) by an overpowering lust. She stepped back from the door, reached down and undid the button of his cargo shorts, unzipped them and pulled them to his knees. "Get in," she said.

He climbed into the passenger seat, somewhat awkwardly in his hobbled state. Sophie reached up under her sundress and pulled down her panties, stepping out of them in the dirt. She kept her boots on. Watching that maneuver was all Finn needed (he was a sucker for a sundress and boots) to be fully ready for what came next. Sophie was equally ready, and quickly clambered into the truck and onto her new husband, burying him in her with a jolt of electric pleasure that nearly made her scream. She grabbed the headrest behind him, then bore down on him with an urgency bordering on mania. He arched his back, slid his hands under the back of her dress and up her hips, grasping her and pulling her down on him hard. It was just about the most desperate and life-affirming sex they had ever had: loud, fast, and in three minutes, over. The truck's windows were steamed over and the air inside was heavy with the musk of their exertions. After coming, she collapsed onto him, nearly limp, then, after catching her breath for a moment, slid off of him, rolled over into the driver's seat with the grace of a gymnast, buckled up, and eased the seat forward. Finn squeezed her hand tight for a moment before they each took one last look at the storm in their rearview. Sophie slid her sunglasses, which had somehow stayed put during their frantic grappling, down from where they rested atop her head, and after checking for oncoming traffic, pulled back onto the two-lane, aiming the pickup at the peaks that rose in pillars of sunlight from the plains ahead.

* * *

FOR THE WEEK preceding their anniversary, the area had been suspended in a weather pattern where the days began in a brilliant sunshine that persisted into the late afternoon, then gave way to thunderstorms of varying intensities, and which lasted anywhere from fifteen minutes to two hours or more. No matter what, though, today's storms will have passed through well before their guests were scheduled to arrive at the studio, where the tables were already set, the tea-lights hung, the deejay's equipment set-up, the bar stocked, beer iced. In the center of the old barn *Finn, Sleeping* swayed gently, suspended from its cables, shrouded in secrecy and a sheet of raw linen. Donatella and a small army of her employees would arrive at six with the last of the food, and a bit later, just before the guests began to roll in, a bevy of college students, hired as waitstaff and bartenders, would take their places, making sure that no hunger or thirst went unsatisfied.

Sophie could not wait for the party to start. For eight furious months she had toiled, alternately wrestling and dancing with the painting in secrecy and solitude. She had hated not showing it to Finn, just as he hated the horrible anticipation of waiting to see it, but if anything, the mystery that enshrouded the painting had made the first year of their marriage even sweeter. If people had any doubt as to her feelings for Finn, those doubts would most certainly be dispelled when they saw the *Finn, Sleeping*. Or at least she hoped they would, for as much as she had poured into the work, as much as she had stretched the limits of her knowledge and her craft, as sure as she was that this was the best thing she had ever made, she could not be positive that others would see it.

Such doubts were a tiny chorus of distant voices, though. Mostly, she was awash in pure astonishment at her life with Finn, the unexpected progress of her art and her running, in the happy anticipation of being among family and friends, many of whom she had not seen in far too long.

Plus, this workout was beginning to *hurt.* Time to think about that a little, too.

* * *

SOPHIE BRUSHES AWAY the droplet of sweat that hangs from her right eyebrow, catches it at the last second before it drips into her eye. She inhales deeply, exhales forcefully, leans into the hill that rears up before her, as intimidating as it is familiar. She pumps her arms, drives her knees high, refusing the limitations imposed by gravity, and runs with a habitual, almost casual focus, the bored technician manning the control panel in her head, intent on nothing but holding the difficult pace. Another part of her, however—the larger part—is simply lost in the grandeur of the moment. The physical discomfort she experiences is but one facet of a morning that glimmers with halcyon feeling. This run, like the evening yet to come, is a celebration of a life she could never have imagined even three short years ago, so she opens herself up to every sensation, rolls in them like a puppy in freshly cut grass. A summer zephyr rustles through the dry vegetation at the roadside, perfuming the air with spicy whiffs of some sunbaked summer shrub. Small creatures titter and caw among the grasses, dart across the road as if daring her to give chase. Boats bob on the lake: a paraglider launches himself into the breeze, soars out over the town, and Sophie is again blind-sided by a love she never saw coming, a love for a man, a place, a body that allows such afternoons as this, alive and at speed, for a brain that purées her senses, hands that smear the resulting goo onto canvas. She has been flattened, resurrected, and filled up with this powerful and perfectly legal performance-enhancing drug. She can feel it thrumming in the blood that gushes from her oversized heart and through the vessels in her arms and legs, engorging her muscles and propelling her pell-mell after the very source and object of this love, who runs along in his own cocoon of pleasure and pain some one hundred meters up the road. Seeing him up there, his yellow shorts, his sweaty and glistening back a beacon growing slowly smaller in the distance, she is aware of not only joy, but a strong and sudden sorrow. She misses him!

Though Finn motors along less than thirty seconds up the hill ahead of her, for a fleeting instant the gulf between them seems immense, unnavigable, and she is drenched in a new, bittersweet emotion, some strange step-cousin to nostalgia. For a few strides, she is overtaken by this feeling, and she accelerates, ratcheting up the pace even further, as if to chase him down, bring him back to her side. For a shadow of a second, she considers calling out to him. Then the feeling passes, and she laughs at herself, a little abashed at her own itinerant emotions, suddenly overjoyed despite the rather marked increase in pain her burst of speed has caused her. And her mood is spiced with anticipation for the party, the excitement at seeing all her favorite people gathered in one place.

Beannie and Gizmo, with Finn's mother in tow, had arrived in a flurry of hugs and happy expletives just before she and Finn left for the run. Evie and Lisette would be there when she and

Finn arrived back home, as would Rex and Rachel, eager to run any unforeseen errands. Martha would infuse the air with charm and the spice of her Ecuadorian Spanish, and Donatella was, at this very moment, Sophie was sure, issuing directives and calling shots. Anais would be driving up from Denver, where she had been in meetings with curators at the art museum, bringing with her, to Sophie's surprise and infinite glee, Ophelia Essex. *A pilgrimage to see the hermit on her mountain, she's calling it,* said Anais when she called earlier that week. Jimmy and Chaim are coming from Boston, and her grandparents and assorted aunts, uncles, and cousins are flying in from sundry points around the globe. Aunt Patsy, though now divorced and not technically a relative, has already arrived from Santa Barbara, and half the running community will be coming, ensuring that things could get happily out of hand. This was not going to be an evening for the faint of heart. Sophie happily attacks the last section of the hill, her delight acting as a counterweight to gravity, to fatigue. Her staccato footfalls sing out, *tonight, tonight, tonight!*

And tonight (finally!) she releases *Finn, Sleeping* into the wild.

For so many months, she has been enfolded in an intimate pas de deux with the painting, holding it close, keeping it from the world, and now, like a new mother, she is going to introduce her most precious and personal creation to the people she loves most. In a few hours, she will roll wide the big barn doors and invite them all in, let them see the product of her passion up close and personal, bear witness as everything that lives within her is brought out into the light, naked and unapologetic on the canvas. The thought of it sends another little frisson of apprehension through her body. It settles atop the pain of the workout like powdered sugar on a cake, noticeable, but mostly ornamental. For this will be the friendliest audience imaginable. There will be good food, music, and the light of a million stars. Their guests will either like the painting or go back to dancing. Her nervousness evaporates as quickly as it had come, replaced by a buzz of happy anticipation.

But first there is this run to finish, a prospect made ever more difficult by the hill, by the fatigue that seems to increase exponentially with every step as she draws inexorably closer to its crest, which up ahead, Finn has nearly reached. She stares at his slowly receding back, latches on as she sometimes does in a race, attaches an invisible tractor beam, and imagines herself being towed up the slope to the summit. The muscles in her legs scream. The bellows of her lungs work with a wheezy rasp in the dry air and she is coated in a slick sheen of sweat. She is pressed to Earth by the heat, the hills, her own mounting exhaustion, but too, she is lifted up, carried along by the unfettered feeling of freedom running has always brought her. The crystalline afternoon, its views of lake, mountain, and town, buoy her, and she flies over the road, rather than landing upon it, invigorated and intoxicated by the cocktail of emotions that course like an electric rainbow through her blood. In extremis, yet completely blissed-out, she toes-off, springs lightly from one step into the next, just another in a series of unremarkable and nearly identical strides that create a sort of stasis, a permanent present that nonetheless keeps delivering her into her future.

And so, unbound from Earth for the duration of that single stride, Sophie finds herself—to her great and infinitely fleeting surprise—lifted up, wrapped in an aurora of the most astonishing blue, a hue into which unspools everything she has ever been, all that she ever would be.

* * *

HER EYES WIDEN in a final millisecond of wonder. Between one heartbeat and the sudden stillness that follows, everything becomes clear: she is a vital thread in an infinite tapestry, a glittering shard in a grand mosaic. She is a singular and beautiful brushstroke streaking across a canvas that stretches forever. This is what she has been reaching for, what she has always suspected was possible. The colors are astounding, and they sing to her in a chorus of pure radiance. She is a stained-glass window, a kaleidoscope spun at the speed of light, a prism made of liquid fire. A mote, she swirls among fellow motes in their dazzling trillions, and freed from the bonds of gravity and mass, she finds she has become pure color, pure light. All at once, she has become *everything.*

* * *

And then, she is nothing at all.

Echo and Interlude

The Murder in her He(art)

(a criticism)

Last thoughts: the
godhead is a fist of light
a pistol and a pestilence my maker
my destroyer I guess I always knew.
I knew names, dates
(and she couldn't have that.)

I knew the paintbrush
was trying to tell me something:
the hum and the buggery,
a thug with some sluggery.
Mayhap it was something
more funny ironic than funny ha-ha

(a smattering of bandicoots)
(a splattering of pigment)
(a fidgety figment)

Sophie sleeps and the trees sing
ding-dong the muse is dead,
the doorstep wolves aslumber,
sated on the lawn:
one red shoe, a dandelion a sonnet
or two,

the shadetree shadow-hung,
the anklebone picked clean.

Part Four: Finn, Sleeping

Finn

AND SO, AN anniversary party becomes a wake. And so Finn's best friend and lover, his partner in art and crime, the future mother of his children, the woman with whom he had planned to be hobbling around tracks and up trails until he was ninety, his comedic sidekick, his voice of reason—goddammit, his *wife*—becomes a memory, a ghost, the contents of a fat baggie in a polished cherrywood box.

I do. I did. Ashes to ashes. Death done did us part.

The Saturday following the accident Beannie, Gizmo, and his mother fold his sedated body into the cream-colored linen suit, the pale chartreuse shirt and plum paisley tie Sophie had bought him for the party (in a lucid moment, he had gotten the word out to the guests: no black), and drive him up the canyon to Sophie's studio, where the erstwhile celebrants wander the property, stunned, as the fairy lights he had strung in the trees blaze up into a duet with the ironic dazzle of a million stars. (The universe would keep making beauty, whether he was in the mood to appreciate it or not). Anais and Donatella do what natural organizers do when the hosts of a party inconveniently die or fall apart: they make sure people are fed, that they have (more than) enough to drink. They borrow easels from the university and display Sophie's paintings, which had been racked in an old firewood bin, in a large, outward-facing circle around the chairs in which everyone will sit, weeping, murmuring to one another in their shared shock, facing the much larger canvas, which hangs, still shrouded, in the spotlit middle of the room.

* * *

THE UNVEILING IS left to Gizmo and Anais, who bring a perfect blend of gravitas and expertise to the task. They know art, they know—knew—Sophie. They had some vague notion of what she had been working on, how to talk about the painting before actually having seen it, how to commandeer the uncomfortable blend of anticipation and anguish that infused the very air, and turn it toward something with an eloquent and appropriate sense of wonder, a feeling that Finn, untethered as he was by Valium and grief, idly wonders if he will survive.

Having taken Finn's decree forbidding funereal attire to heart, the lovers—whose May/September relationship, to those in the know, was proving surprisingly durable—present a picture of muted, reverent elegance, Gizmo in a summerweight navy silk suit, linen shirt of the palest sky blue, and yellow tie and pocket square patterned in navy, the square with paisley, the tie with tiny polka dots. Finn looks at his lifelong friend, manages a sad chuckle at memories of Sophie, who never failed to give Giz shit about being such a peacock. (Look at Mr. French Country, she would have said tonight, a nod to his color-scheme—What, no little roosters or fleurs-de-lis?) Though she gave him a lot of good-natured crap and was always ready to take him down a needed peg or two, still, she made it clear she was impressed by his sartorial splendor. Anais is again dressed in yellow, her modest butter-colored sleeveless tunic accented by a silk wrap (Hermès, no doubt) adorned with abstract swirls of periwinkle and navy, and draped lightly

around her shoulders against the chill of a mountain summer evening. Finn closes his eyes, holds onto the image of Anais and Gizmo as they speak about the painting, which is still shrouded in linen and mystery, and tries to imagine how this might have gone had mother nature not so cruelly intervened. Ophelia Essex, who Finn rather likes, has worn black—a tailored seersucker jacket, though over a short dress of raw, pale-green silk festooned with dark green dots that complement her early-to-grey hair—stands at Anais' elbow, ready to help with the actual unveiling.

The words that spill from the lips of his friends do not quite reach Finn's brain. It is as if somewhere between where Giz and Anais stand flanking Sophie's painting, and where he sits, adrift in his lonesome fog, the words are stripped of their contours, the sharp corners of consonant and vowel sanded away, the sensical shape of syllables eroded and worn as smooth as stones in a fast moving stream, and by the time they reach him, they are as inert and featureless as dying balloons. Even so, he gets the gist, of which he is all too aware: the painting is for him, of or at least about him, that she had done many smaller studies, had planned and choreographed the work for nearly two years before launching into the eight month-long symphony and dance that would result in the painting they were all about to see for the very first time.

It takes Finn a moment to realize that Gizmo has stopped talking and is looking inquisitively in his direction. The studio has fallen into so rapt a quiet that the distant hooting of an owl is clearly audible. Grief has given way momentarily to a nearly unbearable anticipation, and half the mourners in the room stare intently at the linen draped painting, the other half at Finn, twenty-nine and a widower, sitting drugged and broken in their midst. He shakes his head a couple of times quickly, hoping to dislodge some of the fog that continues to accumulate there, pulls back his shoulders and looks over at Giz, who smiles him a familiar smile, all reassurance and love, and nods as if to say, Now?

Finn extends his hand, palm up toward his old friend, all the flourish he can manage, and nods once. He feels his mother's hands tighten around his left forearm, feels Beannie's do likewise around his right, as if they have no idea what he might do when the cloth which enshrouds the painting falls away. Which makes sense, he thinks idly, as he has no idea himself.

Later, after the shock and awe has receded just a bit—after the power of Sophie's painting has eased its grip maybe a little on her gathered friends and family; after they've had some time to come to terms with the immensity of her gift, the sheer magnitude of her accomplishment; after Finn gives up for the moment trying to sort out and name everything he is feeling; after the collective gasps and sobs have subsided, the astonished murmuring dissipated to silence; after he watches Giz grab Anais' hand and hold on tight, the look of mute astonishment on her face, the single tear she blinks from one eye and then the other; after the wave of...what...awe? Joy? Pride? Disbelief, surely, and around the edges, the shadow of a black and killing emptiness, failing for now to crush and carry him away—after all of this, but before the realization that this is it, that neither they nor the world would ever be graced with another such miracle from her hands, Finn gathers himself, pulls himself like a balloon down the string at the end of which he had drifted in a detached narcotic haze. He owes her this much.

He takes himself in hand, stays coherent long enough to bring everyone in the room back to their feet and back to tears with an impromptu ode and elegy. He walks a wire between oratory and incoherence, saying this public goodbye, though clearly not believing she is gone. He paces, takes long pauses, longer looks at Finn, Sleeping, then spins his memories, his nearly unendurable pain, into melody, unspools sentences and paragraphs that paint pictures on the evening air, auditory brushstrokes that roll from his throat in cadences that have the gathered mourners mesmerized, swaying as if to song. He recites two poems from memory, Hopkins' "Spring and Fall"—Sophie's favorite—and his own "Nude Descending a Staircase," which he had written for her early in their relationship upon finding that she loved Duchamp's signature painting of the same name:

Moonstoned in the depths of the Ambien hours,
she flows—bedroom to kitchen to bath—naked,
gravity-lover downstairs dancing,
unembarrassed as whitewater in a kayaker's dream.

Sleek and dangerous, she hypnotizes: my Salome,
my mistress of hydrodynamics and dance.
Swamped in veils, in waves and brush strokes,
oh what can I do but founder: twee playboat
capsized in her aftermath, shouting out, not waving,
but drowning!

O shapeshifter, sharpshooting mad under moon,
descend untouched, untouchable, slip aqueous
through my luckless grasp—liquidshimmery,
lickety-split—lost in new ideas of what is face,
what is form where current is king.

No mudpuddle Narcissus, I only have eyes
for the rushing by, the burning too quick

for retina to register, for beauty in fleetest form
setting the millworks afire,
out beyond the rainglossed highway,
where muscle cars whoosh puddles into oilslicked
masterpieces, streetlit abstract expressions:
four hundred horses of paintbrush, one hundred
thousand Duchamps dancing on the head of a pin.

Ah, the hunger in your eyes, the shiny fish
writhing under your skin!
Shiver me your undulation, modulation,
your ballet, your hipsway, your come-thee-hither
from upstairs down.

For you I breathe deep, dive deep
into your sizzle and froth, scream you a song
you carry only to lose to a bigger river.
Another voice in the drowned-boy chorus,
another lullabye gone home to sleep in the sea.

As he recites, he looks at the stairs that spiral from the loft to the barn floor, steps that he had watched a naked Sophie descend on more than one occasion, and it is then that something grabs him in its fist and begins to squeeze.

Even before his last line echoes from the rafters and wafts into the mountain air, Finn's carefully cultivated composure evaporates, and only the quick reflexes of Gizmo, who has moved to Finn's shoulder during the eulogy, keep him from collapsing and tumbling into the front row of mourners. Giz and Rex each take an elbow, guide Finn out of the barn and among the parked cars lining the pine-smelling barnyard to get some air, followed quickly by Beannie and by Finn's anxious and agonized mother, as Donatella takes over inside, leading Sophie's many friends and family members in offering up a story, an anecdote, a memory of the one who had left them far too soon.

Later still: Beannie strapped to her Stratocaster, eyes bloodshot and fierce behind mascara wrecked into a rock and roll masterpiece. As she steps up to the microphone a sort of sob escapes her throat and vaults into the amplified air, a guttural, animal yowl of unmitigated anguish. She takes a deep, shuddering breath, leans into the mic and whispers, "Sophie, baby, this one's for you." Another breath, this one calmer, more assured, and then: "Now, motherfuckers, you dance."

Beannie, Lisette, and Evie rip into a blistering version of "Pincushion Heart," and the gathered mourners, who had been pressed to their chairs by the weight of their sadness, the wonder at Sophie's painting, do what they are told, feeling something different now, as they rise as one and begin to move, to thrash and pogo as Beannie tears chords from her Fender and casts them into the throng like shards. Sadness still clings to every surface like a greasy fog, but as Beannie windmills at her axe, jerking and thrusting its neck as she snarls and screams lyrics about love and loss, another feeling grips the mourners. Whether they are dancing or moving about the barn looking at the ring of paintings, an electric and savage emotion, one that uses their sadness for fuel and feeds off of it as it grows, begins coursing through every neuron, flashing across every synapse of every nerve in the room, and soon the barn is a well-appointed mosh pit, and now those who had gathered to celebrate the life and work of a woman they had loved lurch and spasm to the music in a spell of communal, if not yet cathartic, rage.

The mood does not reach Finn (though it would soon enough), who, along with Gizmo and Rex, picks his way among the starlit silhouettes of rocks, nearly a half mile away up Flowers Road, the music that chars the ears of those inside the barn reduced to a dull and distant throb.

As three men in suits pick their way along a starlit trail, back inside, the runners, whose vitality had gone unquestioned, and who knew better, but had felt like together they had drunk from the fountain of youth, as though hard training and high-tech footwear would let them sprint away from black death, the runners, whose delusions had been torn away like a blindfold or a Band-Aid, tapped into a communal grief, an affronted and angry howl, Beannie directing and choreographing their rage from the low, makeshift stage. They danced and cried, cried and danced, until they had danced away their fury, cried away (for now) their despair, and then, taking one last look at the painting, which now dominated the room, said their goodbyes and silently departed.

Eventually, Skirtchaser stops playing. Evie and Lisette each take one of Beannie's hands, and as they stand, silently watching the mourners depart, Nikki Desmond joins them, wrapping a familiar and consoling arm around Beannie's waist. Nobody notices, nobody cares. Finn's mother casts nervous glances at the door as she is comforted by Aunt Patsy, as Donatella and Anais attend to Sophie's dazed relatives. Chaim and Jimmy have another beer, keep their own counsel as they stand looking at Finn, Sleeping.

* * *

IN THE MORNING, they run, those hungover, erstwhile Lost Boys and Girls, led by their gaunt and haunted Peter Pan, joining Sophie one last time for a sunny out-and-back along Flowers Road. The run is a sort of relay, a memorial, and celebration, each of them briefly carrying then passing on the polished box that held all that was left of the corporeal Sophie. The forty-odd runners, who had spent countless mornings and afternoons moving together along so many stretches of trail and roadway, had only intended to run three miles, spend twenty minutes or so in what was for many of them the closest thing to church, before returning to those waiting at the studio for a final short memorial. Twenty minutes was not enough, though, not for any of them. So they moved deeper into the mountains, nobody talking, until, at the crest of a long, gentle hill, Finn stopped, took a long look at the peaks that rose to the west, and turned, leading them back down the mountain, returning to the studio nearly ninety minutes after they had left.

The ceremony was short. Pretty much all that could be said had been said the night before, so it was a silent and haggard crew who stood in their shorts and T-shirts around the lightning-struck lodgepole and watched as Finn poured Sophie's ashes into the simple, biodegradable box, and nestled the box snugly between the tree's roots at the bottom of the small, deep hole he had dug as the sun rose that morning. One by one, they tossed a sad shovelful of earth back into the hole, murmuring a silent farewell before passing the shovel to the next mourner in line. When the hole had been filled, with Finn tamping the compacted earth into a small mound, and after everyone had placed the flowers they had brought onto the fresh little grave, they each hugged Finn and walked slowly to their cars, because, as Frost had written all those years before, "...that had ended it./ No more to build on there. And they, since they/ Were not the one dead, turned to their affairs."

In the years that followed, after Finn had leased the barn to the university, to house the writers and artists awarded a Sophie Ringrose McGuinn Residency, which had been endowed in perpetuity by Finn, Beannie, Gizmo and Anais, the lodgepole would come to be known as Sophie's Tree. Marked by the small stainless steel plaque Finn affixed to the tree that morning, and a carved wooden bench made by a friend, the spot became a favorite place to read, to picnic, reflect, and meditate for the poets and novelists, the painters and sculptors who lived and created for a time there under Sophie's roof.

* * *

ANVIL LIGHTNING ORIGINATES in the very top, or anvil, of a thunderhead, the seething, cosmic blacksmith's shop where the most sinister storms are made. More dazzling, deadlier than other types of lightning, it launches itself upward and away like a javelin, to land in the lap of the unsuspecting like a postcard from the end of the world. Finn had done his homework, made himself an expert. He knew what lightning could do. He knew that forty thousand feet above the ground, in the violent heart of a stormcloud too far off yet to see, forces had conspired like evil thoughts in the noggin of some trickster god, thoughts made manifest by the million-volt flash that had lashed out, plucked Sophie at random from the ranks of the living. It was the classic "bolt from the blue," a sucker punch from out of a clear Colorado sky on a sunny day when Finn and Sophie, hand in hand at the apex of their young lives, could see with crystal clarity the future that awaited them, beckoning and bright.

And now, seven years later and a thousand miles to the east, Finn sat on the edge of his tub, staring at his bloody and ointment-slickened knees, and marveled at how—despite the miles, despite the years—what a short distance, really, he had traveled.

You see, despite the years, The Glimpse had not abated. If anything, it had grown crueler, more erratic, sometimes blowing up his day with shock treatments and pornographic freeze-frames, sometimes lying sneaky and still, allowing him a cringing handshake or hug. His latest therapist had tried to get him to find a pattern in the kind of contact which would cause a burst and the kind which would not. But no pattern had yet emerged, so he continued on, living his life as warily as a fawn lost in a forest of wolves.

And, as his wounded knees would certainly attest, the lightning had not stopped luring him into storm-shattered evenings and afternoons, enticing him towards a final, searing tango. Was he suicidal? Well, the jury was still out on that one, though he had to admit that for nearly a year after Sophie's death his fondest wish was to die. He had endured each moment in the secret hope that it would not be followed by another, and though he never considered actually taking his life, neither did he want to continue living. The panicked, nerve-immolating grief which had for the first few months ripped him from sleep or at random waking moments torn through him with a bolt of pure adrenaline, gave way to a heaviness that coated his every cell with a substance somewhere between molasses and wet cement, a sadness so thick you could stir it with a stick. His friends assured him things would get easier over time. The smoking crater in his chest assured him he would feel this way forever. So every night as he lay, simultaneously fearing sleep and craving the oblivion it would bring, Finn prayed to the God in which he had never believed that he simply not awaken the next morning.

His prayers, alas, went unanswered. The sun kept coming up.

* * *

MAYBE THIS WAS why, late in the spring following Sophie's death, his brain spawned the demons, who came up with a juicy gambit that aimed to make moot the whims of capricious, if nonexistent, gods. Thus, ten months later, on an unsettled and blustery Thursday in mid-May, as he sat in his kitchen nook, a half-graded stack of final exams on the table before him, Finn felt himself gripped by a nimbus of weird electricity, an irresistible force that grabbed and made of him its puppet, working the wires that sent him hell-bent-for-leather into the lightning-licked maw of an oncoming deluge. Suicidal? Maybe, maybe not, but when viewed from a certain angle, and in tandem with the newly acquired torment of The Glimpse (Beannie called them his superpowers), it could certainly be argued that his newfound survival mechanisms were seriously fucking with his chances for actual survival.

* * *

YOU'RE A DUCK in a shooting gallery, aren't you, sport? You take a deep breath, shapeshift yourself into a tasty target. You weave, you bob, you run the ridgeline all badass, rope-a-dope the bolts with a come-and-get-me quickstep. Ain't no hitch in your get-along, is there, amigo? Your sweet stride strobed by clouds that spit forked tongues, split the sky with a sizzle that aims to strike? You are exposed, unprotected. You don't know it, but you are begging to be bitten. You are suddenly smitten, aren't you, in love with the notion that maybe you can follow, that similar highways might seek the same destination, if only you can roadmap them right. So you shove your thumb into the traffic of oncoming clouds, hail and hitch a lift in the only direction that matters, take a hard, last run, chasing your love down breakneck road. But you get no takers, do you, pal? You holler, you yell, you wave your arms at the flame-painted chassis of passing thunder, but today you're invisible, today you get nothing but wet.

So you sprint past the eyes of animals that glimmer in flashes, ascend the switchbacks at silly speeds. Midnight's crashed hard into the center of afternoon, shuttered-up the sun. So you dance over rocks lit but by the lightning whose kiss you crave, trip onto blacktop slick with splash and boom. The wind spits its hailstones in your face, blows hard enough to bend your back 'til it breaks. But nothing can slow you, can it, sport? You're a million-volt cowpoke, you live to rodeo that bright blue bolt. You don't feel the hail, don't notice the dark. You lean into the wind, run as if by Braille through an electrified blindness of your own making, your feet dead certain where they are going, though your mind, my friend, your mind is surely lost.

* * *

AN HOUR AND nearly twelve miles later, Finn stands in a puddle of muddy water in the middle of his kitchen, clad only in shorts and trainers, shivering with cold, no idea whatsoever how he has come to be here. His heartrate is north of two hundred. His chest heaves, and his legs, mud-spattered to the waist, throb and wobble as only after the hardest workouts or races. It is dark, though he doesn't think it is night yet. He flicks the light switch.

Nothing.

Lightning strobes the room, followed a second later by thunder that shakes the walls, rattles the dishes in the cupboards. He cringes involuntarily, takes off his shoes, socks, and shorts, leaves them puddled in the middle of the kitchen floor, then feels his way down the hall to the bathroom, where he gropes around until he finds an old towel, and dries off, wipes the mud from his legs, his teeth chattering. From the top shelf of the linen closet, he pulls down the quilt that still smells like her, wraps his shivering and goosebump-covered body in its folds, before stumbling back down the hall to the living room, where he curls up in the fetal position on the couch and watches the lightning play shadow puppets on the wall, numbly listening to the rain.

After a while, his shivering abates and his breathing returns to normal. He stands, pads to the kitchen, picks up his soggy shorts and socks from the middle of the floor, rinses and wrings them out into the sink. He fills a glass with water, chugs it as he stands naked at the window, watching the flickering of the receding lightning illuminate the dripping leaves of his backyard lindens. The day grows gradually lighter as the storm retreats eastward. He removes his damp clothes from the sink to hang them on the line, slipping into a pair of sweatpants before opening the back door and stepping into the early evening sunshine. Behind him, the fridge clicks on and begins to hum. The microwave beeps. Power has been restored. He wishes he could say the same for his equilibrium.

He clothespins his running shorts and socks to the line, then surveys his yard, stooping and gathering the twigs and small branches that the rain and hail has cast about, stretching the muscles in his traumatized legs and lower back. Attending absently to these details, his muddied mind begins to clear. It is obvious that he has gone for a run—apparently a long and hard one—in the middle of a raging thunderstorm. The wet clothes, his mud-spattered and aching legs, the now-silenced racing of his heart, hint at a wild afternoon of dancing on the red line. Also clear is the fact that he had sprinted away into the tempest at the behest of a will other than his own. It must have been an incredible workout. He's sorry he missed it.

Gizmo

SOPHIE AND I had our issues, sure. *Lovely girl, I thought when we first met, but a bit too blithe a spirit for me.* I remember her saying she was "totally geeked" to come to London; I mean, *come on.* Her chipper mood was almost unassailable (though God knows I tried to assail it), even more so than Finn's, whose relentless good cheer always seemed to me at least in part a spell cast against encroaching darkness. I should have seen that her determined positivity came from the same place. I was a jerk. So sue me.

As to her abilities as a painter, however, I never equivocated. She was the real thing, and it was the immensity of her talent that eventually triggered the sexual attraction I came to feel for her, that stupid, drunken kiss. I swallowed those feelings, of course, just like I do with every other convoluted, inappropriate thing I feel about Finn or Beannie or any other good thing in my life and focused my general dickishness on other people.

Anyway, *Finn, Sleeping* is as breathtaking a contemporary painting as I have seen in a long time. Huge, at seven feet by nine, and abstract, at least mostly—perhaps a bit more so than de Kooning's *Woman I,* with which it shares a distant kinship—it offers up the merest ghost of a figure. Sprawled akimbo across the canvas, the form (think love-child of Pollack and Alice Neel on acid) lies haphazardly cocooned in a nest of riotous brush-strokes—some wide, assertive and solidly physical, some spaghetti-thin and seeming to linger as lightly upon the canvas as the fading echoes of a dream. In places, calculated drips lead to an almost Frankenthaler-esque wash, as if those dreams are about to lift from the canvas and waft away. Areas of Richter-like scrape seem to expose the viscera that lies beneath the dream, an inscrutable cosmic clockwork. The painting is done mostly in a palette of purples, from periwinkle to regal to an indigo bordering on black, (picture the darkest Iris) and, as with that flower a mystery made of deepest purple—veins of brilliant, orange-infused yellow are etched into the tender flesh at its most private center, drawing the eye inward in an act of breathtaking intimacy.

And then one's gaze is forced gently outward to take in the work again as a whole, this time aware of how the yellow, though only present there at the center, somehow imbues the whole canvas with an otherworldly glow, like neon ghosting over from a bar around the corner. It is only now, aided by this new light, that the eye catches the subtle and bewitching greys and greens and fuchsias that seem to dance and shimmer across the sleeping figure. (*How have we missed that up until now?*) The figure—now solid, now nebulous—is indeed sleeping, and peacefully, but across him bristles a nimbus of energy, as if a globe of ball lightning had burst over the sleeping body, covering it in crackling light, a light that I can only interpret (and yes, I am far from objective) as the love of the painter for the subject. As the picture draws the eye in, then pushes it away to see the work once again *in toto*, we begin to notice the colors that seem to writhe and tango across the slumbering figure, and suddenly the whole thing seems to pulse with an energy that is overtly sexual; throbbing; almost auditory. One would have to be made of stone not to be nearly undone by the pure erotic power of *Finn, Sleeping*. Like an iris spreading its petals, the sleeping figure is naked (or at least seems to be) and without shame, aslumber in a place light-years from where modesty remotely matters. Unashamed also is the painter, whose hand, as if by some kind of alchemy, makes love to the subject and the canvas at once, using her colors to evoke a palette of emotion ranging from the sweetest tenderness to the most wanton of passions, all without resorting to bombast or sentimentality. The picture is as much about the artist's own pulsating, burgeoning, rapidly evolving feelings as it is about the hinted figure asleep on the canvas, and these feelings are there for anyone who would care to spend five minutes with it to see.

And this is mostly what I will say about Sophie's best painting, in the catalogue for her posthumous, one woman show at New York's Anais Fleischer Gallery. The painting is such a tour de force of love and eroticism and tenderness that it makes the very air in front of it vibrate, as with song. I don't know how Finn can be in the same room with the thing.

* * *

TO UNDERSTAND FINN, you have to know about Sinead.

Saint Sinead, beautiful Sinead, Sinead pale and doomed; Sinead who walked on water, the ripples changing to wine beneath her feet—I am not trying to be a dick here, I am just trying to make it clear how large she looms in Finn's memory—Sinead, the protector; the big sister. Sinead, who died of leukemia at eleven, leaving a sister-shaped hole in both the little boy Finn was then and in the man he has become. Even now, when he talks about her, he gets this dreamy look on this face, as if the curtains have parted and his big sister is with him again.

Despite the passing of nearly three decades, he fills his stories of his lost big sister with the kind of uncanny detail that is either the product of his skill as a writer or the inspiration for it. First, he will describe her: tall for eleven, and strong, yet thin and waif-like, with straight, white-blonde hair that reached her waist, her wrists always encircled by silver bracelets or leather cords or chains made from the stems of dandelions and daisies. She was pale, with high cheekbones that flushed easily and bright green eyes that blazed like emeralds when she laughed, which according to Finn, was often. And indeed, every picture I have seen of her shows her laughing in delight or grinning with wicked amusement. Even in the photograph taken in the month of her death, bald and gaunt from the failed chemo, she smiles down at the little boy reading at her feet, her face the very picture of benevolence, not a hint of the fear and pain and sadness she must surely have been feeling.

He will tell you of their trips into the woods behind their barn, seeing how many kinds of mushrooms they could find, or how many animals they could spy. Sinead would draw them in the sketchbook Finn would beg her to let him carry, and which he still keeps. He still talks of her joyfully racing ahead down a trail, her hair flying behind her in two long braids, and how, when she would disappear around a rock outcropping or into a thicket, Finn would find himself utterly bereft, then overjoyed as he rounded the next bend to find her, breathing hard, waiting for him, dappled in leafshadow and light. He says this is his strongest memory: Sinead sprinting effortlessly along the wooded trails, both ethereal and animal, disappearing into the woods as he dashed pell-mell after her. I am absolutely sure this is why Finn took up running and why he became so good at it. I think he is still that four-year-old boy, chasing after the sister he loved above all others, convinced somehow that if he can just run far or fast enough, he will get to that place where he will find her laughing still, waiting for him in a pool of sunlight, head encircled in a wreath of leaves like a victor's garland.

* * *

FINN IS ALWAYS chasing ghosts, both Sinead's and Sophie's, and fast as he is, they always elude him, flying along together just out of sight around the next bend in the trail. And with a life circumscribed by the affliction he has come to call The Glimpse, ghosts have become his closest companions. He is visited by shades, mocked by demons that drive him into electrified embraces and thickets of deadly lightning. He is stoical, and good-natured as always, but haunted in the truest sense of the word. He wears his suffering lightly around the eyes, in a certain wan smile when he thinks he is not being watched. At dawn and dusk he appears almost translucent, nearly a ghost himself, like a saint in a painting by Crivelli. It is as if the effort he has put into retaining some semblance of his jocular, friendly self in the months and years since Sophie's death, and in the face of The Glimpse, has made it a struggle for him to remain completely corporeal. And thus, in certain slants of light, he seems little more than an apparition, a wisp in search of its old, solid form. He haunts, even as he is haunted, a specter sometimes even to himself. Yes, Sophie haunts him surely, and on most days in a good way, as does Sinead, but so too does his father, whose body Finn and I found.

* * *

IT WAS A clear, frigid February night during our senior year—a Friday or maybe a Saturday, the stars electric, fresh snow knee-deep on the ground. Finn and I were just returning from a night out—a basketball game, or perhaps a movie; Beannie must have had a secret rendezvous—and when we entered the blessed warmth of the McGuinn kitchen (our standard American tribal uniform of letter jackets and watch caps being woefully inadequate to the task of warding off the Vermont chill), Finn's mom called down for us to go out to the barn and retrieve Dr. McGuinn. The other Dr. McGuinn—from long habit I addressed them both by their professional titles, despite their pleas for me to use their first names—who as usual had lost track of time tending to his kiln, and whom we were sure we would find ensconced in a chair next to the kiln's warm glow, deep into a book and a good bottle of cognac. We reluctantly went back out into the cold, hurrying along the shoveled brick walk from house to barn, our path lit by small globes hanging from the trees, intent on quickly and dutifully retrieving the delightful, yet somewhat absent-minded physicist and potter (and perhaps scoring an esophagus-searing snort of Prunier), before raiding the fridge and playing a little ping pong before turning in.

By this point, I was spending more time at Finn's than at home, as things with my old man had become intolerable. Beannie stayed over a lot too, since her parents couldn't be bothered, one way or the other. Heck, we were there so much that we both had beds in the guest room, our own dressers. The closet was full of our clothes. The dinner table was always set with places for both of us. More grateful than we could express at the time, Beannie and I secretly called the McGuinn's house "The Orphanage."

When we entered the barn, we found his father on his knees in front of the open kiln, into which he had been feeding the wood he had spent the summer cutting, splitting and curing for the purpose. A new batch of ceramic moons, comets, planets, and stars, from which he made beautiful mobiles, wall decorations and wind chimes, and sometimes, from tiny ones, charms to be worn on necklaces, bracelets, and earrings (he had made Beannie an exquisite, purple and green figure, a mermaid gazing at the moon, which he had hung from a silver chain; for me a softly glowing, multi-hued Saturn on a leather cord), and which he painstakingly shaped and fired, had been glazed and placed on racks in the kiln for a second firing, and now he was adding the wood to bring the complicated (to me) stone and brick beast to a temperature which would turn the liquid glaze into many-hued glass, the shaped bits of clay into jewelry.

We knew to enter the barn silently, so as not to startle him, which could cause an accident. When we came into the room, the kiln had been fired and Dr. McGuinn seemed to be resting briefly between feeding pieces of wood through the open cast-iron door of the specialized oven, which took up a large section of the barn's rear wall, and which the professor had built himself. The fire through the open door sent a devilish ballet of orange light and dark shadows dancing across his kneeling form and upon the walls of the old stone barn. We stood in the delicious warmth for a moment, waiting for him to move or to acknowledge us.

"Dad?" Finn said.

His father did not answer, so he called a little more loudly. Still nothing. Now Finn and I both knew something was wrong. We both moved quickly to the professor's side.

"Dad?" said Finn again, this time gently grasping his father's shoulder. Finn immediately recoiled, turned to me, shouted, "Oh God...quick, Giz, call 911!"

I ran to the wall opposite the kiln to do just that, but as I did so, I could see that it would be no use. Now that my eyes had adjusted to the flickering orange light, I could see what Finn already had: his father's hands fallen uselessly to the floor, his chin hanging past the open top button of his heavy flannel shirt to his chest. He had balanced himself perfectly, heel to haunch, fed one last hunk of wood into the maw of the kiln, and died. Stroke or heart attack, it must have happened some time before, as Finn could not get his father unbent from his final position on the hard dirt floor of the barn. It was quite clear that it was too late for CPR. I explained all this to the dispatcher on the other end of the line. Finn stood, turned to me with a numb, disbelieving look on his face, and said in a hoarse croak, "Stay with him, please. I need to go get my mom before the ambulance comes."

He left the barn like a man walking underwater, while I stood helplessly in the subterranean light, unable to take my eyes from the form kneeling before the open door of the kiln like a supplicant saying a final prayer to a god of fire.

Finn

HOME AGAIN. HAMPDEN College, Hampden, Vermont—two days before Thanksgiving, his fifth since Sophie had died, and yeah, holidays still pretty much sucked. Killer workout on the windswept tundra of Hampden College's The End of the World, but first a late morning and early afternoon spent roaming the galleries at MASS MoCA, stopping to stare for an hour or two at *Finn, Sleeping,* reacquainting himself with it, losing himself again in its layers, its bursts of music, its auroras and pulsars, its story lines that all end in lightning bolts, every time. The painting unzipped him like a chainsaw, and as always, laid a live wire in his guts. His senses exploded. It was as if through this painting, Sophie's anniversary present and last bequest, she had passed along her synesthetic gift to him. Or maybe it was The Glimpse. Maybe the two were related in some way he had not yet come to understand. Whatever it was, being in the presence of the picture made his senses come fully alive, made the walls between them dissolve.

The painting itself became three-dimensional, and he dove in, swam and spelunked its brushstrokes, bathed in its palette of purples, let the oranges and yellows rip through him like jolts from a cattle prod, its lavenders and fuchsias whispering along his skin like a silk scarf. In its presence, he smelled damp earth, mock orange, Russian olive. He inhaled the honey and sunflower that had emanated from the nape of her neck, the musk of her body after making love. The hair on his own neck stood up under the painting's command, his skin played over by caresses, the feeling of teeth gently biting the flesh over his hipbone, his cock enfolded in a grip that made him hard. Arpeggios and glissandi unfolded like fireworks in his head, whole symphonies ran roughshod along his spine. Padded hammers banged out punk hosannas upon the xylophone of his ribs.

This was the seventh or eighth time he had visited the painting, at one museum or another where it was displayed on loan over the five years since Sophie's death, and in that time he had learned to endure, make a wary peace with, then to embrace what seeing it did to him, to let go of himself and succumb to the picture's weird power. He was nowhere close to ready for it the first time, for the magnitude of its effect on him, which was much the same as The Glimpse: a sensation the strength of which had nearly caused him to very publicly collapse. But now he simply got comfortable, stood loose-limbed as a willow or sat on the bench in front of the picture and let the big canvas do to him what it would. He tried to come to the museums on sleepy, early weekday afternoons, when the galleries were lightly populated and he could have the painting more or less to himself, because even though he was now more at ease with the various effects the painting had on him, he was never quite fully in charge of his movements, the tremors and twitches and shudders, or of the sighs and moans and whimpers that escaped from him when he was in its grip. On busier days, or when returning to the painting for a second time after visiting whatever exhibition was currently on display, he would approach the painting more obliquely, or study not the picture, but rather the effect it had on others.

For he was not the only one to come under the painting's spell. Though not nearly to the same cataclysmic degree as Finn, who was a tuning fork, struck and vibrating in its presence, others too were particularly sensitive to *Finn, Sleeping*'s powers. These fellow pilgrims would stand rapt in front of the canvas as if transfixed, uttering little cooing noises or singing softly to themselves. They would shiver, their hands would lift from their sides to flutter in the air like helpless birds or fly to their mouths to cover the gasps that escaped from them. Some would simply sway, as if the painting were singing, rocking from side to side for long minutes as the crowds parted and moved around them. He loved them, these fellow souls, who were somehow made of the same stuff as he, these finely-tuned antennae, seemingly born to receive the messages Sophie, through her painting, was sending.

He had thought about keeping *Finn, Sleeping,* but Gizmo and Beannie had helped him come to his senses. If he had lived with the painting, they said (not that he had a wall big enough for it anyway), he would have been crushed by its psychic weight. And of course, they were right, the painting would have driven him mad. So he and Anais had put their heads together and found a way that he could share it with the world, yet visit whenever he wanted. The gorgeous, old industrial site that housed the North Adams museum, just twenty miles from his childhood home, made perfect sense. It was actually Finn's mother who helped Anais work her magic—*No,* she said, *the magic is all Sophie's*—who sold the painting to a rich Hampden alum (who immediately donated the painting to MASS MoCA) at a price a bit lower than they could have negotiated elsewhere. The museum, which had no permanent collection, then loaned the painting to other institutions before taking it back in, displaying it in its own little alcove among the exposed beams and pipework of the old factory. Finn made up for the loss of commission by giving Anais a pair of album cover-sized paintings outright, which she protested, but eventually, being, after all, both lover of the work and a businesswoman, accepted.

The museum was all but deserted on this raw, pre-holiday midday. No one had wandered by as he sat on a bench under the building's exposed guts, facing a section of three-quarter wall in the middle of the gallery, and communed with Sophie in the only way he still could. As always, he marveled that her hands had touched this canvas, built this transmitter, this radio starship time-machine. Her fingers had filled it with the fury of her love, and her mind had translated her vision into a portal that took him someplace different every time he slipped across its threshold. Her cross-wired brain had shown her what was possible; her eyes had told her hands how it could be done. Her sweat had mingled with the pigment, strands of her hair had become stuck in drips of dark purple and curved strokes of cornflower blue. Her actual molecules lived on among fleeting flashes of Lapis Lazuli.

A couple of years before, while studying the painting a bit too closely for the comfort of museum employees, he had noticed a strange, fibrous clump near the vaguely figurative center of the canvas. Upon closer inspection, the clump turned out to be a lock of hair. *His* hair. Sophie had apparently done a bit of barbering one night as he slept, collecting a key ingredient for the spell she had spent a year stealthily conjuring, his DNA mixing with hers amid her oceans and rivers of pigment, her brushstrokes weaving an incantation that brought a sleeping thing to life.

He wonders if she had any idea just what sort of spell her conjurings had woven.

* * *

IT HAS NOT snowed, but the mud beneath the dead grass is frozen hard beneath his spikes. Clouds droop treetop-low and mix with fragrant fireplace smoke that evoke warm feelings but bite his lungs in a manner less than conducive to the task at hand. He has marked the corners of the big field in front of the Commons with four of the ever-present Adirondack chairs that litter the Hampden College grounds, and around which he will run his intervals: six times five minutes, just a tad under a mile and a quarter each, a tad more than three complete circuits per rep. A nowhere-near-long-enough minute of jogged recovery await between each effort. His warmup has taken him over the covered bridge and out into the muted and leafless countryside, to the old church graveyard, where he had a quick chat with his dead father (it seemed to be the day for such conversations) before making the return trip up the hill to campus to begin his labors. The warmup has not only flushed the detritus of travel from his legs (he had driven from the airport in Albany straight to the Museum), but has at least partially chased the post-visitation fuzziness from his head. It is at times like these he is most grateful for running. To be able to apply himself to something so overtly physical forced him out of himself, didn't let him get too cozy in the cloying and troublesome spaces he occupied after spending time with Sophie's art.

He likes that running is such physical work, how, much like building a wall or digging a ditch, he can put in his daily portion of labor, then measure, at least in retrospect, how far his effort has brought him. The last year had garnered him surprising (at his age) personal best times at the half marathon, twenty-five kilometer, and marathon distances, along with some welcome cash, and less welcome press. Despite the 2:13 he had run to finish second at Twin Cities, he knows perfectly well that if everybody were to toe the line at next year's Olympic Trials, healthy and full of run, he has no chance whatsoever of making the team. *The trials are still fifteen months away, and why in God's name is anybody even talking about them?* He just wants to show up, throw down, and go home, happy he has given it his best. But now, after a decade of racing a notch or two below the world class level, squeaking onto a couple of World Championships cross country teams (best World's finish, 47th), he is being mentioned by the geniuses on the new running websites as a dark horse to make the team for the Athens Games.

Ridiculous. Yet here he is on this grey and fading afternoon, grinding body and spirit against the wheel of the improbable, as always, a sucker for the difficult task. At 34, he still loves running, he just hates thinking about it all the time. He still loves racing: the loosing of the hounds, the answering of questions that cannot be answered any other way. Sure, he still hates that last few minutes before the firing of the gun, the exquisite tension, the illogical fear, but he loves more than ever the racing itself, the marshalling of reserves, the life-size ambulatory chess match, the miles of cat and mouse before committing to an endgame that would inevitably prove devastating. But for whom? Well that is the question, now isn't it?

Yes, there is a marathon to run, somewhere out there in the mists of time, but Finn has more pressing fish to fry: another U.S. cross country championship awaits, just three months away, on the sacred, scarred turf of Boston's Franklin Park, and today's workout is designed with that race clearly in mind. He sits in one of the Adirondack chairs, takes off his trainers, eases into the slipper-like racing spikes; snug and feather-light, all the traction he would need on the grassy field coming from the nine-millimeter stainless steel spikes adorning the underside of the shoes beneath the ball of his foot and toes. The nines are maybe a bit long for the hard winter ground—sevens would have been better—but he'd had no way of knowing the grass would be so short, the frozen mud so hard.

He stands, pulls off his windproof softshell pants, catching them, of course, on a spike and nearly falling—why in the world did he never remember to take them off before donning the spikes? He wrestles free from the pants and matching jacket, from the breathable hooded sweatshirt with his shoe company sponsor's logo on it, wadding them and tossing them in a ball onto the chair. A slight breeze has come up, and it cuts through the thin long-sleeve shirt and tights he has stripped down to. He is still moving in a cocoon of his own heat from his warmup, however, and once he begins this workout he will generate more than enough warmth to keep the late November chill at bay, and besides, the effort he will be putting forth will relegate cold to near the bottom of the list of discomforts he will be enjoying. The tights and snug-fitting tangerine-colored shirt, the stretchy gloves and green and orange ski cap, with its jaunty Nordic tassel will keep him plenty warm enough, while helping his aerodynamic frame to slip through the breeze with as little resistance as possible.

He faces the center of the empty field, does a couple of last, quick stretches, then, taking a deep breath, begins the series of strides, gradual accelerations that will get his heart rate up, fire the motor neurons in his muscles and send blood coursing to his legs, priming the pump for the extended bout of hard effort to come. He begins at an exaggerated, high-kneed trot, careful not to catch a spike and stumble, then accelerates over the course of eighty or ninety meters to a full sprint, before easing off and slowing gradually to a walk. Now in the middle of the field, he walks for a moment, bends to touch his toes, noting happily that the hint of hamstring soreness that had been nagging him for a few days has abated, then repeats the process back in the direction from which he has come. He's breathing hard now, each exhalation sending a cloud of steam into the sub-freezing air. After six strides, his body is primed for the exertion that will now commence, his working muscles drenched in oxygen-rich blood, the bellows of his lungs working effortlessly. A quick frisson of electric adrenaline signal that it is time to begin the less pleasant part of the program. The part that both he and his demons like the best.

* * *

IT GETS REAL simple, real fast, doesn't it, sport? Only two minutes in, and here it comes, that *what the fuck* moment. And there goes the mind, just like always, panicking about the signals coming in from the frontier. Outposts in the legs and arms and chest send telegraph messages warning of imminent collapse, buzzers and bells go off, messages are screamed over neural loudspeakers: *We are in extremis here; the center will not hold; meltdown coming; shut this hombre down!* Conventional wisdom says listen to the body, ease off the throttle or things could get dire. But you hold no truck with conventional wisdom, do you, pal? Instead you get all Zen and shit, turn down the volume on the Chicken Little act in your cranium, decide the discomfort is well within the acceptable range, decide, in fact, that it might be a bit more comfortable if you *sped up* a couple of seconds per mile.

Still, it hurts a little, though, doesn't it, sport? Pushing every system nearly to failure: the rhythm section of heart and lungs, concerto of viscera in your flashing legs *this close* to devolving into a cacophony of clashing muscles, tendons, and ligaments that will leave you collapsed and twitching on the dead grass like an exploded calliope. But you've got this, don't you, *Kemosabe*? The din between your ears is old hat by now, the burning in your legs and chest almost like some shitty old song on the radio, one you used to hate with a fiery passion, but is now merely background noise, elevator music serenading you in the calm, moving bubble you have created for yourself. Sure it hurts, the aging rubberbands in your calves and quads and hamstrings propelling you over the frozen ground at a little under thirteen miles per hour, your lungs wrenching every last molecule of oxygen from the frigid air, heart firing that sweet oh-two like a drug through veins and arteries and capillaries and out to the desperately elongating and contracting muscles. The truth though, is that you have been through this rigamarole more times than you can count. You know the drill, sport, you know the discomfort is mostly a hollow warning, that sooner or later the voice telling you to slow down will just shut the hell up. It's not that the pain the voice keeps yammering on about isn't real. It's just that you don't freakin' care.

Round and around you go, don't you, amigo, gaudy hamster on an invisible wheel. You chase after the ghosts of races future, races past, under the darkening sky, under the occasional gaze of a down-swaddled and vaguely curious students hurrying across the grass toward the dining hall. Your spikes send a flurry of dead grass into the air with every stride, your breathing audible at some distance now, the white wraiths of your every exhalation streaming behind you, ever more visible as dusk descends.

* * *

IT'S GOOD TO be home. Nearly full-dark now, and the thoroughly, yet pleasantly shattered Finn eases out of his spikes, into his warmups and into his cooldown, staying mostly on campus, traversing the lanes and well-lit parking lots, the lovely dirt path past the pond and carriage barn, the music building where Shirley Jackson had written *The Lottery*, and which was said to be haunted. In high school, he and Beannie had spent several nights wandering the building until dawn in a semi-serious attempt at ghost-busting, never catching a protoplasmic peep. Gizmo scoffed at such ridiculousness, staying home to play Scrabble with Finn's parents until bed.

The pain in his legs receding, he feels his way along the darkened trail past the guest cottages and through a brief woods, his feet seeming to remember the location of every root or embedded rock that might trip him up, until he reaches the far campus gate and the road that would, were he in the mood to make the climb back to campus, take him down the hill into North Hampden and its general store, which is one of Finn's favorite spots on Earth. *Not a chance*, say his legs, so he raps his knuckles against the metal ball atop the stone gatepost (an enduring harmless tradition he and Gizmo and Beannie had instituted as adolescents), then reverses his course, encountering groups of students, now fed, hurrying off through chatty breath-clouds to sundry lecture halls, studios, or to dorm rooms that, unbeknownst to the current occupants, house the randy ghosts of Finn's amorous awakenings. A memory of a particularly gymnastic evening with a talented dance major appears before him like a hologram, and he is not sure whether he should laugh or cry. My, how things have changed.

He shakes his head, throws in a quick burst of speed as if to distance himself from the erotic phantasm, and hurries on back to the field where he had run his intervals, coming to a stop at the end opposite the infinitely-photographed commons building at the center of campus. Breathing deeply, but regularly now, he stands at the edge of the steep drop-off that tumbles away from the flat field into tangled mass of denuded greenery, and which is known far and wide as The End of the World. As he has done countless times before, he stands atop the low stone wall marking the brink, gazes out across the valley to the line of rounded old mountains etched black against the darkening sky. The mountains, stretched across the horizon at dusk, have always appeared to him to be a woman lying on her back in repose, a sunbather beside a summer swimming pool: knees bent slightly, long thighs gracefully descending to the hint of pubic bump; then the flat belly, slight rise of ribcage, until finally, the inviting, yet modest swell of breast, on top of which winked, to Finn's never-ending dismay, the red light adorning the top a radio tower. Like a gaudy pasty twirled on the nipple of the sweet girl-next-door, to Finn it just seemed *wrong*. He laughs to himself. Which did he need more desperately, a hot shower, or a cold one? The first hint of a chill worries along his spine, and with a shudder and a nostalgic sigh he drops from the wall and trots off, a spiked shoe in each hand, completing a final lap of the empty field, tapping the backs of its Adirondack sentries as he passes, before turning in the direction of the grand old Commons, hurrying through the darkness past its bulk, and honing-in like a lonely moth on the welcoming light burning in the window of his mother's campus office.

* * *

HE SLOWS TO a jog outside the Barn, the old, red wooden horseshoe with its honeycomb of benign bureaucracy and insanely clanking radiators, and which houses the office his mother has inhabited for more than twenty years. By this point the cozy space, with its paintings, plants, and gently battered furniture, is more like a well-worn and comfortable set of clothing to her than a room. Finn pauses briefly outside the office window and watches her work. She sits at her desk, cup of tea at her elbow, nose nearly touching her computer screen, her glasses forgotten and pushed back on her forehead, forcing her stylishly-coiffed grey hair into a cresting wave. Across her keyboard her fingers tap and pause, tap and pause. Her lips move slightly as she types. Then she notices him standing outside her window, starts briefly, then bursts into a wide smile. *Come in out of the cold,* he lip-reads as she beckons to him with one hand, the other still tapping away. He gives a quick thumbs-up, trots twenty feet to the door, and gives himself over to the building's familiar, warm embrace.

* * *

HIS MOTHER FINISHES the email she had been composing, and then they drive to Price Chopper for groceries, supplies for the Thanksgiving feast, taking his mother's Outback (the same model as Sophie had driven, same color, but three or four years newer: the world was full of forgotten old booby-traps and emotional land-mines), and leaving Finn's rental parked next to the guard shack on campus. To the accompaniment of Christmas carols for which he is nowhere near ready, though he guesses José Feliciano is not *too* bad, Finn pushes the cart up and down the aisles as his mom rather maniacally fills it with enough food to get a regiment of Cossacks through the long weekend. Beannie and Giz will be driving up from Boston the next morning, which has her amped with delight (she still referred to them as "my kids," still remembers all their favorite foods), but what really has her on happy edge was the other guest who would be coming for the holiday. It seems his mother has acquired a boyfriend.

* * *

SHE HAD MET Tomaž, a Slovenian Kafka scholar, at a conference in Vienna. He had, it seemed, wandered by mistake into a lecture she was delivering on lyricism in Thomas Mann's *Tonio Kröger,* and transfixed *(Transfixed! His actual words!* She laughed. *Can you imagine?)* by her manner, had stayed. Afterwards, he had persuaded her to join him for some coffee and a pastry. They talked for hours (mostly in English, but also in

German and Italian, in which they were both fluent, and which she had far too little opportunity to use) in a small café on the Philharmonikerstraße, eventually moving on from coffee and Sachertorte to wine and dinner, their reluctance to part growing as the evening deepened.

He too had lost his spouse before turning fifty, and had never remarried, instead dedicating himself to his teaching, his work on Franz Kafka, and his passion for collecting rare British records from the early days of rock and roll. He was positively giddy at the recent acquisition of a bootleg recording of a Düsseldorf concert by The Kinks, which had been pressed onto vinyl by an intrepid Czech—*In an edition of less than one hundred, and much to his own peril!* Tomaž whispered conspiratorially, as waiters lit candles against the deepening gloom. By the end of the evening, when he walked her back to her hotel, long slumbering feelings had begun to awaken in both of them; old notions began to thaw and emerge from hibernation. When he walked her home again the following evening, she asked him up for a nightcap. "The rest, as they say," his mother tells him with a glibness totally at odds with the tone in which she had been speaking, "is history."

Finn gasps in manufactured shock. "What a tart! This is the woman who raised me? Picking up strange men in foreign countries?" She swats him with a stalk of celery. He kisses her on the cheek.

They talk, the cart fills with greens and root vegetables, fixings for stuffing and three kinds of pie, plus assorted drinks and football-watching snacks. (Finn, a lifelong Nebraska Cornhuskers fan, had picked up the obsession from a favorite uncle who had attended college in Lincoln. He was fairly certain he would be the only one in front of the TV when they played archrival Oklahoma on Friday). He interrogates her about Tomaž, and she holds forth in a breathless, slightly bashful rush, displaying a girlish side of her he has never seen, and by the time they reach the meat department to pick up the fresh organic turkey she had ordered, she is positively glowing. Finn is delighted and enthralled, this being the first real talk he has had with his mother in years. It carries over from the grocery store to dinner at the Hampden Station, where he feels like a bit of an idiot, still dressed in his warmups from after his run. He passes on the waitress' offer of a drink to start, opting for water and a cup of tea to chase away the post-run chill.

"Fantastic, then you're the designated driver." She then orders an expensive tequila without needing to look at the menu, and hands over the car keys. *My, my,* he thinks, *the surprises just keep on coming.*

The conversation stays lively, turns to her work editing a new collection of letters between Mann and Carl Jung, which, once she has sipped the tequila, clearly savoring both the smoke and fire of it, she talks about with real excitement. "God, Tommy, the power of those two minds, the ideas they bandied about, the sheer glory of their prose. Everyone talks about Jung's correspondence with C.S. Lewis." She shakes her head as if disgusted. "Not even in the same ballpark." As if for emphasis, she tosses back the rest of the tequila, signals the passing waitress to bring her another, then says, "Oh listen to me going on, I must be boring you silly. And you've had such a long day."

And he has. He had arrived at the Humphrey Terminal in Minneapolis at five a.m. that morning, everyone still getting used to the new travel restrictions, their attendant delays, that had been in place since the terrorist attacks the preceding September. And though the flight from the Twin Cities to Albany had been an easy one, and the drive to the museum in North Adams uneventful, his time with *Finn, Sleeping* had been as intense and exhausting as ever, and the workout had been a killer. So yeah, he is bone-tired, but he is having a fantastic time, enjoying dinner out with his newly animated mother, who is talking to him like a familiar colleague, or even a friend.

"Mom, no, you are not boring me at all! I've always loved Mann, his lyricism, the ferocity of his interrogation of art. Reading your copy of *The Magic Mountain* when I was in ninth grade changed everything!" His mother beams. "And Jung. Wow. I can't wait to read the book."

"It should be out a year from this spring, God willing, but I'll send you a copy of the galleys." She takes a long, slow sip of her drink. "And hey, I don't think I ever told you, Todd Margoulis is using *your* book this semester. Both he and his kids are crazy about it!"

His third collection, *Don Rickles Sings the Blues,* had been released by Copper Canyon in August, to modest hoopla, good reviews, and, for poetry, strong sales. "That is very cool. Tell him thanks for me. If he wants, I could come back before Christmas break and talk to his students. I'm giving a reading at Williams, so I'll be just over the hill."

He was on sabbatical fall semester, traveling, giving readings from the new collection, running massive mileage weeks, and working on his new book, a novel this time. The last two volumes of poetry had been like cutting out organs—without anesthetic—so tackling a novel had thus far proven a refreshing, if intimidating, enterprise. He spent a few weeks in August and September in Colorado, checking in with the university on the residency program at Sophie's studio, spending one night, as he did every summer, in a sleeping bag under the stars beneath the lightning-struck lodgepole, telling Sophie everything that had happened over the previous year. It was silly, he knew. There is not one piece of him that believes some sentient phantasm or heavenly emanation drifted nearby, listening to him ramble on. Still, it made him feel better, if terribly sad, to converse with the darkness, and that was reason enough.

His mother takes all this in, listening intently, the age lines in her forehead deepening as she concentrates. Finn takes a little break to attend to his halibut, savoring a crispy bit of skin, (God, he is starving!) and they eat in silence for a time before he goes on, telling her about his month living in a condo on the slopes in

Steamboat Springs, the ski resort deserted between the summer and ski seasons, running trails deep into the mountains and hammering away at the novel, a bildungsroman called *Sleepy Eye*, after the central Minnesota town of the same name. The book is a about a high school hockey hotshot torn between his desire to escape town on a college scholarship or stay and protect his mother from a brutal second husband.

"And how is that project coming?" his mother asks between bites of grilled salmon.

"It always sounds so boring when I describe it, but I think it has a chance to be okay—you know, family as a metaphor for the dying American towns in which they live, societal decline in the era of late capitalism, that sort of thing. An update on Sinclair Lewis, who hailed from the area." She nods her head, considering this. "Plus, there's hockey. You can never go wrong with hockey."

"I'm just glad I was able to raise such a good little socialist." She smiles and squeezes his knee. No Glimpse; God was that wonderful.

She asks, so he talks a little about The Glimpse, how it had never really abated, complains wistfully about the women at readings, particularly grad students and occasional faculty at schools to which he is invited, who, having read his books and familiarized themselves with his sad story, attempt to bring him cheer through the comfort of their bodies, a maternal/predatory approach that both arouses and leaves him a little nonplussed.

"Jumping back like I've been attacked with a cattle prod and screaming works pretty well as a rebuff, though I prefer the appreciative, but very sad, *I'm just not ready yet*, approach." He gives his mother an exaggerated pouty lip. "All depends on how much time I have to get ready for being touched." He shrugs, wishing he had a drink after all. "My life in a nutshell. I'm like a comet. I kind of orbit people: I drop in, share a little gravity, but never crash or kill any dinosaurs. Then it's back into the empty reaches of space, towing my shiny tail of poems and ice." He finishes with a flourish, makes a toasting motion with his tea mug.

His mother merely shakes her head, her eyes shining. She stays silent as they eat their dessert, taking tiny bites from her wine glass of chocolate mousse while he attacks his apple pie and cinnamon ice cream. When they have finished and are back in the car, she finally speaks, her words coming freighted with sudden sobs that are as unfamiliar to him as her earlier girlish effusiveness.

"Tommy, I'm sorry. I know I haven't. . .I mean I never. . ." she gives up, looking at him with a gaze of miserable supplication.

"Mom?" He lets the car run, the whoosh of the heater the only sound other than a sniffle or two from the passenger seat. "What's going on? Why are you apologizing?"

She takes a deep shuddering breath. "You have been suffering so much, and so bravely since Sophie died. Just like you did after Sinead. And you were just a little boy." Her face is twisted in anguish. "Your father and I were so devastated after Sinead died, I think we sort of forgot about you."

"No, Mom, you didn't!"

"We did. Well not forgot, maybe. But we pulled away, protected ourselves from being hurt like that if something happened to you, just let you fend for yourself." Finn is stunned. He had always thought of his childhood as idyllic. The freedom he had to run the woods with his friends, to pursue his academic interests, to make adolescent mistakes and learn from them. And always, he felt safe, like he had the softest of spot to land if he were to fall. He tells his mother this, but she just shakes her head.

"And when your father had the stroke and died, it was you who took care of *me*. Oh Tommy, I have been so selfish!"

He figures that some of this is the two tequilas doing the talking. His mother is a tiny woman and had never been much of a drinker. But given the intensity of her outburst, he gathers that she has been thinking about this for some time, that the tequila has just made a soft spot in his mother's reserve, allowing the pent-up feelings to come bursting through. Again, he tries to assuage her guilt.

"Mom, I had the best childhood a kid could want. Okay, I always knew you and dad had your own little club that I could never be a member of, but I always just figured that was how all parents were. And what about Beannie and Gizmo? They practically lived with us after junior high. You were far better parents to them than their own parents were."

She shrugs. "Well, that's not saying much, now is it?" She forges ahead. "And in the years since Sophie's accident, I have had no idea how to help. I just let you dive into your writing and running, told myself that was what was best for you. And maybe it was, but I could have done research, talked to experts…talked to *you.* And I just worked harder, wrote more, traveled more…I have been worthless."

"Mom, no. Where did I come the Christmas after she died? Who brought me back from the very edge? You did, Mom. You and Beannie and Giz. Without the three of you, who knows if I'd even be sitting here right now?"

She shrugs again. "Well I should have done more. From the time you were a little boy until right now, I should have done more." She takes his face in both hands, turns him toward her. "But you've always been the very most important thing in the world to me, Tommy, to your father, too. I have always loved you more than anything else there is."

"I know, Mom. I know. It's okay. And no apologizing. You are a great mother…and besides…" Now he breaks into a grin; "Just look at how great I turned out! Right?"

"You have," she says solemnly. She changes the subject, snaps back into being the mother he knows. "Amanda Sue is bringing a friend." She always refers to both Beannie and Giz by their given names, maybe the only person on the planet to do so. "Have you met her?"

He has not. He doesn't know anything about a new flame. In fact, Beannie has been strangely mum about her love life of late, which is very suspicious, a situation Finn will soon be getting to the bottom of, you'd better believe it. He sighs. Everyone, it seems, is hooking up but him. His mother, Gizmo—whose relationship with Anais has cooled back to friendship, and who is now making tabloid headlines with a Scottish concert promoter—and as always, Beannie, who falls in and out of love with shocking regularity and ease.

The next afternoon he sits, feeling a little bemused, in his father's old chair in the barn, wearing a flannel-lined barn coat of his father's, reading the 1919 first edition of *The Wild Swans at Coole* he had found among his father's books, and drinking a pint of local hard cider. His mom is off to Albany to pick up Tomaž, and as he waits for the arrival of Giz, Beannie, and her mystery guest, he figures nobody Beannie could bring home would really surprise him.

He is wrong.

When he hears tires crunch on the gravel drive, he eases from the chair and walks around to the front of the house, to greet and help with bags. Gizmo emerges from the driver's side of the new Volvo Cross Country wagon with a wave, followed by a grinning Beannie, who more or less leaps from the front passenger's side, turns, and opens the rear door, through which emerges...*Nikki Desmond.*

Well fuck me, thinks Finn, overcome by a sensation he can only describe as wonder.

* * *

"WHAT FRESH HELL is this?" he says by way of greeting, recovering, he thinks, rather nicely from his shock.

"Very funny." says Beannie, still grinning. Nikki smiles nervously over Beannie's shoulder. Gizmo, per usual, just stands there smirking.

After a few seconds of awkward silence, Finn opens his arms and Beannie steps into them for a long hello hug, followed by a manly, back-slapping embrace with Gizmo.

"So," chimes in Nikki in her Northlands accent, "do I gait a hoog too, or will it, like, kill ye?"

Finn, who like Nikki, remembers their last embrace all too well, smiles anyway. "Welcome to Vermont," he says, then wraps her in a hug that indeed brings a jolt, but not, this time, an X-rated electrocution.

Beannie leans in close, whispering in their ears, "There'll be no threesomes, sorry guys," then, cackling, tosses her daypack over her shoulder and marches toward the house. "What do you have to eat around this joint? I'm fucking starving!"

Neither Finn nor Nikki are surprised enough to blush.

* * *

"WE EXCHANGED OUR hearts over coffee and tarts!"

They are all completely charmed by Tomaž. Tall, lean, and silver-haired, his face cracking often into a crooked-toothed and delightfully disreputable smile, he carries himself in a manner that is an irresistible mix of Old World gentleman and bomb-throwing revolutionary. Finn understands immediately that his mother never had a chance. Tomaž has just finished giving, in his mesmerizing Slovenian accent, his version of the events Finn's mother had described to him two evenings before, the table around which they sat covered in the remains of the scholar's first Thanksgiving dinner. He delights them all, answering Gizmo's questions about to the works of Slovenian painter and mosaicist Jože Ciuha, with whom Gizmo had recently become enamored, with great clarity and enthusiasm. He is even more thrilled to talk music with Beannie, who after dinner breaks out her vintage Martin acoustic and, to his infinite delight, does her best Pete Townshend impersonation. Finn's mother, overjoyed with how all the ones she loves are getting on, simply sits and glows.

The next day, as Beannie, Gizmo, and his mother take Nikki on a sightseeing drive through surrounding the area, showing her all of their old haunts, Tomaž even sits and watches the football game with him, peppering him with questions and seeming to enjoy the experience as much as Finn does. Earlier in the day, the four runners had headed into the countryside, the natives showing Nikki round a circuitous ten-mile route they had long called the Seven Bridges Loop for its eponymous covered bridges. They return from their run to a rustle of activity from upstairs, Finn's mother momentarily appearing on the landing, smoothing the front of her sweater, Tomaž following behind her looking suspiciously nonchalant. *The old dog! Grabbing a quickie while the kids go out and play!* Beannie whispers in Finn's ear.

Later that night, as the others play Scrabble, Finn and Tomaž sit drinking cognac in front of the fire, talking about another Tomaž—Šalamun, poet and a countryman of the old scholar, whom he knew well enough to have a story or two. This development delights Finn to no end, as Šalamun's enigmatically surreal, sad, and humorous work often inspire Finn's own poems. Tomaž asks to hear a poem or two of Finn's own, so he finds a copy of *Don Rickles Sings the Blues* on his mother's bookshelf, thumbs through, looking for something appropriate, and begins to read. The others come in from the dining room and sit on the rug in front of the hearth to listen in. Earlier volumes are found, and Beannie, Gizmo, and his mother keep him busy for an hour, refilling his glass frequently as they request favorites. Even Nikki has an old one she wants to hear. Finn finishes by coaxing Beannie into strapping on her guitar once again, and together they sing "Maybe Tomorrow We'll Know," a bittersweet, minor-chord ballad she had made of a poem he'd written in grad school. By the end, everyone in the room is in tears. Even Gizmo has to wipe his eyes. Then they all bid one another goodnight and wander to their various bedrooms in a shared state of pleasant melancholy. They are all quite drunk.

There are more tears on Sunday, as Finn tosses his bags into the trunk of the rental car in preparation for the drive to Albany, where he will catch his flight home to Minneapolis. He hugs his mother and Tomaž, then Beannie, Nikki, and Gizmo, who stand next to the Volvo, which is loaded for the trip back to Cambridge. More hugs all around and promises to return for Christmas, then it's off into the grey late morning, the first flakes of winter whispering down as he looks in his rearview, watching his mother and Tomaž waving from the porch. He hasn't felt this good, this whole, in a very long time. He had even hugged Nikki without needing medical intervention. Maybe there is hope for him yet.

Finn

IMPRESSIVE," ELISE CROONED, surveying the scabbed lacerations on Finn's knees. "Like you fell on the playground and went boom." She reached out and gently touched the scab on his left knee, somehow without setting off too big a flash grenade in his skull. A good sign. They sat at a table in a secluded corner of Saloon 67, a more-or-less respectable Nordeast dive at which she had long bartended, and which she now co-owned. A licensed chiropractor, her offices occupied the second floor of the two-story stucco structure a couple blocks from the river, hard by the glow of the Grain Belt Beer sign. It was a slow Tuesday night, giving Elise time to take a long break with Finn, whom she had for the last few months referred to as her "favorite customer," the implication of which she had long ago made perfectly clear to him.

The invitation in those words was one he had for some time wanted desperately to accept, but the almost certain pyrotechnics, the scary and embarrassing repercussions for all concerned, had kept him from making a move. Yet here he was, seated with her under a fierce-looking, nearly three-foot long mounted muskie, reportedly (and disconcertingly) pulled from Lake Nokomis, the southernmost of Minneapolis' Chain of Lakes, and in which Finn, who lived a block away, often swam after hot workouts. The big fish's ferocity was somewhat mitigated, he had to admit, by the wraparound shades it wore and the stogie dangling from its jagged teeth. Finn pondered this ludicrous bit of taxidermy as he nursed his third Dr. Detroit of the evening, pleasantly zoned from the combined effects of alcohol and his afternoon ten-miler, chatting more or less comfortably as Elise idly stroked his wounded knee.

The "Dr. Detroit" was a drink Elise had invented in his honor when she had learned about his addiction to Dr. Pepper (he blamed his mother; it was all she could keep down while pregnant with him—*Hey, I'm like a crack baby,* he had said when he told her), a refreshing pint glass of soda imbued with a generous shot of citron vodka, a signature cocktail (which was also an ironic tip of the hat to the dreadful Dan Aykroyd movie of the same name) that was becoming quite popular among the artists and hipsters who populated the neighborhood and frequented, along with its traditional blue-collar clientele, the increasingly popular little bar.

He had been coming to Saloon 67 for a little over a year. It was noisy enough to invigorate, with its boisterous crowds of artists and salvage workers and shopkeepers, its occasional live music and eclectic jukebox, but quiet enough, especially a bit later on a weekday evening, to have an interesting conversation or settle in with a new book of poems. The jukebox, with its vast selection (and which at that moment played Marshall Crenshaw's "What Do You Dream Of?") was the centerpiece for one of the many odd little habits, quirks, and pastimes Finn had developed as countermeasures to his strange and solitary existence. He called it audiomancy, and it basically involved using the jukebox as an electronic fortune-telling device. He would sit down at the bar or his customary table under the muskie, which he had named Cedric—long *e*—and write out a series of questions (*Should I jump off the Lake Street Bridge? Should I order a cheeseburger? Does Elise find me mysteriously alluring, or just weird? Will the Colorado Rockies ever win a pennant?* Or simply, *What the fuck?*). Then he would put a few dollars in the jukebox, press random buttons, and let the songs answer his questions. Several weeks earlier, the question had been, *Should I ask that woman* (a leanly muscular redhead in her mid-thirties wearing a freshly dirty softball uniform) *to shoot some eight-ball?*

"Stupid Boy," said the jukebox.

The writers and metalsmiths he talked to, the students and waitresses with whom he sometimes shot pool, the ubiquitous poetry he read amid the tempered din of the bar, made him feel a lot less lonely, almost made him forget what a freak he had become. The gentle buzz of two or three (never more; he had a hunch he could grow to like the freedom that buzz brought him just a little too much) Dr. Detroits didn't hurt either. Nor did the presence of his proprietress, Dr. Elise Halvorsen, who had recognized him from a television news snippet he had done before the Twin Cities Marathon the previous fall, welcoming him into the fold with a cold Grain Belt Premium.

Over the months and across the bar, they had come to be friends. As she made orders or polished glasses, he would tell her about growing up in Vermont, his running, his writing. She would bring him a sandwich or a bowl of pretzels and talk of her childhood on a farm northwest of Fargo, her close-knit Scandinavian family (*Swedish, Norwegian, a dash of Finn—I'm a total mutt*), the omnipresent Lutheran reserve that made her crazy to light out for more exciting territory, (the Twin Cities, it would turn out, where she would, coincidentally enough, play basketball for MacGillivray, the very college where Finn taught). He talked about Sinead and his father, and eventually she told him about her abusive ex-husband, a high school history teacher she had met at a T-Wolves game, about the hospitalizations and miscarriages, the calls that brought intermittently sympathetic police officers, tearful apologies, flowers, and vows of change. And eventually, restraining orders, jail time, and a divorce.

"It's an old story, but a boring story," she intoned with self-mocking gravity, in the dulcet tones of the narrator of a documentary on the Discovery Channel, as she sat across from him beneath Cedric, nursing a Grain Belt late one Wednesday, doors locked, the last customer gone home.

"I'm just glad it's an old story," he said, taking a chance on placing a sympathetic hand on hers where it lay resting atop the bar. He received only a moderate jolt, a headful of sparks. He had gotten good at masking the small ones; she didn't notice a thing. She rolled her hand palm-up, held his tightly for a moment. The current amped up a few notches; a muscle in his bicep spasmed. The sparks threatened to become Roman candles.

"I'm glad you decided to wander into my bar, sailor." She smiled, but her eyes were full of question marks.

He almost kissed her then. Instead, he did something even riskier. He told her about Sophie, the lightning strike, his subsequent acquisition of The Glimpse, and the resulting lifestyle choices, which to Finn didn't feel much like choices at all. His propensity for sprints into the teeth of lightning storms. She didn't bat an eye, just squeezed his hand more tightly, which turned up the juice to near finger-in-the-light-socket levels. Disquieting pictures began to flicker to life behind his eyes. This time, she did notice, loosening her grip on his hand just a little. But she didn't let go.

"Is this okay?" she nodded at their intertwined fingers. "Am I hurting you?"

He shook his head no, lied, said it was noticeable, but okay. She asked him to describe what he was feeling, and so he did his best to explain what it was like to be him. "Well," he said in conclusion, "I must seem pretty pathetic now."

She took his hand, which she had never released, in both of hers, squeezing tightly. Electricity roared up his arm; the Las Vegas Strip blazed again to life in his cranium. She shook her head, looking at him with flashing eyes.

"I think you're heroic." She stared into his eyes for a moment, the tender intensity of her gaze never wavering, and continued. "Look, the horrible things that happened, you didn't ask for them, any more than I did in my life. And this thing, this Glimpse, you didn't ask for that either. Jesus, Finn, most people would have given up—killed themselves, gone insane, crawled inside a bottle and never come out—but look at you; college professor, professional runner, successful writer…" She looked down to where his fingers lay enwrapped in hers. "Holder of hands. Yeah, I think heroic about covers it."

Heroic was about the last thing he felt. Ever. But it felt good to hear her say it.

To his surprise, she was crying a little. And unless his allergies had gotten worse all of a sudden, he was pretty sure he had gotten a little weepy too. Nothing like a little inebriated catharsis on a Wednesday night. Other than Beannie, Gizmo, his mother, his doctor, and assorted therapists who specialized in grief and PTSD issues, he had never told anyone. Not in seven years. And most certainly, he had never told anyone whom he was attracted to. Those people he avoided like the plague.

"Finn," she was looking at him fiercely, almost defiantly. "I like you. A lot. And I'm fairly sure you like me too"—he squeezed her hand despite the voltage; of course he liked her— "so what I propose is that we try to figure a way around, or through, or over this. Your shit and mine both." She lifted his hand, still gripped between both of hers, to eye level. "See, we've already made some progress!"

And she was right. The current running up his arm was now a more than tolerable buzz. Maybe she was onto something.

"Stand up," she said, dropping his hand and standing up herself. He did so. "Now I am going to hug you, if that's okay." She said this like a doctor who was about to perform a painful procedure, which, when he thought about it, she was.

***

ELISE HAD A plan. It was a good plan, a sensible plan. It was also a scary plan, but if it worked, it would carry them slowly and methodically to a place where they could, she said, just maybe find themselves lovers.

"Have you heard of graduated exposure therapy?" she asked him, after their first hug had been negotiated without the need for smelling salts or paramedics.

"You mean like when someone is afraid of dogs, they cure the phobia by having the person hold a stuffed puppy, then move to a guinea pig, then a bunny, then a real puppy, and before you know it, the patient is rolling around with a pack of Mastiffs...like that?"

"Exactly like that. Which makes me, all naked and sexy and stuff"—she smirks at him lasciviously— "your personal pack of Mastiffs." She makes a face at the analogy. "Well, at least your example did not involve spiders, and..." she said, her face brightening into a smile, "we've already gone from stuffed puppy to guinea pig stage, just tonight. From hand-holding to a fully-clothed hug, now that's what I call progress!" She grew silent for a moment, her face suddenly serious. "So it's really been, um, six years since, well, you know..." then seizing upon the salvation of a movie quote, which rose like a koi from the pool of her brain "...you bagged a babe?"

He looked at her, nodded, trying to grin, trying not to blush. Her face, though, lit up once more.

"Gosh, it will be like I'm deflowering you. How fun!" She pulled him into another quick hug, and, before The Glimpse could even think about returning, whispered in his ear. "It's been a while for me, too."

Elise finished locking up the bar, and he walked her to her ancient, rust-eaten Honda, her hand wrapped in his, his fingers tingling at only a slightly higher level than what he would call pleasant. When they got to her car, he turned loose her hand so she could unlock the door. She turned back to him, looking into his face searchingly and with a slight sadness. "I want to kiss you," she said.

"I know. I want to kiss you too...badly."

She laughed, said, "If you're going to kiss me, buster, it had better not be badly!" She rose up on her tip-toes, pecked him playfully—and ever so quickly—on the tip of his nose. It registered like a flashbulb exploding, the pain level somewhere between the pop of static electricity and a minor bee sting. The look of surprise on his face made her laugh. "Okay, maybe a couple more steps before we try that again." She slid behind the wheel, rolled down the window, and slowly eased from the curb, her voice ringing out into the darkness. "We will have a plan, my friend. And it will be a great and glorious plan." She accelerated, extended her arm from the car, and waved, her hand fluttering like a pale dove in the glow of the streetlight as she drove away.

The next afternoon, she had surprised him after class. Since she had finished with patients for the day, and since it was her night off at the bar, and as he had a couple of hours to kill before his weekly massage, after class, he found her waiting in the hallway outside his classroom.

"Hey sailor, how about a date?"

They ate a late lunch, sitting outside under a cheerful umbrella at a new South St. Paul café, watching runners and cyclists stream by on the twin paths which snaked along the tops of the bluff overlooking the Mississippi. A pair of barges bobbed, nose to tail, on the river below, waiting their turn to pass through the lock and onto the next stretch of river. They shared a turkey sandwich bedecked with exotic and expensive lettuces, and a huge basket of sweet potato fries, and—Elise producing a pen and notebook—got to work on the plan. She proposed, somewhat sadly, that they stick with holding hands and hugging for a week or so, before moving on to some Eskimo kisses, face-stroking and such, and then progressing to kisses on the cheek, nose, and forehead, while caressing a bare shoulder, or perhaps a knee.

"Getting hot yet?" she asked bobbing her eyebrows and spearing a couple of fries. "Yeah? Me too. And once that gets doable, some cuddling, maybe with me in my frillies."

She wrote it all down in no-nonsense, blocky letters, like she was prescribing a stretching routine. "And here," she said with deep mock seriousness, tapping her pen on a spot two-thirds of the way down the page, "is where kissing, actual kissing on the mouth, becomes, I'm afraid, unavoidable."

He shrugged, his palms in the air, as if to say, *Well, whattaya gonna do?*

Elise forged ahead. "From there, there's no avoiding it, really"—she shook her head, pretty brow furrowed—"we're simply going to have to get nekkid and start touching the naughty bits, kissing a little farther afield, lingering a little longer over tender spots." She sighed dramatically. "Until there's nothing left for you to do except, you know," here she paused for effect, "penetrate me."

Which he wanted to do, immediately and right there among the condiments, which, alas would probably render him quite dead and her under arrest, so he decided they should probably stick to the schedule she had down on her legal pad. He must have let out a moan, or a little whimper of frustration, because she patted him on the hand, said, "I know, sweetie, believe me, but slow and steady wins the race."

He nodded, though he knew from vast experience that was simply not the case.

She chewed her pen and frowned. "Longest goddamned foreplay in history. And I loooove foreplay, don't get me wrong, but this is a little beyond the pale." She let out a deep and dramatic sigh. "Good news is," she continued, much more happily, "we can start with the phone sex pretty much whenever you want."

As the afternoon passed, they reveled in their increasing intimacy, talking about things of no great import as the shadow from their table's umbrella stretched farther and farther into the street, until, to his profoundest regret, Finn had to leave for his massage, a variation of physical contact which strangely brought no dire electrical consequences (*Yeah, what's up with that?* Elise said, then, winking, *Hey, maybe I should give you an adjustment, speed things up a bit...*), maybe because deep-tissue work was already so inherently painful that The Glimpse would have been redundant. As they parted outside the restaurant, Elise, in her enthusiasm for the project, unthinkingly gave him a hug and quick nip on the earlobe. Finn made a little strangling sound, staggered backward as if he had been tased.

To her immeasurable credit, Elise did not freak out, which helped a great deal, and just said, "Oops, sorry dude." Then, with a jolt-inducing squeeze of the arm, "Slow and steady, love, slow aaand steady," then turned and sauntered up the sidewalk.

* * *

ELISE HAD NOT been kidding about the phone sex. Within minutes of his returning home after his massage, she called. "Are you still all oiled-up and slippery?" she asked without preamble, her voice husky. "Because I'm pretty darn slippery myself."

An hour later, he was curled under a blanket, exhausted and murmuring sleepily into his cell phone, not wanting to fall asleep, wanting to keep at least her voice there in the room with him for as long as he could. It wasn't the same as having her curled up with him in bed, her head on his chest, as she asked him to imagine her to be. It wasn't nearly the same as being physically together, of course, but to Finn, even this level of intimacy was like the sweetest water to a man who had been wandering alone in the desert for the last seven years. He fell asleep, replaying the erotic adventure she had taken him on, her imagination having proven at least the equal of his own, which was saying something, indeed.

Evenings at Saloon 67 became jovial affairs, the bones of poems appearing more easily on the pages of his drink-ringed red Moleskine, his conversations with the bar's patrons coming with greater ease. The air was spiced with anticipation of amorous adventures to come, the implementation of the next step in the plan, and the promise of his eventual deliverance.

* * *

"DO YOU LIKE watching me?" Elise lay facing him on the large Oriental rug in the center of her large downtown loft, the river outside the window reflecting the Minneapolis skyline, her voice coming in a husky pant. She was completely naked, and like him, covered in a glaze of sweat from their exertions, the breeze from the ceiling fan raising gooseflesh on her slick skin and further stiffening nipples already erect from excitement and the touch of her own fingers. "Do you like it when I do this?" She slid her hand down her slick belly and between her thighs, arching her back with a gasp, never taking her eyes from his.

Elise was tall, maybe an inch beyond Finn's five-ten, and powerfully built, with long, muscular legs that on the court propelled her down the floor quickly and allowed her to jump high enough grab the rim, and which now, on the floor across from him, flexed and relaxed, coiled, uncoiled, and spasmed in reaction to her ministrations. Her ass was hard from years of workouts, her shoulders were broad, her tattooed arms thin, yet defined, and her abdomen rippled with muscle. Her breasts were perfect to him, smaller than he had pictured them, and swelled above her visible ribs, her nipples small and pink and responsive to her every lecherous thought, to her every caress, to his every word. Perfect, too, was the rest of her, from the tousled dirty-blonde of her hair, to her calloused feet. Her visible hipbones beckoned to his hands and lips. God, how he wanted to touch her. But for now he had to be satisfied with watching her own hands move over those sweet hipbones and thighs, over the copious yet compact swell of breast, watching them linger at her nipples and throat, watching one hand go to her mouth as she bit down, moaning at the pleasure the other hand was bringing her as she worked it among the wet and intricate places between her spread thighs.

"Oh," she said. "God." She gasped again and arched her stomach toward the high ceiling. "Unnhhh…yesss," she hissed. "Do you like it when I do this?" she breathed again.

"God. Yes." His own voice came in almost a moan, his own hands similarly occupied.

"I like watching you, too," she groaned. "And keep talking. Tell me what you are doing to me."

And so it went, each of them exercising their imaginations, as intimate as two people could be without actually touching, each watching rapt as the other spoke, stroking and caressing themselves, each talking to the other, touching themselves with hands guided by the voice of the other, making unspoken declarations, promises of what was to come, all through elaborate performances that left them both spent and shuddering, lying as close as they possibly could without touching, the electrified inch between their naked bodies a yawning, and for now unnavigable, no-man's land.

And though these long nights of mutual self-satisfaction, the advanced and elaborate autoerotic storytelling, left them feeling equal parts sated and frustrated, there was no questioning the progress they had made. And though Finn often found himself frustrated nearly to tears at his inability to yet touch her more than fleetingly, he was infinitely grateful to have found her, for her patience, for how she had delivered him from the arid desert in which he had been lost, and led him to this promontory of sweaty limbs and promises whispered on a thick, old rug, to this new and exciting shore, from which he could just see the fog-shrouded beachhead of their eventual consummation.

* * *

SO THEY HAD a plan. It was bold, yet cautious, incremental, yet relentless. Terrifying, yet comforting. It was a terrific plan, and it worked exactly as they had designed it. Right up until the point where they kissed and blew the whole thing apart.

* * *

THE KNEE SHE caressed throbbed with an electric hum even after she removed her hand, a succession of electric pulses emanating from beneath the healing scab and sweeping across his nerve endings like a beacon at a small-town airport. When she stood to return to her spot behind the bar, she bent, saying softly into his ear, "I think maybe you should hang around, come over to my place after I close up. I think it's time to move on to...let's see." She pulled a battered sheet of yellow paper from the back pocket of her faded Levi's. "Step five on the list. And in case you've lost track"—he most definitely had not— "that means kissing, *finally*, right on the mouth, like teenagers, with tongue if the stars are aligned right, and oh, while partially disrobed. You think you might be ready for that, cowboy?" She looked down at him with a look of theatrical lust tempered with genuine concern.

"Only one way to find out." He leered up at her, trying to convey an ease a few notches beyond what he was feeling.

She was not fooled. "Stay put," she said. "I'm going to get you another drink."

* * *

WHEN HE AWOKE the next morning, his head throbbing and filled with the ghosts of terrible dreams, Elise was gone. He opened his eyes and spots swarmed his vision. His fingers throbbed and his whole body flashed with tiny muscle spasms, and his cock, holy Hannah, his cock felt a little like he had closed it in a waffle iron. He was desperately thirsty. It took a couple minutes for his eyes to clear, his body to calm down. He took a few deep breaths, inhaling and exhaling with exaggerated slowness, then propped himself up on one elbow and looked around her bedroom. His clothes were folded and stacked neatly on the chair next to the bed. On the nightstand was a glass of water and three brown caplets. Ibuprofen; she was a saint. She had also left a small plate with a bagel, some cream cheese, and a mottled Bartlett pear. Based on what little he could remember from the previous evening, such consideration seemed well beyond what he could reasonably have expected. Had he merely dreamed it all? Beside the plate was a note.

Dear Finn,

I have patients this morning so had to run. I hope your sleep was peaceful, and I am so sorry if I pushed you too fast, that I couldn't see you weren't ready yet. But I am kind of crazy about you, cowboy. I think we can get through this. It will be okay. I just know it will.

xoxo

Elise

So it hadn't been a dream. But the thing was, it wouldn't be okay, not ever. He knew that now. He folded the note, put it back on the nightstand, and flopped back down on the pillow, squeezing his eyes shut against the hopelessness of his predicament, then stared for a while at the ceiling. Then he sighed, stood, tossed back the Ibuprofen, and guzzled the water. He dressed, made the bed, and carried the plate with the pear and bagel to the kitchen and ate them standing over the sink, running the previous evening through his mind on repeat. Everything had gone so well—shockingly, preposterously well—right up until that final moment, until, *Jesus,* apparently he had lost consciousness (but not, given the evidence, before coming).

Fuck.

Could this be any worse? He could only imagine how terrible it had been for Elise, could almost feel her horror as he pictured himself, at the moment of consummation, thrashing about uncontrollably atop her, mumbling some weird-ass gobbledygook, and unceremoniously ejaculating as she lay there helplessly or scrambled to get away.

Fuck. Fuck, fuck...FUCK!

He cared about her. A lot. Hell, he might even be falling in love with her. But he couldn't allow her to fall in love with him, would not put her through another nightmare like last night must have been. He wouldn't do that to her.

He tossed the pear core out the window for the squirrels, rinsed the plate, and put it in the dishwasher. He returned to the bedroom, found a pen, and appended his own note to the bottom of hers:

Dearest Elise,

You deserve so much better than this. I just can't, won't do this to you.

I am so very sorry.

I wish you all the happiness in the world.

Humbly,
Finn

He placed the note upon her pillow and left the apartment without looking back.

* * *

THAT NIGHT AFTER her shift, they had tumbled through the door to her apartment in a delirium of desire, and when she kissed him, it was like having his tongue clipped to a car battery. But in a good way. Sort of. Her lips were like flames, and when they opened, he burned. They dumped their clothes like November trees in a gale, and Elise, being in command (as Finn could by this point in the festivities neither speak nor see), decided now would be a fine time to jettison the plan, damn the torpedoes, full speed ahead. Klaxons and red warning lights went off in his head, but he was way past being able to act on them, as the walls had already burst into flame. Her tongue searched his mouth like a live wire as she stepped from her jeans and tugged him towards her room.

There were words coming from her mouth, but he could not hear them through the roaring, only sense their desperation. He was a sapling in an inferno and the last sensate part of him could feel how bad she wanted this. And he wanted it equally as badly, so he held on like a doomed man, strapped in and soon to meet his maker, and kissed her harder despite the forked voltage seething behind his eyes. He filled his fingers with her hair despite his blood having turned into a river of fire. He held on for dear life as she pulled him onto her bed and into her, at which point his head simply exploded.

* * *

YOU FEEL LIKE an asshole, don't you, sport? Well, you are an asshole. You're an asshole for believing things might be different with Elise, an asshole for going along with her plan, when you should have known all along you were freakin' doomed. You're an asshole for going to her apartment, for kissing her, for getting into her bed, an asshole for believing in something too good to be true. You're an asshole for subjecting her to The Glimpse, the ridiculous, stupid Glimpse, when all she wanted was to make love like a normal person, to be held, to wake up in the arms of somebody who would never hurt her. And what could you ever possibly do, amigo, but hurt her?

* * *

AND RIGHT NOW, late in the afternoon three days later, a storm blooming and barreling in from the west, its irresistible gravity already building in his blood, he was most *definitely* an asshole. He ignored his cell phone, playing "Cherry Bomb," which Elise had programmed in as her personal ringtone, on the desk next to his computer. *Hello Daddy, hello Mom,* it sang, as it had ten or twenty times each of those three stupid fucking days. With every fiber of his being he wanted to answer that phone. Or throw it out the fucking window. Instead, he turned his back on the ringing, on the woman who was somehow crazy and wonderful enough to still want to talk to him, until finally it stopped. Immediately it started up again, this time playing Elton John's "The Bitch Is Back." Beannie. Whom he was also for the moment ignoring, able only to answer the call of the storm flickering at the western edge of the city. Even so, he was most assuredly still an asshole as he double-knotted his running shoes and stepped, a deaf, dumb, and blind boy, into the teeth of the oncoming gale.

Beannie

I'M GOING TO give the motherfucker a piece of my mind. That is, if he'd ever pick up his goddamn phone. The weather alert for Minneapolis just went off on my phone, and like Pavlov's fucking dog, I'm on the horn, attempting once again to babysit his sorry ass from a thousand miles away. Seven years this shite has been going on. *Seven fucking years.* God. Okay, as you've probably guessed, my bark will be worse than my bite. I mean, it's not like he hasn't tried, right? Fucker has had therapists out the ass. Grief counselors, PTSD specialists, Freudians and Jungians, lions and tigers and bears, oh my. Serotonin reuptake inhibitors and benzodiazepines and yakkity fucking yak. But seven years later and his itch is still a bitch. No touchy, no feely without bringing the hammer down; no thunderstorm without the mad willy-nilly. And wouldn't you know, there is no such thing as a doctor who specializes in treating lightning strike survivors. Almost impossible to set up a study, and besides, there's no money to be made, it'd never lead to a pill.

After the accident, Giz and I, we thought he was a fucking goner. He had put all his eggs in Sophie's beautiful basket, and when she died, he went all Vesuvius and shit. Our sunny, happy-go-lucky Finn was a screaming wreck for two straight months, off the fucking rails and burning in a ditch, sending off clouds of toxic smoke. After the screaming came the movie marathons and long babysleep drives; after the drives, the talking jags—days and days spent wired and crying—then days of nightmares and fucked-up sleep. Then the pills kicked in and he was the star of his own zombie flick: a couple more months of walking into walls and drooling and shit, followed by the drinking binge over Christmas, me and Giz and Finn's mom walking on fucking eggshells the whole time, keeping an eye on the sharp objects, not knowing what the hell to do. Then January comes and *boom,* he just picks himself up off the fucking floor and goes to work. He teaches his classes, he runs, he slips back into a pre-Sophie sort of life, impersonating himself almost convincingly. Our boy has become comfortably numb.

But it doesn't take to long for shit to get weird. A month later, his asshole friends drag him to a club, he runs into Nikki, the world explodes, and all of a sudden, every physical encounter sets off some psychedelic firestorm in his melon, applies a cattle prod to his nethers, fills his head with scrambled porn and the voice of Kingdom Come. And if that ain't quite enough, come the rainy season, his busted brain sends him out to dance the Saint Vitus boogaloo, try and conjure down that last bright bolt. He spends his days either in thrall to one thunderous deity or hiding out from another, completely in the fucking dark one way or the other.

So which theory are you buying? Come on, there are plenty to choose from. Did the strike that killed Sophie scramble his eggs, do some serious cellular-level shit, cross up his wires in a way that will never get uncrossed? Or are you down with the hypothesis that the grief's the thang what fucked him up, says he's semi-subliminally suicidal, paying court to death, while at the same time allergic to the touch of the living? Or maybe he's gone full-on X-Man, flush with useless superpowers, uncaped crusader sprinting the rainswept city in his lightning-bolt underoos.

My own theory? Glad you fucking asked. See, Sophie was the be-all and the end-all, alpha and fucking omega. You have no idea how happy our two lovebirds were. King and Queen of Neverland, all the Lost Boys and Girls basking in their reflected glory in a sunsplashed Rocky Mountain paradise. And our boy, maybe he finally accepted his own good fortune, maybe he just stopped waiting for the other shoe to drop. So when it did, it crushed him like a bug. And Finn being Finn, he only allowed himself to wallow for so long. Then one day he figured he owed it to Sophie, to his friends, to his students to be strong. So he stuffed his guts back up under his ribs, zipped himself up like a duffel bag, and stepped back up to the fucking plate.

He teaches, he runs like a motherfucker, and writes like a fucking fiend. The running allows him to function, burns off some of the swamp gas given off by the sadness that churns and seethes inside him, makes the chaos go quiet for a bit. For an hour or two each day, he goes all Zen and shit, finds the stillness at the heart of movement or whatever, out there on that empty road. Sometimes, the stillness sticks around and he can sleep.

I pity the fools who had to race him then, the poor motherfuckers who felt the force of his infinite rage. You see, nothing could hurt him: he didn't care if he lived or died. And when the gun went off, he wanted to make you suffer, too, motherfucker, though he felt bad about it later, and yeah, he got pretty good at it, too. And that made him a demon on the racecourse. Best times and victories piled up; his bank account got a little fatter. But did he give a shit? No, my friend, he did not.

And the poems, when they finally came, gushed forth like blood and vitriol. They spilled from the slit wrist of his psyche and torched the page, singed the hearts and minds of those poor fuckers who saw themselves in the rubble of his shattered stanzas. So yeah, he ran; he wrote. He kept himself busy and he kept himself tired, but in the end, he could not make himself whole. All the stuff he packed back inside, all the evil shit it emitted, could not be vented with running and writing alone. They say when sap hardens inside a tree, the tree begins to die. When the stuff inside Finn began to harden, things got weird as fuck.

Nikki and Finn both told me about that hug in the club in Colorado, the first detonation to rock his ideas of reality, the first paroxysm of the psychic entropy that pinwheeled out from Sophie's Big Bang, rewrote his personal laws of physics. Between Finn and Nikki, I saw it from inside and out, and either way it looked fucking whack. To our boy, everyone is packing, ready to tase his ass into twitching oblivion, which naturally freaks everyone the fuck out. So, he finds himself a hidey-hole, hangs out until the next fucking thunderstorm comes, and teases him out into another little dance with death. The big question, of course: is he going to be this way forever?

* * *

COME ON, FINN, pick up the phone. I've got some news, motherfucker, and it's going to blow your fucking mind. Aaaaaand of course he's not home, what with the need to indulge his suicidal tendencies and all, but okay, check this shit out. Guess who I just got off the phone with? Give up? Are you sitting down? Quentin fucking *Tarantino*, motherfuckers! Yeah, out of the blue I get a call from the director of my favorite all-time film. Are you fucking kidding me? At first, I was sure that Lisette was having one over, but nope, that voice, I *knew* that squeaky fucker sounded familiar. Okay, yeah, Quentin fucking *Tarantino* is on my phone, and get this. Somehow—friend of a friend of a friend-type of shit—he hears "Freshly-Fucked Look," a song from the new album—not even released yet, mind you—and wants to use it for the soundtrack for his next movie, called—get this—*Zed's Dead.* Some brilliant, weird-ass sequel to fucking *Pulp Fiction*, only my favorite movie ever, and the man wants to use *my* fucking song! Again, are you fucking kidding me? And he told me this: he said he could picture exactly the scene in which the song would be playing. Said it would be *pivotal.* Pivotal, bitches!

So pick up the phone, Finn, goddammit! Because he's got to be the first person I tell, you know? Good news or bad, Finn's *always* the first person I tell. Ever since I realized my parents were fucking junkies. We were in seventh grade, and I came home early from school one afternoon sick, just in time to find my dad shooting up my mom in the living room, the surgical tubing around her arm gripped in his teeth, the needle in her vein, her head back in a kind of pre-ecstatic trance. That explained a whole hell of a lot, let me tell you. It was like catching them having sex, only way more fucking horrible.

I happened upon them in a moment of extreme intimacy, I mean, Jesus Christ, technically he was actually *penetrating* her. The candle they had used to liquefy the junk, or whatever it does, was burning on the table next to the sofa, like some surreal fucking parody of romance. They were so into it that they didn't even notice me standing there. When he finished emptying the syringe into her, my dad said, "Now you do me," his voice low and husky and full of anticipation. It was then that I backed through the front door, in which I had been standing, and went outside to throw up into the bushes.

Then I ran straight to Finn's and cried all over him for about five hours. And he was still there seven years later, with Gizmo, holding me up as they put what was left of my parents into the ground after they got high and burned the house down. So much for the mood lighting. Up to then, they had been pretty functional for heroin addicts. They went about their lives and I went about mine. Live and let, well, you know. Anyway, so yeah, Finn is my go-to, happy or sad. And I want to tell him my good news, *right fucking now!* But no, his goddamn phone, it rings and rings. Best day of my whole fucking life, and the fucker is probably out there running five-minute miles through the worst fucking storm of the summer, as always, doing his damnedest to get himself killed.

And tell me, just who will I fucking talk to then?

Finn

He didn't want to die, at least not anytime soon, though he had to admit that his therapist's question was as valid as it was obvious. Anybody who could see him now, though, running at world-class speeds through horizontal sheets of rain down Minnehaha Parkway toward the river, untroubled by the lightning strikes that every few seconds ripped through the sky, or the tornado sirens wailing even louder than the wind, might beg to differ with his analysis. Sitting in Leslie's small, comfortable office at his last session the week before, clad in cargo shorts and a T-shirt, his hair still wet from a post-run shower, he had shown her the ropy new tissue that augmented the original scars on his knees, which had led her to ask—not for the first time—about his dangerous sojourns into a world of meteorological mayhem. Leslie Wayman, a therapist who specialized in Post-Traumatic Stress Disorder and grief issues, had put him immediately at ease. Even the first time she had shaken his hand, The Glimpse had barely registered: a low-grade jolt up his arm, one tricolored burst of fireworks in his head. She had noticed him flinch, of course.

"Want to start by telling me about that?" she had asked gently.

So he did. That first session he told her about both The Glimpse and his thunderstorm fartleks, to which she responded with "Interesting," and "Tell me more," while taking copious notes on a yellow legal pad. Her complete lack of shock at his story, her warmth and genuine curiosity reassured him, made him maybe a little less resigned to his fate. So he kept seeing her. He had gone back a few days before the kiss that blew up his life, and sat, the white noise machine outside the door threatening to put him to sleep, telling her again how it felt: the force that compelled him, like a firm hand in the small of his back, out into the maw of every oncoming thunderstorm.

"I have a theory," she said. "Would you like to hear it?"

"Well, that's why I pay you the big bucks, now, isn't it?" He grinned; she cocked her right eyebrow, as if to say *Can we be serious for a moment?* "Okay, let me have it, doc, I'm all ears."

"This might sound a little goofy at first, more metaphysical than psychological, but hear me out."

"Of course." He knew this was going to be right up his alley.

"I think that at the base of it, you are on a quest."

"A quest?"

"Exactly. You lost something vital to you: the love of your life, your purpose, your future. A part of you knows that there is something out there that will fill the hole that Sophie's death made in you, and that voice, which is the psychological component to this, has sent you on a kind of epic quest to find what fills that void, and since—now bear with me here, I'm thinking aloud—a part of you feels guilty about wanting to move on, to leave Sophie behind, your mind has come up with a series of tests you must pass to prove yourself worthy of a new life."

She watched him for a moment, letting it sink in. "You're Odysseus, Galahad...Quixote. You're tilting at windmills, or in your case, power poles, looking for your Holy Grail, your meaning of life, your Dulcinea." She paused once again. "I also think that there's a physiological component. I think that you were probably hit—splashed, they call it—by the same strike that killed Sophie, and that it literally fried your brain just a little, maybe even permanently. The physiological, psychological, and metaphysical possibilities here are myriad, really, but the quest idea makes a lot of sense to me. The trick is to get you to that magic chalice before you get yourself killed. Just a working theory, but it rings true to me. How about you?"

It had rung true indeed, as soon as she had said it, though it was possible it merely appealed to his literary side. Still, it had given him a measure of hope that he had not felt for a very long time. And since he had always found the very idea of an afterlife, the thought that Sinead and Sophie and his dad were somewhere waiting for him in all their corporeal glory ridiculous, he knew it wasn't the desire for a literal reunion that drove him into the deluge. So, the quest theory made much more sense to him. But he also knew that a part of him—up until he had met Elise, at least—looked at his life and recognized that he had done pretty much everything he had ever wanted to do: run fast times, traveled, made good friends, read and written books, and that it had all culminated with his marriage to Sophie. Her love was the great achievement of his life, and with her gone, there really hadn't been much more he wanted to do. He was treading water, and he told Leslie so. So, yeah, a search for something new, something meaningful, made lots of sense. And then he had met Elise. A new chapter was added to the epic.

Leslie had been thrilled to learn of his new flame. And she had listened excitedly as he told her about Elise and his plan for achieving physical intimacy.

"Graduated exposure, what a fantastic idea! This girl's a keeper," she had enthused when he had told her about Elise and her plan. "In the biz, this is what we call a breakthrough. But keep it slow and steady," she warned. "If you can manage that, your great quest may soon be coming to an end."

But slow and steady went out the window with that first kiss. And where did it leave him? Right back where he had started, as far from his holy grail as he had ever been, witlessly sprinting through a storm that was more than capable of putting an end to his quest once and for all.

If any of these thoughts passed through his head as he tore along Minnehaha Creek toward Lake Nokomis and the Mississippi, they did so as if at a great height, like a biplane towing a banner with a message he could not quite read. He was even less aware of his thoughts than he was of his surroundings, though in the hours after he returned home, drenched and groggy, they would surely return to him just like always, with stunning clarity, which was something Leslie had found very interesting. Maybe, he thought, though the thought barely registered, she could help get him back on track when he saw her again next week. But for now, he had a storm to play in.

* * *

DREAMS COME TRUE, right, sport? 'Least, that's what they've always told you. And so, once again it's onto the dancefloor, driven by the voltage ribboning the treetops, the static crackling in your head. Oh, you're pretty as a picture, aren't you, pal, up there on your toes and sprinting? Skinny, silent messenger, you take to the rain-lashed streets, keeping your weird-ass counsel. You carry a postcard meant for a specter, pray for a valentine sent by a ghost. You're absent. You present yourself to be plucked, like a flower, like a banjo string. Your footfalls make the music of disappearing. The heavens open up and you're an angel of the Apocalypse, singing "Glory, Glory," and ain't that a shame. It's the end of the world as you know it, my friend, so down the flooding bike path you fly, over the river and into the woods, in search, once again, of your wolves and their teeth of flame.

Atmospheric flashbulbs strobe you over the bridge, the river below you lost in gloom. Trees toss and wires sing in the wind. The sky seethes and whatever wields the whip drives you harder, the kids in the minivans all agape as you sprint past streetlights that flash to mark your passing. Don't Walk signs are not the boss of you. They flicker on and blaze in afternoon's indigo midnight; still, you run blind. You run deaf, and the wind's no hindrance. The hailstones have no bite and the cars that drench you don't even register.

You hear nothing, see nothing. You only have eyes for the flash that calls last dance, the midnight liplock glimpsed inside a fireball. Flying blind, for a minute you outrun the gale, staccato your steps down city streets unkissed by a single drop of rain. The wind's at your back, the cloudwall thunders down, and you slip between buildings like a wish, your prayers all gone unanswered, your yearning skin unstroked by fingers of flame. You sleep; perchance you dream, then once again, you wrap yourself in a blanket of rain. Air masses collide, playing their calamitous funk. But the din fails once again to wake you, so you somnambulate the city at a pace to wake the dead, racing, you crazy bastard, your demons down the road you hope might carry you home.

Because you heard somewhere that wishes are granted, lotteries won. The downpour catches up, threatens to engulf you once more. Pedestrians huddle under umbrellas, declare you batshit as you race your reflection across storefront windows and streets made mirrors by rain. Flashes fill the clouds, and just how long must you be patient? Oh you're the lonesome last duck in the shooting gallery—aren't you, pal? —and dammit, it's time for your reward. So, when at long last the sky offers up the singe, that sweet release, you do not refuse the meeting. Another breath, another stride among millions. For a millisecond, you hang in low Earth orbit, you fill your lungs with wet, sweet air. Then lightning flashes and the pedestrians beneath their bumbershoots gasp as you twist and embrace what you've been wishing for so hard.

So tell me one last thing, sport: can you see the bright, blue bolt whose arms enfold you? Can you taste the kiss of heaven, hotter than the surface of the sun?

Rancid, Gladys

I am not radio friendly. I am not frequency,
I mean frequently tuned-in,
seldom turned on, (no hummable hooks) but still
I broadcast my etudes my little ditties,
which may someday be received
by sensitive mechanisms. Pseudopodia will tap,
antennae will wave, and thus will I be big
on Alpha Centauri the way Night Ranger is big
in Japan. If I am buttons, the zeitgeist is a zipper:
efficient, sure, but bereft of anticipatory fumbling,
no sweaty palms, her voice going
suddenly husky, and just as the tastiest sandwich
is the pilfered sandwich, the tastiest kiss
is the kiss stolen behind the drapes at the party,
lips devoured like canapés, the feasters groping
backlit unknowingly on someone's terrace
where lightning licks the last morsel of song
from the throat of the nightingale.
Is it a love song, the note stuck behind the refrigerator
magnet, the note that says the milk is rancid, Gladys,
but the raspberries are sweet?
Is it still a love song if she leaves for the market
and never comes back,
everything you ever said to her lost,
spinning off into the galactic nevermore like slang,
already out of date where syllables coalesce
into slaggy gibberish and stagger off to die
behind the fridge? Lightning licks kiss-shaped

shadows from my wall. Thunder mumbles
its incoherent odes, while the canary, bright
on her perch of flame, stands mute.
Across the alley a party flares dimly, while inside
me someone begins singing. Somewhere far away
a spaceman starts tapping his feet.

Epilogue: Lightning Strikes Twice

Nayalix

"COME ON, BABY, *breathe.*"

Nayalix Pedraza, fresh off a shift assembling new Pinarellos at Freewheeling Bikes, was running late for her statistics class at the U. She emerged from the shop just in time to see the flash and watch the running man collapse to the street. Without thinking, she sprinted to where he had fallen, between (and she would always remember this) a new, white Camry and a beaten, red Dodge Ram pickup with a vanity plate reading "GOFRZ" next to a bumper sticker bearing the insanely smiling visage of Goldy Gopher, the University of Minnesota mascot. The runner's head had missed hitting the curb by only a couple of inches when he fell—arms akimbo, his body bisecting the small distance between the two vehicles almost perfectly—and he lay awkwardly on his right side, his head in a small patch of gravel in the gutter's cement verge.

Rain had begun to fall now, in the kind of huge, slow drops that always presaged a true downpour, with deafening claps of thunder exploding, one on top of another all around. She took the man's wrist in her right hand, put her ear to his lips—no pulse, no tickle of breath—before rolling him onto his back, placing his arms at his sides, his head tilted slightly back, and began quickly and rhythmically pumping her clasped hands, palm-down, against his sternum.

She had spent her high school summers lifeguarding at a Minnetonka country club and earned work-study money at the University pool as an undergrad, so doing CPR came to her automatically, though this was the first time she had ever performed it on anything other than an armless plastic dummy, or some dummy she was dating at the time. Every sixty strokes she would pause, inhale deeply, cupping the back of his head with one hand, while closing his nose with the other, and put her lips to his, blowing the held air as hard as she could into his lungs. By her second cycle, others had gathered on the sidewalk, drawn first by the flash, crash, and subsequent wail of car alarms, then to the sight of the young woman performing CPR on a fallen runner.

"Hey!" she turned to the gathering crowd and shouted as best she could between fast little exhalations as she continued to bear down. "Somebody call 911. He's been struck by lightning."

For four endless minutes, she persisted, working rhythmically as the rain came down in sheets, silently praying for the ambulance to hurry. *Fuh-fuh-fuh,* came her breaths as she pumped, switching her gaze back and forth from the man's face to the ever more deranged looking rodent on the rusted bumper before her. Just as fatigue began to deaden her arms and a burning tightness began spreading across her shoulders, the man shuddered and jerked under her hands, coughed once wetly, and inhaled with a long, raspy wheeze. He blinked two or three times, then opened his eyes, which were dilated, and furrowed his brow in confusion.

"Whaaa...?" He tried to speak, to sit up, but she eased him back onto the pavement, tucking her messenger bag beneath his head, which would make him more comfortable, and possibly keep him from drowning there in the quickly filling gutter, but would also most likely render the textbook and binder full of notes within a total loss. She stroked his shoulder with one hand to comfort him, while the other she wrapped around his opposite wrist, checking his pulse, which was erratic and way too fast, but strong. "Just you relax, baby, everything is going to be just fine."

He seemed to consider this for a second or two, looking at her quizzically before closing his eyes and once again losing consciousness. At that moment the ambulance rolled around the corner, siren wailing, and crunching to a halt in the wet gravel next to where she knelt at the runner's side, his wrist still cupped between her fingers, as the paramedics burst from the ambulance and began to go about their efficient business of keeping him alive. They asked Nayalix a few questions as they put the man on a back board, got an IV running, and hoisted him into the rear of the ambulance. "Are you okay?" one of them, a wiry and serious-looking woman, asked her.

"Excuse me?" Nayalix asked, not sure what the woman was talking about until she looked down at her hands and realized she was shaking. During the long minutes tending to the man on the street she had been focused, all business, but now the stress of the encounter had begun to descend, and she was more than a little freaked out. Plus, she realized, she was soaked to the skin. "Oh. Uh, yeah, just a little weirded-out; a little tired...and a bit cold." She took a deep breath, rolled her neck, shook out her arms. "But yeah, I'm fine."

The paramedic handed her a bottle of water, tossed a thick blanket over her shoulders, and asked if she would ride along, fill them in on what had happened as they rode to the hospital.

"Sure," she said, "of course." She threw her messenger bag over her shoulder, her books probably ruined and temporarily unnecessary anyhow, and clambered in next to the EMT, thinking to herself, *Best excuse for missing class ever.*

Finn

HE CAME TO in what appeared to be a hospital room, after vague dreams of kissing, with an unfamiliar young woman reading in the chair at his bedside and absolutely no idea how he had come to be there. Wires and tubes ran from numerous places on his body and were connected to IV bags and various beeping and whirring monitors. Every inch of his body ached or throbbed or did something worse. His feet burned like hell. He felt like some modern Rasputin: poisoned, set on fire, and thrown in front of a train. Who had done this to him? When he tried to move, his limbs responded sluggishly and on a delay, the commands from his brain sent thousands of miles across the windswept prairie over sagging telegraph wires.

He looked around the room again, at the strange woman staring at him from the chair. Maybe she knew what had happened to him. Someday, when he had the energy to speak, he might ask her. His pain was real enough but seemed to come from far away. He guessed that powerful pharmaceuticals were at work. Idly, he studied the bland, framed landscapes on the walls, the impressive array of machinery surrounding his bed. A thunderous rain pounded against the window across the room and lightning strobed through the curtains, projecting quick, Burtonesque horrorscapes across the wall. He tried to put together a coherent thought, coming up with nothing. He wanted to remember. He vaguely recalled sitting on the rattan chair on his screenporch, brushing out the dogs, drinking from a bottle of Gatorade and singing along to the new live R.E.M. album (if he remembered correctly, the song was "Boy in the Well"). He recalled a rumble of thunder off in the distance.

"Oh fuuuuuuck," he croaked. He was beginning to have a pretty good idea what had brought him here.

"Well, well, Lazarus rises from the dead," said the woman in the chair, a crooked grin lighting her face, giving her dimples that, even in his current state, he wanted to touch. Maybe in a year or two, when he could move without shattering into a million pieces.

He pondered her mysterious and improbable existence for a moment, then croaked, "Cheeky, you are," to which she burst out laughing. Now he was a bit put out. Here he was, dying of dengue fever for all he knew, yet still—if you asked him—managing a devastating charm worthy of James Bond, only to have some strange woman, looking a bit like a half-drowned puppy in obviously borrowed scrubs festooned with out of season candy-canes and Santas, begin laughing at him.

"At just what"—wheeze— "are you laughing?" he rasped again, and again she erupted into hoots of laughter, this time actual tears coming to her eyes, then sensing his consternation, reigned it in with a final snort.

"I'm sorry," she said, still not able to completely subdue the giggles that shook in her chest. "It's just that you sounded exactly like Yoda."

Finn considered this a moment while he plumbed the cotton candy that was his mind for the origins of that familiar but elusive name, and when it finally came to him, he realized she was possibly right. He attempted a smile, an expression which quickly turned into a grimace, as the act of smiling felt like someone was splitting his head with an axe. Unable at the moment to speak, he gave her a little thumbs-up, and it occurred to him that if some stranger was sitting at his bedside giving him shit, he might not actually be dying.

* * *

IT TURNED OUT her name was Nayalix, and she came to visit each afternoon for the first three days after he was struck. She was small and kind and would talk with him about her life until his head once again filled with cotton, a mammoth fatigue overcame him, and he dropped suddenly into a deep and psychedelic sleep. She was a bike mechanic and Ph.D. candidate in epidemiology at the U. She had planned on doing her dissertation on farming injuries to minors, but after the lightning strike, she had gotten curious, discovered the dearth of research in the field, and had abruptly changed her emphasis, much to the chagrin of her adviser. She asked Finn if he might agree to be a research subject for a couple of years, and since she had saved his life and all, he didn't see how he could refuse.

On the fourth afternoon, he awoke to the sound of voices. Nayalix was talking to someone in the hall outside his room. The new voice was familiar, husky, full of smiles and sex, but in his condition, it took a moment for it to register.

Elise.

Elise

WHEN I SAW him there, asleep and broken in that hospital bed, bags and beeping machines nourishing and draining and monitoring his battered body, all the fury I had been nurturing over the previous five days, my resolve that if he was going to give up at the first setback, then to hell with him, vanished in an instant. Nayalix, the girl who had saved him, had gone to his house, fed and comforted and cleaned up after his frantic dogs, then found his phone and called me, since my number appeared thirty-seven time in a row on his phone. She ushered me into the room by an elbow, then squeezed my arm reassuringly at whatever sound escaped me when I saw him lying there. I guess I was probably crying.

"It's okay, really. He is going to be just fine. Let me go get a nurse, or find the doctor, they can explain everything to you. But he's good. Really"

In the few moments I stood at his bedside, just watching him breathe, all of my hurt, all of my anger evaporated and was replaced by a bottomless tenderness, an infinite gratitude. I decided then and there, he was never again leaving my sight. And when his injuries healed, I was going to kick his scrawny ass.

Finn

SUMMER WAS HAVING a tough time handing off the baton to fall, but though it was still way too hot for mid-September, the humidity was mostly gone and the heat dissipated as the sun descended and evening came on. The Twin Cities Marathon was just over two weeks away and Finn bore down in the middle section of his last truly hard training session before the race, a seventeen-mile "progression" run, a type of fartlek wherein the fast sections within the longer run got progressively shorter and faster as the workout went on. The idea behind the run was both to test his fitness for the upcoming marathon and to prepare him to run his fastest when most tired. Ideally, he would be able to run away from anybody still with him in the last two miles of the race. Leg speed was also a very handy arrow to have in the quiver on a course which ended with a half-mile long downhill stretch.

The temperature had dropped steadily as he ran, a product of the setting sun and a cold front that had moved in from the northwest. The cooler air refreshed him even as his muscles warmed up and his pace gradually increased. He clicked his watch as he finished the second of two mile-long surges, twelve miles into the workout. He had run the gently rolling mile in 4:22, exactly the same as his best high school time for a single mile. He was a bit stunned at how great he felt. Rather than destroying his hard-won fitness, the ten days he had missed after the lightning strike had allowed for a much-needed rest, and after a few transitional days to get his legs back under him, he had felt refreshed, his legs zippy. He hit workout times that he had never run before. His feet were still a bit sore from the (according to the doctors) surprisingly minor burns he had sustained there, and he still had some muscle aches and spasms, along with bouts of dizziness and brief attacks of vertigo, but in general he felt strangely buoyant, lighter. Which was, of course, almost entirely due to the fact that The Glimpse had disappeared.

That wonderful development had become clear to him the afternoon Elise had appeared at his bedside a few days after he was struck. He had awakened to find her staring at him with possibly the tenderest gaze anyone had ever bestowed upon him. Indescribable warm fuzzies began at the tips of his toes and percolated up through his body, taking root somewhere around his sternum, overpowering even the pain of his injuries, to become a nearly all-encompassing joy, and even though smiling still felt like it might break his face, under the circumstances it could not be helped.

When Elise saw his eyes flutter open and his lips break into a smile, without thinking, she more or less leaped into the bed and covered those lips with kisses, forgetting until a little too late that kissing had contributed to his being in this hospital bed in the first place. Finn, still groggy and absolutely delighted to see her, had amazingly forgotten to cringe in anticipation, and just let the kiss happen. When her lips and tongue found his, no twitchy firestorm ensued, no x-rated video played in his head. Oh, there were plenty of sparks, to be sure, but only the kind to be expected when new lovers start kissing.

* * *

HE WAS RELEASED the next afternoon under orders to take it easy, write a journal of his recovery for research purposes (which he did—in verse), and stop running during thunderstorms. *Good luck on that one,* he thought. Elise drove him home, and after a frenetic and joyous reunion with Seamus and Frank O'Hairy, as well as a blissful, long shower, she took him straight to bed.

"The doctor said for you to take it easy," she said, pushing him onto his back and straddling him, "so I guess I'll have to do all the work."

Finn went back to teaching classes the following day, returned gently to running less than a week later. Elise packed a couple of bags, told him she was coming to nurse him back to health, which mainly consisted of spending every moment they were not at work making love to him, after which they lay entwined, talking. Sometimes they worked out together. She rode her bike alongside him on his last twenty-miler, handing him a water bottle from time to time. He loved having her along, and found he was completing his runs feeling better than usual, though he was actually running a few seconds per mile faster. She cheered wildly at his last race before the marathon, and he returned the favor as she dominated her city league games at the South Minneapolis YMCA, executing perfect picks that left her open for long jumpers, which she drained with stunning regularity, and to which he shouted, every time, and much to her embarrassment, *String music!* He loved spending long late evenings with her in the MacGillivray gym (he had a key, a perk of being the athletic star on faculty) rebounding for her as she shot her hundred free throws and assorted jumpers. After her drills, she would school him in games of one-on-one, after which they would return home, shower, and engage in a different version of one-on-one, a game that was just as sweaty, and in which everyone came out a winner.

The lightning strike seemed to have cured him of The Glimpse, though of course medical science could provide no reason why. Leslie proclaimed his quest successful and had suggested a few couples sessions to help Finn and Elise make the transition into a life together. Elise officially moved back to her own apartment, though in reality they rarely spent a night apart. They both assumed she would eventually move in with him for good, but for now there was no hurry. Finn returned to doing some of his writing at the bar while savoring a Dr. Detroit or two, as well as playing rounds of audiomancy, where he found his questions answered with a weird frequency by New Pornographers songs.

Finn and Elise became friends with Nayalix and her new boyfriend Gus, a bicycle courier and professional mountain bike racer. Nayalix and Gus spent many evenings at the bar or at Finn's house, and were both Scrabble fiends, good enough to be a near match for Elise and Finn. Finn's mother and Elise hit it off immediately over a quick weekend trip to Vermont, where the two had disappeared together for hours into the woods behind the barn, a hike from which Elise returned knowing all sorts of embarrassing details from Finn's childhood. Elise's parents were reserved, but seemed to like Finn just fine, and he bonded with siblings and cousins over driveway basketball, an outing to a Twins game, and a lefse-making marathon in his own kitchen, which had never known such happy chaos. The dogs were beside themselves with joy.

He still missed Sophie, of course, sometimes intensely enough to cause physical pain. He thought of her every day and hoped he always would. But no longer did he feel haunted, no longer did he feel the need to chase after her ghost, follow it down the dead-end and demon-infested streets of his mind. Gone too were the ghosts of his father, of Sinead. He was happy to surrender them, every ectoplasmic nuance, every sub-atomic particle, to a universe he could not help but share with them anyway. He felt lighter, young again. His senses seemed to be operating fully for the first time in years. Sounds were sharper, colors deeper, the autumn air alive with what he called "cross country smell," the aromas of the first decaying leaves and the last mowing of grass. The future seemed, well, like the future again.

* * *

FINN FEELS KISSED by some strange magic, as one by one the streetlights flicker then wink to life along the bike path ahead. The lake reflects a sky that fades from brilliant blue to navy to indigo, the brighter stars already beginning to glimmer in the heavens and dance on the breeze-riffled water below. Tackle clinks in the rigging of the sailboats that bob in the marina, crickets serenade him from the grass, and out over the western suburbs unseen thunderheads build and rumble, a hint of lightning flickering above the trees silhouetted against the purple sky. With every flash, Finn feels a frisson of muscle memory, a quick hit of adrenaline, a brief tidal tug. Then nothing. Only the burning of his muscles, his mounting fatigue. He grins, breathes deeply of the cool evening air, then jacks up the pace another five seconds per mile. If he hurries, maybe he can make it home before it begins to rain.

The Smell of Something Burning

This time lightning strikes the house
in your heart where your dead still party,
raising the roof in rooms of crash and light.

Walls buckle, ceilings cave. Interrupted
is the sing-along, the ghostly call
and response,
but your dead, they simply start to dance:

Suicide Johnny jitterbugs with a strobelit, murky hum,
Grams and Gramps mosh before rising as one.

Your dead they hippie shake, they shimmy,
they spill forth sleek in gowns of glimmer,
suave in suits of flame.

Sweet conga sizzle, and blown
by the bellows in your breast,
they flare a filigree: naphtha scrimshaw
on a November sky star-bereft, but xmas-lit,
action-painted by your posse of fireflies,
your chorus of living

(but not living)

sparks.

And ascending, they sing again,
burn their torrid semi-quavers
onto the retinae of passersby.
It's the blues, baby, and it stings but sweet
the eyes the ears of strangers,

the drunks and somnambulists
to whom you croon your speak like tongues.

True-blue flames lick like lightning
at notes that leap from your throat,
hiccup upward, glissading; innumerable.

Darkly angelic, these choristers:
boogie-boys bell-ringing long-dark storefronts,
girl-groups freestyling sequined harmonies,
bidding their funky farewells.

Alley winds stoke trashcan fires,

so sure, why not? One last doo-wop
on streets where dreams die
and flaming, are born again
—then off, rising, singing their gospel
of smoky soul.

(There's a sweet-ass chariot coming
for to carry us home.)

And doesn't your own heart swing
a little sweeter now you've finally set them free:
Raggedy choir flown the coop like a plague
of pigeons (coo-coo-cachou), gone, daddy gone,
dauntless squadrons hoodooing home,
aloft on wings of ash.

—for Sophie

Acknowledgements

Many more eyes and ears than mine went into making the tome you are holding in your hands. I offer my deepest gratitude to the possessors of those sensory organs, each of whom read at least part of, commented upon, and made this a better book. My thanks go to Tasha Leffingwell, Maria Kunda, Carole Baran, Cindy House, Sydney Ayers, Paul Eberle, Dan Donaghy, Kellie Cathey Archuletta, Anthony Mendes, Ashlee Konow, and Andrew Beutel. Extra huge thanks to Jill Alexander Essbaum Peng, who found the beginning of this novel buried somewhere in chapter two. That first sentence seems pretty obvious to me now! Thanks also to all of my students, friends and colleagues who formed a huge cheering section and always lifted me up when things looked bleak, A hearty thank you as well to Summer, Jay, Caitlin, and everybody else at Unsolicited Press for believing in my work and making this wee sleekit beastie into the gorgeous art object here before you. Frank and Terry? Damn! And finally, to my sister and biggest cheerleader, reader of forty-seven revisions, Leslie Humrich: no amount of thanks will ever be enough.

About the Author

Brent Terry has been an elementary school teacher, coach, running store manager and semi-elite runner. His poetry has won several awards and his poems, stories, reviews and journalism have appeared in many periodicals. He is the author of three collections of poetry and hundreds of unused band names. He has more pairs of running shoes than small beaches have grains of sand, and his love of Dr. Pepper is legendary. Terry lives in Connecticut, where he teaches creative writing and literature at Eastern Connecticut State University. This is his first novel.

About the Press

Unsolicited Press is a small press in Portland, Oregon. The team publishes poetry, fiction, and creative nonfiction by award-winning authors.

Learn more at www.unsolicitedpress.com

CPSIA information can be obtained
at www.ICGtesting.com
Printed in the USA
LVHW031623200220
647643LV00004B/803